Story Overview

Born and raised in South Boston, Nicole is tougher than most. Fearless some might say. Even in light of the fact she might be going deaf. Then her courage is put to the test when her Broun lineage introduces a whole new reality. Time travel exists. Evil awaits her in medieval Scotland. And the newfound Claddagh ring on her finger? It means she has no choice but to travel back to the thirteenth century. Straight into the arms and under the protection of a man she would rather never see again.

Cousin to the Laird, Niall MacLomain wants nothing more than to keep the future King of Scotland safe. Regrettably, that also means keeping safe a headstrong lass from the future. But his honor means everything. No matter how exasperated, he swore no harm would come to Nicole. However, protecting the feisty redhead ends up stirring his blood in more ways than one.

When Niall and Nicole come together, sparks fly. Excitement. Strife. Desire. But not love. Never that. Determined to work as a team to keep little Robert the Bruce safe, they embark on a non-stop adventure. With help from the MacLomain's Viking ancestors, they might just stand a chance against Brae Stewart and her villainous partner. More than that, they could very well discover that they fare far better together than they ever did apart.

Honor of a Scottish Warrior
The MacLomain Series-Later Years
Book Two

By

Sky Purington

Dedication

For Nicole.

We lived out loud.

You died young, but I kept living for us both.

I will *never* forget you, my friend.

Edited by *Cathy McElhaney*
Cover Art by *Tamra Westberry*

Published in the United States of America

Chapter One

North Salem, New Hampshire
2015

"YOU THINK YOU got me, eh?" Eyes never leaving her enemy's dagger, Nicole evaded.

"Are you going to fight back or what?" he growled.

She would eventually. Meanwhile, let him sweat it out. When he thrust, she crouched fast and swiped his foot. He jumped. She rolled. But not fast enough. The next thing she knew she was flat on her back with a dagger to her throat.

"How many times do I have to tell you?" he said. "If you're hitting the ground you better move a hell of a lot faster than that."

"Hey, in my defense I've only been training for a week." She grinned up at Darach Hamilton. "Most of which you weren't here to help me."

"Aye, true enough." He pulled her to her feet. "And I'm sorry for that."

"Don't be," Jackie said softly from the rope swing. "It sounds like you've been busy enough."

When Darach and Jackie's eyes caught, Nicole grabbed his hand and pulled him toward the house. "C'mon. Let's go grab a cold one."

Well aware of Jackie's infatuation with Darach, Nicole kept trying to head them off. Mostly because she was undecided whether or not she wanted him for herself. Sure, that might sound selfish but it was what it was and she made no apologies. He was hot. And she was single.

Since arriving here a few days ago, she had been stuck on overdrive. Who could blame her? Like her three friends with Scottish Broun blood, she had learned that another whole reality existed outside of this one. A reality over seven hundred years in her past.

One that *existed* in medieval Scotland.

It all started when she and Cassie showed up here at Leslie and Bradon's home. Within hours, she knew ten times more than before. Apparently there was an unending romantic connection between the Broun and MacLomain clans. When Cassie vanished the same day they arrived, Nicole soon learned why. She had traveled back in time and as it turned out, fallen in love with Logan, the current MacLomain Laird…of a thirteenth-century clan.

Yet there was far more to the story than that.

Darach unscrewed the cap and handed her an icy cold beer. When they sat on the couch, she yanked off her shoes, plunked her feet on his lap and grinned. "You *so* owe me a foot rub."

"I suppose." He smiled and rubbed her feet. "Though I'm not sure you earned it."

"Oh, I earned it all right." She leaned her head back, closed her eyes and groaned. The man had some seriously strong hands. "Two hours of standing on my feet and crossing daggers with you was more than enough."

"Never enough," he murmured.

She cracked opened her eyes. "I'll be okay ya know."

"So we hope," Jackie murmured as she joined them. As always, she sat in a chair by the fire, a book tucked neatly on her lap. "Me? I applaud Darach for pushing you so hard."

Jackie was one of those types nobody ever judged correctly based on her personality never mind her appearance. Most would think she was full of herself. With naturally platinum blond hair and deep brown eyes, she was flat-out beautiful. And though soft-spoken with an extremely reserved nature, she was blunt to a fault. To the point that sometimes it took a great deal of patience to tolerate her.

Like every other hot-blooded man, Darach's eyes were ensnared by Jackie. "I'd offer to get you a beer, but I know better."

Jackie offered one of those tempered, soft smiles she had perfected. "Thanks but I have water brewing for tea."

"Of course you do," Nicole muttered and wiggled her toes so that Darach remained focused. "One of these days you've gotta loosen up and try alcohol." She swigged her beer and winked. "It's not half bad."

"So you say." Jackie's brows perked. "But I'm far more interested in how confident you feel going up against what's coming."

Nicole groaned and closed her eyes again. Jackie referred to her role in their upcoming saga. And it was just that. A dramatic set of events unfolding in medieval Scotland. Apparently, when Cassie traveled back in time, she became part of a quest to save King Robert the Bruce when he was a kid. If that wasn't enough, it seemed that Nicole, Jaqueline (AKA-Jackie), and Erin would also be entrusted to look out for Robert.

"Seriously, Nicole," Jackie said. "We all know that you'll be traveling back in time soon. In fact, the bad guy is determined to kidnap *you* to get to King Robert."

"Yeah, yeah." Eyes still closed, Nicole took another swig of beer.

Darach's hands tightened on her feet. "You're taking this all too casually, lass."

Nicole yawned, determined to seem unaffected. The truth was she was scared shitless.

"You were taken against your will by black magic and thrust back in time already," Jackie reminded with an edge of worry to her voice. "Into the heart of a battle no less."

Nicole took another sip. "Blah, blah, blah."

Darach pushed aside her feet and was in her face so quickly she barely had time to react. There was a dangerous glint in his bluish gray eyes as his brogue thickened. "I ken yer need to hide yer fear, but this cannae be taken lightly. 'Tis yer life and that of many at stake." Worry and anger met his words. "At any moment ye could be yanked back and when it happens 'tis verra likely 'twill be into the arms of the enemy."

"Yeah, I got that," she said slowly, anger building. "Hence the shit-show I landed in before."

Though not there long—and pretty damn drunk because of Bradon's whisky—she still remembered every moment with vivid clarity. The wide meadow. The vicious Scottish clansmen determined to take her.

And the one determined to save her.

Darach—as he was so good at doing—almost seemed to read her mind, his accent lessening. "Niall means to protect you, Nicole. And never was there a more stubborn Scotsman."

She flinched and groaned, pushing Darach back so she could polish off her beer. "That brute needs to stay the hell away from me."

"That *brute* is not only one of my best friends but my cousin," Darach reminded.

Because Darach, of course, was from medieval Scotland as well.

"Good enough." Nicole stretched. "That doesn't mean I have to like him."

Darach muttered something under his breath that sounded a lot like, "Nor do I think he's all that fond of you."

Nicole narrowed her eyes. "What was that?"

"So how much time has passed in medieval Scotland?" Jackie interrupted, clearly on purpose.

"Over a month," Darach said, downing his beer.

Strange how that worked. Time went by much faster there than here. Some speculated that it was the past trying to catch up with the future.

Jackie was about to comment when Leslie and Bradon walked in the front door. Leslie was a modern day Broun who had hooked up with Bradon, her medieval MacLomain. Theirs was a strange tale in that Leslie's cousins had ended up living in Scotland with their men and were now in their fifties where she wasn't a day over thirty. Bradon's kin, those called the Next Generation, were also much older, but he had stayed young when he decided to remain here in the twenty-first century.

Darach and his cousins were the children born of the Next Generation.

So Darach, Logan, Niall and Rònan made up the men apparently meant for her and her friends. Daunting thought. Well, not so much Darach because he was a sweetheart. And not Logan because he evidently adored Cassie. Rònan? She didn't know him in the least. Niall? Forget it.

He was meant for Nicole over her dead body.

"Hey there." Leslie smiled at them. "Wanna grab some groceries out of the car?"

"Sure," Nicole and Jackie said at the same time.

So everyone set to helping out. Nicole grinned at Bradon as she set her bags on the counter. "Jeesh, if I were a wizard like you and Darach, I'd just snap my fingers and have all this stuff brought in and put away in an instant."

Leslie winked at her. "And what makes you think we witches couldn't do the same thing?"

Right. There was that. "I'm a newbie witch." Nicole shrugged. "I have no clue how to use my powers yet. What's your excuse?"

"I like to watch the men work." Leslie eyed Bradon with appreciation. "Though a few cartons of milk doesn't make those arm muscles flex too much."

"Mayhap not milk." Eying her with equal appreciation, Bradon yanked Leslie against him and grinned. "But I can think of all sorts of other ways you could get my muscles to flex."

Nicole rolled her eyes and shook her head. She knew exactly what muscle in particular he referred to. "I'd tell you guys to get a room, but I know you've already got one. It's been damn near impossible to sleep at night since I got here."

Leslie shrugged and nuzzled her face against Bradon's neck, words muffled and non-apologetic. "You can always stay at a motel."

"*Or*," Darach said. "You could travel back in time with me so we can keep you safe at MacLomain Castle."

He had been badgering her on and off to do that, but something held her back. Not just the obvious fear of potentially traveling through time, but more. For some reason, she felt safer here. Maybe it was just logical considering this was where she belonged. Or maybe it was something else altogether.

"So if you and your cousins can travel back and forth through time, why is it that you're the one trying to protect me and none of the others?" Nicole asked Darach as she put a carton of eggs in the refrigerator.

An annoyingly soft smile came to Jackie's lips. "You mean why isn't his cousin who swore to protect you here?" The smile took on a smirk-like quality. "Brute that he is."

"Oh, he'll be here soon enough if you dinnae agree to come," Darach said. "Up until now Niall's been busy helping Laird MacLomain fortify the castle so that we might keep the future King and his mother safe."

"And that doesn't fall into your job description?" Nicole asked, shaking her head at her own words. They sounded too much like she cared which cousin was here.

"Aye and nay." Darach shoved some canned goods in the cabinet. "I help when I'm there but I'm a Hamilton so I have to travel to my castle as well."

"Busy boy." Nicole shot him a grin. "Not that I'm complaining."

"It *almost* sounds like you are, though," Jackie pointed out softly as she poured hot water into a mug then added a tea bag. She slanted a look at Nicole. "Maybe you're just hoping a MacLomain will toss you over his shoulder and force you to travel back in time."

Jackie, of course, referred to what Niall had done to Nicole the first time they met. "Don't be a wiseass. Besides, he didn't get far with that."

Darach chuckled and tossed Nicole another beer. "You've yet to arrive at MacLomain Castle and already you've earned a reputation."

Nicole cracked open the beer and snorted. "Right, I'm the *lass* who brought a mighty Highlander to his knees with one good pinch." She bared her teeth and offered a dainty chomp. "Just wait till they see what I can do with a little nip to the right area."

"Oh dear God, you're bad," Jackie murmured, biting back a grin as she tossed her tea bag in the trash.

"I think it'd be wise to keep Nicole away from Rònan," Bradon said, slapping Leslie on her rear end when she turned away. "Those two might throw the whole damn country into havoc if they meet."

"It's hard to imagine a man who rivals you, Nicole," Jackie said, yet there was fondness in her eyes. "But maybe too much intensity for anything that could last."

"I dunno." Nicole shrugged and took a gulp of beer. "Birds of a feather, after all."

"Last I read, dragon-shifters don't have feathers but scales," Jackie remarked.

"Ha ha, because Rònan's part dragon. Quick comeback." Nicole patted her on the shoulder in passing. "Looks like I'm finally rubbing off on you."

Nicole didn't wait for a response but headed out to the barn. Autumn was peaking and the late day sun ignited red, yellow and orange in the surrounding forest. Never one to pay much attention to nature, she headed inside and inhaled the fresh scent of hay. Barns and horses weren't really her thing either but something about this place, better yet the horse in the first stall, kept drawing her. Oddly enough, like Cassie's horse had with her, the one Nicole kept admiring shared the same hair color. Dark red.

As always, the minute she stepped in, Vika trotted over. Apparently her name meant 'from the creek' in Scotland. Hopefully, she would not have the same ominous outcome that Cassie's horse Athdara did. Meaning 'from the oak ford,' Athdara didn't end up doing so well at that location.

"Not you, though, eh, girl?" Nicole murmured, patting Vika's muzzle when she thrust it over the stall door.

Nicole flinched when she caught sight of the Claddagh ring that had ended up on her finger the night she arrived. In no way, shape or form had she put it on. Nope, it was simply there when she awoke the next morning. With nothing at its center but a clear stone, she soon learned that it was one of the original Claddagh rings created by a Celtic god. What was worse? It evidently brought together a Broun and her one true love MacLomain.

"*True* love. Yeah right." Nicole shook her head and kept patting Vika. "Stupid concept."

Vika tossed her head and neighed as if she agreed entirely.

"I dinnae know." Darach joined her. "'Tis a thing love. It has a tendency to hit those who dinnae believe in it the hardest."

"There's that ancient kick-ass accent." She smiled. "You whip it out when you feel like it, don't you?"

"'Tis far more comfortable on my tongue." He patted Vika as well. "Your accent is difficult."

"You don't speak with my accent in the least," she said. "But nice try."

"Aye." He grinned. "Because you *pahk* your *cah*, right?"

"Yeah, I'd *park* my *car* if I had one." Nicole laughed. "Jesus, hon. Whateva you do, don't *ever* try to mimic my Boston accent. We all but get rid of our r's where you definitely embrace them with your Scots brogue." She nudged him. "And trust me, it's sexy as hell."

Darach chuckled and responded, but all she heard was a low buzz. Damn it. Her eyes fell to his lips to try to follow him but his medieval way of speaking made it difficult. So she nodded then refocused on Vika. The horse's nostrils flared and she neighed, but all remained silent. Vika stomped her front hooves a few times, eyes wild.

When Darach touched Nicole's arm, she ignored him, turned away, and headed down the middle aisle between stalls. More and more, her hearing had been faltering but she refused to admit it. Just a little time is all she needed. It always came back. *Always.* Sure enough, a low buzz started. Soon after, the sound of horse's hooves, the wind outside and even Darach following her became clear.

"It happened again, didn't it?" Darach asked, frowning as he came alongside.

"I don't know what you're talking about," she muttered and refocused the conversation on the horse two stalls down. "Eara seems agitated."

Eara, as it turned out, had a mane and tale as white blond as Jackie's hair.

"Aye, no doubt because things aren't so good east of us."

Eara, naturally, meant 'from the east' in Scotland.

And Scotland was east.

"Is that really why she's acting up?" Her eyes narrowed on him. "Or are you just bullshitting me?"

"Nay." He stroked Eara's muzzle. "This lass is from medieval Scotland and a gift from the MacLomains so 'tis verra likely she senses trouble around the clan."

"Ah." She leaned back against Eara's stall and eyed the horse across the way. "It's still so weird to think four horses were left here when four of us Brouns are coming."

Darach walked across and patted Tosha. The third horse remaining, she was different from the rest. Silvery gray with a jet black mane and tail, she was unusually calm with an almost eerily wise look in her eyes.

"She reminds me so much of Erin," Nicole whispered.

Darach grunted something indiscernible. "The friend who can't be bothered to come."

"She was here for a few hours then had to go." Nicole shrugged when his brows lowered at her. "Hey, you can't blame her for wanting to take care of her horse back home."

"The lass needs to be here." He shook his head. "Does she have no one else to care for the beastie?"

16

"Erin isn't really the trusting type. Let's just leave it at that."

Darach's jaw hitched, but he gave no response. Instead, he pulled a saddle off the wall and headed in Vika's direction. "Time to go riding, lass."

"What? Why?" She frowned. "The sun's setting. I thought we'd kick back a few more beers and watch some TV."

"You can kick back a few more in Scotland." He started saddling up Vika, who pranced a little as if eager. "Time for you to go."

"Uh, *no.*" She started for the door, but Bradon appeared, arms crossed over his chest. He had no intention of letting her pass.

So she put her arms over her chest as well and kept frowning. *"Really?"*

"Do you not want to see your friend Cassie again?"

"Oh, stop it," Leslie admonished as she walked by him. "Bullying isn't your thing." She hooked arms with Nicole and led her in the opposite direction. "Up for a chat?"

"Do I have a choice?"

Leslie seemed to consider that before she bluntly said, "No."

"Super." Nicole scowled. "Gotta say, it super sucks that I'm not being given any say in this."

"Yeah, that's one way to look at it." They had nearly reached the opposite side of the barn when Leslie stopped and turned her way. "But there's another way altogether to look at it." Her eyes narrowed. "Right now, your story could very well start out like mine but in a *really* bad way. One that you probably wouldn't survive."

"Right. Taken by the enemy," Nicole said. "Then saved by my MacLomain."

"I was taken by a bunch of filthy MacLeods that didn't know their asses from their cocks." Leslie's eyes rounded slightly. "And saved by a MacLomain with far more gumption than yours likely has."

"Screw that. I don't have a frigging MacLomain." Nicole's eyes rounded as well. "And you better not be referring to that bulldozer, Niall."

"Bulldozer?"

"Just *plows* things over."

Leslie pressed her lips together and grinned. "Yeah, that sounds about right."

Bradon's exasperated words floated across the way. "Focus, Leslie."

"Right. Anyways." Leslie lost the humor. "You've got a double whammy heading your way." She held up one finger. "The first, not numbnut MacLeods but true evil trying to get its hands on you." She held up another finger. "The second, a MacLomain with nothing but war and lasses on his mind determined to protect you."

Nicole scrunched her nose. "I don't get why it can't be Darach or even Rònan."

"Don't whine," Leslie said. "We Brouns are made of stronger stuff than that." She shrugged. "And maybe it will be one of the other guys."

"I hope so because Niall's—"

"My cousin is a damn fine lad," Darach reminded as he headed their way with Vika.

"And one of the fiercest warriors walking medieval Scotland," Bradon added. "You might be surprised by what he's capable of."

"Highly doubtful." She was starting to feel ganged up on again. "Listen, guys, you have no right to force me to go anywhere I don't wanna go."

"No, but we have every right to do whatever it takes to keep you safe," Darach said. "And that means getting you to the castle."

Eyes narrowed, she walked backward out of the barn door. "You all need to chill the fuck out. *Seriously*."

"Ye've a mouth on ye, aye lass?"

Nicole froze when strong hands landed on her shoulders. *Hell no*. She knew that voice.

Niall MacLomain.

"Bulldozer, my bloody arse," he muttered. Before she knew what hit her, he scooped her up and plunked her on Vika. She barely caught a glimpse of him before he swung up behind her and spurred the horse.

"Let me go," she cried then made sure those left behind heard her. "You guys totally suck!"

"Shut your—"

"Don't you *dare* say it," Nicole growled as she tried to shift sideways and slide off the horse. One heavily muscled arm locked around her waist and his strong thighs clamped tightly on either side of hers as Vika picked up her gait.

Niall's deep voice rumbled close to her ear. "Keep quiet, lass. *Now.*"

"You'd like that, wouldn't you, you big—"

When his hand clamped over her mouth, she bit.

"Och, ye bloody crazed lass." But he did not remove his hand, words seething soft. "'Twill be but moments before they sense ye, then 'tis a race for yer life. So *quiet*, aye?"

Nicole was about to chomp down harder on his obtrusive hand when the sunlit forest ahead started to shimmer. Her hair blew back as desert hot wind washed over them. What the? Her ears popped as the pressure seemed to drop. While she definitely didn't experience pain, there was a strong sense of discomfort as the forest changed. Gone was the foliage. Now? Green leaves. A slightly different landscape.

Vika slowed down.

Oh, crap. She knew. Just knew.

Somehow she had arrived in medieval Scotland.

Nicole grabbed Niall's wrist and tried to yank his hand away, but he was immovable.

"Will you remain quiet?" he murmured.

Her eyes narrowed at his modern day Scottish accent. She knew they switched from ye to you to make it easier for twenty-first century women to understand them. When she started to dig her nails in, he gripped tighter, words stern. "You've traveled back in time. Get over it, lass. What you need to ken is that an evil far beyond your comprehension is all around us and I mean to keep you safe." She felt the tension of his body against her back. "So *please* remain silent."

Nicole grappled with his request. Did she believe in evil? Not in the least. Did she believe that he believed in evil? Yes. And that said something given her opinion of him.

"Fine," she mumbled against his hand.

"Aye?" he whispered, not budging an inch.

"*Yes.*"

Ever so slowly, he peeled his hand away. But there was no need for him to be tentative. She felt whatever he did in their surroundings. Something was very, very wrong. The forest seemed to darken then lighten as they moved forward.

"Shh," he whispered close to her ear, the sound more of a slow release of air.

If she wasn't mistaken, Vika was purposefully walking with care, her hooves navigating around the rocks. She stepped on soft pine needles rather than dry leaves. When men clad in yellow and black plaids melted out of the forest and fell in around them, she knew they were friends. Allies who were seemingly escorting them somewhere. Long haired and vicious looking, their eyes scanned the forest.

Not prone to theatrics, Nicole was surprised to feel chills race up her spine. This was intense. Scary. But exhilarating too. She supposed she shouldn't be feeling that way. Still. Way to go stealth. If that was what this was. Totally James Bondish in a Scottish what-the-hell's-gonna-happen-next sort of way. Eyes narrowed, she started to scan the forest as well.

Anything to ignore the guy at her back.

Yeah, fine, he smelled nice which made no sense in this day and age but...he did. A bit of spruce mixed with cinnamon maybe. If Jackie were here, she would be more precise.

"He smells like walking into a house at Christmas," Jackie might say. "An apple candle mixed with cinnamon sticks. Spruce being heated on the mantle above a fire."

"Too cozy for my taste."

When Niall whispered "shh" sharply in her ear, Nicole flinched. Obviously she had voiced her thoughts.

"I know," she whispered back, irritated despite their circumstances.

His arm tightened. A warning. So she scowled and kept eying their surroundings. The trees had thinned considerably, giving way to a jaw-dropping view. It took a lot to shock her, but this did. A wide expanse of jagged cliffs lined an angry ocean. But that wasn't the kicker. No, that would be the impressive behemoth of a castle sitting on its edge. It almost seemed alive with its stalwart turrets weather worn just enough so that she swore it glared at the sea in defiance.

No sooner had they broken from the woodline when the whistling wind and crashing waves dulled. Oh no. That annoying buzz in her ears made everything fade away.

Then something strange happened.

What was usually white noise became something else. Whispered words.

"She's here," it said, the octave almost feminine. *"Get her, now!"*

Nicole frowned, confused as the buzzing faded and sound returned. What the heck? Was she hearing things now too? But it didn't much matter because what happened next made strange disembodied voices the least of her worries.

Chapter Two

Northern Scotland
1281

"PROTECT HER!" NIALL roared as he spurred the horse into a run.

It took Nicole several long, discombobulated moments to realize that he referred to her. The men who had been escorting them were suddenly clashing swords with other long-haired men on horseback.

"Oh *Christ*," she muttered and leaned forward to grab Vika's mane when Niall withdrew his sword and started slashing.

Strange chants echoed around them. Or was that just the wind whistling on rock? Impossible to tell. She squinted when dark shadows started whipping down from the sky. *That* couldn't be good. Though she was still trying to wrap her mind around the idea, those had to be the *Genii Cucullati* sent by the bad guy. And a bad girl in this case. An evil couple determined to not only get ahold of her ring but kidnap little Robert the Bruce.

Apparently the *Genii Cucullati* were entities that hung out with the Celtic gods. Nasty soul-eating critters that hovered around births. Nothing she wanted to get to know better.

One swooped toward her but shimmered away when Niall chanted something and rain started gushing over them. Just them. That's right. Wizard that he was, he controlled the element of water. Not daring to release Vika's mane for a second, she sputtered and cracked open an eye.

After that, everything became a blur of activity. Loud roars. Cries of pain. Darkness and light. Niall spurred Vika to go even faster as something massive rose up in front of them.

Then the rain stopped.

Holy frigging *hell*.

What swooped overhead was beyond her wildest imagination. Huge, intensely beautiful, with shimmering emerald green scales and gigantic talons, it could only be a dragon. She peered up as the long belly passed over before a roar unlike any other had her gritting her teeth. Renewed cries of anguish rent the air behind her.

Niall chuckled—*chuckled!*—as they flew beneath the first portcullis and sailed over the drawbridge. By the time they made it to the second portcullis, she could smell burning flesh on the wind. Not pleasant. But at least the bad guys seemed to be getting their asses handed to them.

Moments after they entered the courtyard, the men who had escorted Niall and Nicole thundered in behind them. Unlike her, they weren't a sodden mess but whooping and hollering as the dragon incinerated the last of the enemy and swooped out over the ocean. It was striking and powerful, its body a glittering serpentine dagger in the sun.

"Where are those damn shadows," she gasped, scanning the sky.

"They cannae get you here," Niall grunted as he swung down. Before he could help her, she swung off the opposite side. Regrettably, Vika shifted and she ended up on her backside. *Sonofabitch.* By the time she scrambled to her feet, Niall was standing in front of her, a heavy frown on his face.

While tempted to look anywhere but at him, her traitorous eyes found their way up his strong body until their eyes locked. No way around it, Niall was handsome enough with his swarthy looks, black hair, and deceptively dark blue eyes.

Those damn eyes.

They had managed to infuriate her before and she could tell by the exasperation in them now that some things didn't change. But she was always up for a challenge. So she wiped a drenched piece of hair from her eyes and planted her hands on her hips. "I suppose you expect me to thank you."

"I dinnae expect a bloody thing from you, lass." Niall nodded behind her. "But he might."

Nicole only meant to glance over her shoulder but froze as the dragon landed on the battlement above. Kind of. Its feet had nearly touched down when the air seemed to compress and shimmer around it. The next thing she saw was a well-muscled, overly tattooed, butt-ass naked man spreading his arms and roaring with laughter.

Her eyes *almost* dropped to his groin, but she stopped herself. Too many women to count were scrambling up the stairs in his direction as people again hooted and hollered with approval. Grinning, he wrapped a plaid around his waist before tucking a woman beneath either arm.

Niall snorted, humor in his voice. "Welcome to MacLeod Castle, Nicole."

Not MacLomain Castle but MacLeod? Super. So the hottie on the battlement could only be Rònan MacLeod.

By the time her eyes shot back to Niall, he was already striding away. Real nice. There goes hero material at its finest. *Not.* Okay, maybe a little depending on how you looked at it. He *had* saved her a few times now. Regardless, she was in no mood to put him on a pedestal.

"There goes my savior," she muttered and patted Vika moments before a boy came and led the horse away.

Always comfortable in a crowd even if it was dauntingly medieval, Nicole tried to ignore her bedraggled appearance and fit in. Not so easy in the cutest damn low-rise skinny jeans she had ever owned. The cleavage-revealing shirt might not help either. But she figured what got her in the end was being down one four-inch strappy sandal. So what if it was chilly back home. It wasn't winter until it was winter, right?

Shoulders back, head held high, she meant to saunter but more like lumbered through the crowd. Step on the sandal, she was five-foot-nine. Step on the bare foot, five-foot-five. Most women in their right mind might remove the shoe but not her. Maybe because she'd paid approximately a hundred and fifty dollars for it alone or maybe because she wanted everyone to see the state she had been left in. Saved then abandoned soaking wet by the mighty Highlander, Niall.

When a deep rumble came from behind that sounded a lot like, "Mm mm, now there's a lass who needs a good ride," she froze.

Spinning on her sexy shoe rather than her filthy foot, Nicole cocked her head at Rònan and raked her eyes over him. "Well, aren't you a whole lotta man." Before he could respond, which would have been lewd based on his cocky grin, she made a tsking sound. "And while I'm always up for a good ride, it won't be happening with you."

"Nay?" His grin didn't falter. "Then ye've a thing for Niall?"

Nicole rolled her eyes when the women he still had under either arm tugged playfully at the plaid hanging far too low on his muscular waist.

"I've a *thing* for no one," she shot.

His brows perked in amusement, but his response was overridden by another. With a voice like smooth black silk and looks to match, a picturesque woman came alongside. "Enough, brother." Eyes as bright emerald green as Rònan's turned her way. "Welcome, Nicole. I'm Rònan's twin sister, Seònaid."

Tall, like maybe five foot eleven, Nicole had never seen another like her. And she had known a lot of gorgeous women. But this one was different. Seònaid's eyes ran the length of her and she knew this woman saw beauty in every creature she looked at. Not to say Nicole wasn't hot enough. She was. In her own way. But even better when seen through this chick's eyes.

Not bashful in the least and grateful for the interruption, she cocked a grin at Seònaid. "Nice to meet you." She looked over the surprisingly modern, slim-fitting dress. "Love the outfit."

The corner of Seònaid's lips curled up ever-so-slightly as she eyed Nicole's shoe. "It seems we both have good taste in fashion."

Before she knew it, Rònan's sister tossed a light blanket around Nicole's shoulders, wrapped elbows and led her toward the castle. Where people might have—okay definitely—shot her odd looks before, now it was nods of approval. Perhaps not for her but certainly for Seònaid. The runway model that obviously had no clue she'd been born in the wrong century.

"I won't let ye keep her for long, sister," Rònan murmured, just loud enough.

"Dinnae mind my brother," Seònaid said. "He tends to forget he isnae always at the heart of every lass's desire."

"Oh, I wouldn't go that far," Nicole said. "I'd say he's nailed most of them." She cleared her throat. "I mean, he's likely pretty cozy at the heart of every girl's desire."

Seònaid laughed as they walked up the stairs to the castle. Her sharp eyes flickered to Nicole. "And will he be nailing ye?"

Nicole released a burst of laughter but clamped her mouth shut when looks were thrown her way. How to answer that? Honestly, she supposed. He *was* pretty damn hot. So she shrugged. "If he plays his cards right."

Seònaid's laughter turned to a low chuckle. "I knew I would like you."

"So you knew I was coming?"

"Was that not obvious when you were brought here?"

"Oh yeah," Nicole murmured, any chance of sounding a crack above mildly intelligent gone when they walked through the front door. "Holy *shit*."

"Like Niall said, welcome to MacLeod Castle," Seònaid said.

"Right, like he said," Nicole whispered, gazing around at the arched ceilings and thin stained glass windows. It was like an elegant beast gone rogue. Mammoth tapestries of oceans with dragons flying overhead hung from three walls. Without a railing, the fourth wall was lined by a wide, broad-stepped staircase lit by torches. Like the rest of the place, it seemed to tempt…do you dare?

"Oh, I *really* like this place," she said.

Though it was clearly summertime, the ocean kept it cool and multiple hearths hosted fires. They had just reached the bottom of the stairs when an older couple approached. The man was tall, blond, sizzling hot and muscled like a thirty-something-year-old.

But it was the woman who froze her in her tracks.

Slim, shorter than Nicole, she had a way of owning the room. Not because she was arrogant but because…well, it was hard to know. Perhaps it was the cut of her eyes as she appraised Nicole with one quick glance. Or maybe the way those around her seemed to hover nearby with respect. Even then, it was far more. Something undefinable. Yet humble.

"Thanks for joining us, Nicole," the woman said in greeting, taking Nicole's hand. "I'm Torra." She nodded at the man beside her. "And this is my husband, Colin MacLeod."

Holy hell. This was Rònan and Seònaid's mom, Torra MacLomain, the dragon-shifter who married the enemy. Or at least everyone thought so thirty years or so ago. She tried to respond, but nothing came out.

"I think this is the part where you say, nice to meet you."

Nicole clenched her teeth and tossed Niall a frown as he meandered by.

"He might be right," Seònaid prompted.

"Hard to imagine." Nicole bit her lower lip and shook her head as she met Torra's eyes. "What I mean is it's great to meet you." She gestured at Niall as he walked away. "He just threw me off." Her eyes went between Torra and Colin. "It's truly awesome to meet you both. I've heard a lot about you."

"As have we about you," Torra said.

"Nice to meet you, Nicole," Colin added.

Nicole was about to respond when Torra looked over her shoulder. "Niall, I need Seònaid. Would you mind showing Nicole to her chamber and filling her in on what's happening?"

As though three-tons of bricks were laid on his shoulders, Niall stopped, hung his head and slowly turned. She didn't miss the slew of women flocking around him. Nor did she miss the discontent in their eyes when they realized he wasn't readily available.

"*Not* necessary," Nicole said. "I can chill until Seònaid is available. In fact, I love to browse old castles."

Now that was a total lie.

Just as exasperated as they were in the courtyard, Niall's eyes met hers and he shook his head. "Ye dinnae give a shit about castles, lass."

Her eyes narrowed.

His eyes narrowed.

"Either way," Seònaid piped up, voice somehow both sultry and peppy as she gestured at the stairs. "My Ma needs me so off ye both go."

Nicole didn't care how long she knew the woman, she muttered, "Way to back a sista up."

Seònaid offered a small, guileless smile and stepped back. Meanwhile, Niall made no move until Torra flicked her wrist at him. That, it seemed, meant an awful lot because not only did he move but he did so quickly.

Not to say a sigh wasn't involved.

The next thing she knew, he had a hand on her elbow and grunted. Apparently that was his way of saying 'follow me' before he started up the stairs. When she tried to shoot a 'you stink' glance at anyone still looking her way, all were gone. Seònaid and her parents had vanished into the great hall's crowd.

"Stop," she said under her breath as Niall pulled her after him. When he didn't pause, she repeated herself. Once. Twice. Third times a charm. She yanked her arm free, stopped halfway up the treacherous stairs and took off her sandal. Eyes narrowed, she debated whether or not she wanted to keep following him.

"Just come, Nics."

If she wasn't frozen before, she was now. "*What* did you just call me?"

She had a thing about nicknames.

She did *not* like them.

Niall's steps slowed, but he by no means made a point of correcting himself as he smirked over his shoulder. "I called you Nics, lass."

"Where's a dagger when I need one," she said, voice threatening.

"A dagger?" He turned around, crossed his arms over his chest and nodded at the wall lining the stairs. "Plenty to be had if ye've the ballocks."

Ballocks? She had the balls all right. Eyes as innocent and compliant as she could manage, she hitched her chin for effect as she walked upward. "Listen, it's obvious you and I don't like each other, but I'm feeling pretty damn out of place, okay? Can you just show me around?"

"You dinnae need showing around any more than I need a lass to tell me where my cock is."

She almost laughed. Almost. Because that was a good one. And damn if she didn't detect a sizeable enough bulge beneath his plaid. No matter. He was on her shit list. So time to carry on.

The corner of her lips hitched. "Are you hoping I'll take advantage of your cock, Niall?"

The corner of his lips hitched. "Nay, not even for a moment."

"Then put those baby blues away and show me the way," she said, her voice super soft and ridiculously compliant.

Would he buy it? Was he that gullible?

His forefinger curled just as lazily as his lips. "Let's go, Nics."

"Nicole," she ground out before she could stop herself. He was obviously trying to get a rise out of her.

Niall arched a brow, his expression far too chivalrous now. "*Nicole*, of course. My apologies."

"Of course," she mouthed, heading his way. Like Darach, he was easily six-foot-five and far too muscular to overpower.

However, as she did with any man, she didn't put much chalk in physical but mental strength.

And Niall lacked in that department.

So she kept moving. One step at a time. Maintain eye contact. Don't let him see your weaknesses. Two steps down, she stopped and put on a sweet face. "Are you ready to show me around then?"

With an unguarded, cordial smile, Niall cocked his head. "Will you not pinch me if I do?"

Ha. Very funny. "I think it's a good idea if we play nice at this point. Don't you agree?"

"I do." He shifted sideways and gestured up the stairs. "Please. Lead the way."

Abso-freakin'-lutely.

Truly, when she planned her next move it had nothing to do with harming him but showing him up. Guys like Niall needed that. So when she sauntered past, shot him a wink then grabbed a dagger off the wall, it was no big thing. Yet it seemed she should have left it at that. A means to keep herself safe.

But no.

Thanks to Darach, she couldn't help but show a little suave with her blade and knifed it Niall's way in a mocking gesture. Unfortunately, she didn't anticipate his reaction.

Half a second later, she grunted when she ended up on her back. He actually had her pinned on the *stairs.* Her eyes widened and the blade teetered in her loosening grasp. She sputtered and gasped when he squeezed her wrist until the blade fell, clattering to the floor below.

"You Goddamned asshole," she hissed, shifting against the weight of his body. She could feel every long, hard inch of him. Niall pulled his face back when she thrust hers forward, angry as hell.

He brought his lips within inches of hers, eyes narrowed. "Dinnae ever pull a blade on me or anyone else unless ye intend to use it and use it well."

Who would have thought he'd have such nice breath?

"The mighty Broun Pincher gets taken down!" someone cried.

"It seems the great Niall willnae be forever dropped by a lass!" another cried.

Nicole grinned to herself. She sort of liked being called the Broun Pincher. But she did not like being so defenseless. When she shot her knee up, he defended. Taking advantage, she slammed her fist into his armpit. A vulnerable yet unguarded spot. Like she knew he would, Niall yelped in pain…and rage.

Time to move.

So she did. Fast and squirm-like, she pushed him aside, shimmied onto the next stair, got her footing and booked it. Laughter echoed from the crowd as she flew up the stairs.

But she didn't get far.

Niall flung her over his shoulder in such a way that her arms were pinned beneath her. He held her so firmly that even flailing her legs was impossible. Yet she'd still managed to hold onto her sandal.

"Put me down, you big brute," she bit out.

"Oh, I will," he assured. There was an unsettling mixture of anger, determination, and slyness in his voice.

"Och, she's a feisty wee thing, aye Cousin?" Rònan yelled up. "Too wild for the likes of ye."

"Aye," Niall yelled over his shoulder. "If ye've a need to have a crack at her, she'll be in the tower."

"A crack at me? You medieval prick." She frowned. "What tower? Is that where my room is?"

Niall gave no response but swiftly walked down a hallway at the top of the stairs before he went through a doorway. Then they were going around and around up what was definitely a tower. And not a large one at that. But tall. Alarmingly so. And he wasn't winded in the least.

"Niall," she ground out, eyes narrowed. "What the hell are you up to?"

Still no response.

Soon enough, he strode into a small chamber with a few narrow windows and tossed her on a cot. Eyes wide, she said, "If you think for a second you're getting any, think again."

"Getting any? Ye could only be referring to sex." Niall shook his head. "Ye are the last person in Scotland I would ever want such from, ye ungrateful crazed lass."

Her eyes dropped to the very obvious bulge beneath his plaid. "I dunno. You must have a thing for crazy women then because I'd say you're at least semi-erect."

Scowling fiercely, he muttered something that sounded a lot like, "Bloody thing has a mind of its own," before he tossed a blanket at her, strode out of the room and slammed the door.

"Oh damn," she said and ran over when she heard the click of a latch. He had locked her in.

"Niall!" She pounded on the door. "Niall, let me out!"

Again and again she yelled, cursing over and over.

Nothing. No response.

She was only met with silence.

Screw the hundred and fifty dollars; she whipped her sandal at the door in frustration.

Voice hoarse, she finally gave up and plunked down on the cot. This *seriously* sucked. The nerve of the guy considering she had just traveled back over seven hundred years in time. Way to have a little compassion.

Nicole sighed and leaned back against the wall. What was with them? She'd never met a man that got her so riled up. Sure, there were the obvious reasons that they had issues with one another. After all, she had pinched him pretty hard when he tried to save her the first time.

But there was more to it than that.

A spark of something she couldn't quite put her finger on. Attraction? Maybe some but that was just normal. She might not like him, but she could admit he was more than just handsome. Chemistry? Maybe some but that was normal, too. Based on what she'd seen so far he was likely hung like a horse and hey, she was only human. The fact that he seemed so honor-bound to protect her? Absolutely not. Because a true hero didn't lock a gal in a tower.

So she sat there for far too long mulling things over before the latch jiggled and the door opened. Nicole jumped to her feet, surprised to see Niall leaning casually against the balustrade, arms crossed over his wide chest. His eyes were hard and his lips set in a frown.

"Were you standing there this whole time?" she said, incredulous.

"When Torra MacLeod requests something of me, I listen." He rolled his jaw. "No matter how much I might dislike it."

"Lucky me."

When she tried to breeze past him, he stopped her with a hand on her upper arm. His words were low and firm. "Neither of us has to like it, but I'm honor-bound to protect you, lass and will do so at any cost."

"Why?" Her eyes locked with his and she cursed her body's sharp response to his close proximity. "Why do you feel so honor bound to protect someone you don't even like? It makes no sense."

"I was the first to go to you when you were almost taken by the enemy. By doing so I made a commitment," he said. "Even if I dinnae like you, I willnae see you harmed. 'Tis not something even someone like you deserves."

"Someone like me?" She stepped a little closer and narrowed her eyes. God, he was huge, but she refused to let his sheer size intimidate her. "What, someone who stands up to you? Someone who doesn't simper at your heels like all the other women do?"

"Nay." One brow swept up. "Like I said earlier, someone who is ungrateful, sharp-tongued and too crass by half."

"Maybe I don't wanna feel like I owe you anything. Especially considering I didn't ask for your help to begin with," she countered, not overly offended by his words. It wasn't the first time she had heard them. "Why did you feel the need to help me anyway?"

"'Twould have been poor of me to leave you out there like that." He shook his head, amazement in his eyes. "Do you *truly* begrudge me saving your life?" His voice lowered. "Are you so unhappy that you would have willingly died? Because that would have been the outcome had you been taken."

"No, I'm not unhappy," she lied. "I just prefer to stand on my own two feet."

"And I took that from you." Her breath caught when he smirked and humor lit his eyes. "When I threw you over my shoulder."

Niall might just go from handsome to seriously smoking hot if a full smile blossomed.

"Very funny. Yeah, you took that from me." She offered a smirk in return. "But then I took the same from you too with a good pinch, eh?"

His smirk vanished. "So you did." Darkness shadowed his eyes. "Something that willnae happen again."

For a second there, she thought they might be heading toward a truce. Evidently not.

"Uh huh." She pulled her arm free and headed downstairs. "Because I intend to keep my feet on the ground in the future."

"'Tis better than me having to carry you," he said, following.

"Jerk," she said under her breath.

"I heard that."

"I sorta hoped you would."

"Yet I suspect even at your quietest you've a good bellow to your voice."

Nicole snorted. What a jackass. "Can't fault a woman for making sure her point gets across."

"'Tis one thing to get your point across and another altogether to have an unnaturally boisterous voice."

"Hey, this mouth gets the job done."

Nicole cringed the minute it came out. That sounded like...

Niall chuckled. "Aye, now there's one way to silence you."

"And here I thought I was the last woman in Scotland you'd have sex with." She stopped and glared at him over her shoulder. "Because it sounded a lot like you were just referring to a blowjob." She perked her brows when he hesitated. "You do know that word, right? Because I can spell it out for you."

"I think he'd *much* rather ye show him, lass," Rònan said from below.

"Och, nay," Niall replied. "She'd likely bite the bloody thing off."

Well, one thing could be said for the Scotsmen she ended up with. They didn't hold back. She had all sorts of quick-witted things she could say in return but wanted out of the stairwell so kept moving.

When she reached the bottom, Rònan was leaning against the doorjamb, a bemused expression on his face. "If he kept you hidden up there much longer I was going to join in."

"It might have improved the situation," she remarked, squeezing by him.

Rònan released a bark of laughter, his comment directed at Niall. "'Tis good we're mentally connected and I knew ye didnae lay with the lass. Otherwise, I might have felt sorry for ye that ye couldnae manage to please her."

"'Tis likely nobody could please her," Niall said. "Besides, 'twould be a battle trying to lay with that one."

Rònan chuckled. "A battle well worth fighting I'd say."

Nicole rolled her eyes, banked a right and started walking. Niall grabbed her wrist and redirected her in the opposite direction. "Your chamber is this way."

She yanked her hand free, wishing she wasn't bare footed and too darn short walking between these two behemoths. "So now that I'm no longer being held prisoner, why is it again that I'm here and not at MacLomain Castle?"

"Because 'tis better for now that you and the wee King are split up," Niall said.

"And none can protect you better than dragon shifters," Rònan added.

"Not even wizards." She slanted a look at Niall. "Better yet, your arch-wizard, Grant Hamilton?"

"'Tis an unpredictable, dangerous magic that seeks you out," Niall said as they turned left down another long, torch-lit corridor. "Rònan is strong enough but his Ma, Torra, is far stronger. To this day, there isnae a power that has been able to infiltrate her lair."

Lair? "You mean to tell me this castle is a *dragon lair?*"

"What else would you call it with two dragon-shifters living in it?" Rònan said.

"I suppose," she said. "I guess I just pictured something more cave-like."

"We're Scotsmen not Vikings," Rònan said with nothing but respect in his voice. "May the gods protect our ancestor's souls."

Viking ancestors? She could see that based on their builds alone. "They were a pretty brutal people."

"Vikings? Aye." Rònan nodded. "The fiercest warriors to be had."

"The best trainers to be had," Niall said.

She looked between them. "Trainers?"

"Aye, lass," Rònan said. "How do you think we became the warriors we are today?"

"Ah, so battle moves were handed down through the generations and that's how you learned."

"Aye, partly with the training from our Da's," Niall conceded. "But not entirely. The rest we learned directly from our ancestors."

"Directly from them?" They stopped at a large, spacious chamber with three windows rounded on top and flat on the bottom. "Yeah right. Whatever you say."

Rònan touched her lower back and escorted her inside. "If you traveled back in time is it such a far-fetched idea that our Viking ancestors might have traveled forward in time from the ninth century?"

He was serious. "*Really?*"

"Really." Niall untied the skins on the windows. "Three of them. Since we were wee bairns."

Nicole became a little too aware of the intimate scene. The low torches. The crackling fire. The way-too-big-for-one-person bed. Then there was the fact neither man seemed inclined to leave. Maybe yapping about blowjobs so loosely with almost perfect strangers hadn't been her best move. Especially considering how lusty they seemed. Rònan, at least. Oh wait, Niall wasn't all that opposed either based on his arousal earlier.

Best to keep the conversation going.

"So your Viking ancestors came just to train you to fight so you could someday protect Robert the Bruce?" she said as Niall dropped the last skin over a window, shutting her off from outside.

"Aye," Rònan said. "Amongst other reasons."

Nicole looked between them as Rònan pulled off his tunic and muttered, "'Tis too bloody hot in here."

Damn. More and more intimate.

"Och, look at her face." Niall glanced at Rònan then nodded toward Nicole. "She thinks we mean to have her."

Rònan grinned, brogue thickening. "It wouldnae be the first time we shared a lass." His eyes twinkled when he looked at her. "Are ye wanting us both then? Because it might help ye relax a great deal."

Play it cool, she preached to herself. "In what reality could I handle you both? I'm good but not *that* good."

Niall snorted. "She makes a good point, Cousin."

"I dinnae know." Rònan contemplated her. "She smelled of arousal when she came down out of that tower with ye."

No, he did *not* just say that.

Niall shot her an irritatingly cocky grin. "Did she then?"

"Aye, she did." Rònan sauntered over. "And she still does."

Nicole decided clever comebacks had no place here. Time for them to go. She nodded at the door as he slowly walked around her, eying her up and down. "Out, Rònan."

"Maybe," Rònan said.

"Or maybe not," Niall said even softer.

Chapter Three

WHAT GODS DECIDED he should be thrust into hell?

Not any benevolent ones to be sure.

Niall had never before wanted to throttle a lass to within an inch of her life. Then again, he had never wanted to be between a lass's legs so much either. It was a pitiful and alarming mix of irritating desires. As he sat outside Nicole's chamber door, he kept mulling over her earlier question.

Why had he felt the need to save her to begin with?

His response had been the truth…but not all of it. Definitely not all of it. The main reason was he couldn't stop himself. She had been so vulnerable and frightened out on that field. So alone. And yes, so damn beautiful that no threat needed to exist for him to head in her direction. Then there was the other thing. What her friend Cassie shared with him and his cousins after the battle. Nicole and her friends were facing life-altering disabilities.

Nicole was going deaf.

And she did *not* like coddling.

He admired that. Respected it. She was a true warrior of sorts. So he was determined to treat her like any other and push her upcoming difficulties from his mind. Never once would she get pity from him.

But it would be damn hard.

Not his lack of pity but having to seem cold when he would rather comfort and lend strength. No one should have to face what she did alone.

When a strange sound came from her chamber, he shot to his feet. Though she thought he and Rònan were going to have their way with her earlier, no such thing had happened. They would never take a lass against her wishes. But how he had hoped for a moment she wanted it…even if his cousin was involved.

Worried, he rapped on the door. "Nicole, are you all right?"

No response. Just that strange sound again. Fear flashed through him. Had the enemy somehow made it past the MacLeod's defenses? His heart hammered into his throat as he thrust open the door and scanned the room.

All was quiet.

Nobody was here.

His eyes shot to Nicole when the sound came again. Arms hanging limply over the sides of the tub, her head was leaning back and her mouth hung open. Hell, the sound had been her snoring. Not a dainty snore in the least, but a gusty sound that would put even the drunkest passed-out Scotsman to shame. And she thought *he* was the brute?

Despite himself, he grinned.

Then his eyes fell lower and he inhaled sharply. He had never seen a better-made lass. Slim-boned with ample enough, nicely rounded breasts, her stomach was small, even slightly muscled. Drawn, he slowly walked over to her. Where only a few faint freckles dusted her cheekbones and nose, slightly darker ones dusted her collarbones and arms. She had inherited a great deal of Irish from her Broun heritage.

When one leg slid up, his gaze traveled lower. Slender and well-toned, even her thigh and knee were freckled. He licked his lips and imagined flicking his tongue over each and every one. Either fortunately or unfortunately, depending on how you looked at it, she released a loud enough snore that she woke herself up.

Head still resting against the tub, she rubbed her nose then slowly opened her eyes. Unlike most people would when they awoke so abruptly, she didn't seem confused or disoriented. She didn't even try to hide her body. Instead, her eyes met his and she murmured, "Enjoying yourself, Niall?"

He kept his expression schooled despite how jolting he found her eyes. Wide-set, thickly lashed, they were the brightest pale cedar he had ever seen. Her stick-straight, face-framing hair was deep red, just beneath chin length in the front and upper-neck length in the back.

Modern and daring.

Just like her.

"Aye, I am enjoying myself." He allowed his gaze to boldly run down her body again. "Who would've thought?"

"Why are you still here?" She fished a bar of soap from beneath the water and nonchalantly started rubbing it over her stomach. Not sensually but practically. "I thought you'd be downstairs by now."

She might act like she wasn't affected by his proximity, but he didn't miss the tightening of her pink nipples. He nearly groaned.

"It's the cold water not you, Brute," she assured as if reading his mind.

"Mayhap." He crouched and slid his hand into the water, enjoying the gasp she tried to hide. With a quick murmur, he heated the water with magic. "Mayhap not."

"Nice trick," she mumbled, lathering up.

"Might ye say thank you then?"

Her brows shot up. "I already thanked you enough by lounging here naked for your nosy eyes, wouldn't you say?"

"I should start calling you 'ungrateful'." He went to stoke the fire. "The name would well suit you."

"Whatever you say, Brute."

"*Ungrateful* it is then."

"That's a shitty nickname." He could tell by her splashing that she was rinsing off. "Get out of here. I need to get dressed."

"My pleasure," he said, trying to bank aggravation. He made sure the fire was roaring again before he headed for the door. "Ready yourself. I'll be waiting."

"Don't feel the need," she started but he shut the door before she could finish her sentence.

Blasted lass.

She might be tolerable if she kept her mouth shut.

As he leaned against the opposite wall, his mind flashed back to her blunt talk of blowjobs. He pinched the bridge of his nose and shook his head when visuals of her mouth wrapped around his cock arose. Hell, that would be awful...in such a bloody amazing way. Those full lips. Those unearthly eyes staring up at him. Those slender hands grasping at his hips, maybe even his arse.

Niall exhaled sharply and cursed his instant arousal. Those were demon lips. Those were deceptive eyes. And those hands? They had biting nails attached to them.

He slid down the wall and resumed his position, all the while reminding himself that Nicole was nothing but trouble. Lasses were good. She was bad. Lasses were soft-spoken and adoring. She was loud-mouthed and annoying. Lasses were compliant and willing. She was rebellious and disinclined.

Though it might have been minutes it felt like ages before the door finally opened and Nicole—in all her glory—stood there with her hands on her hips. Niall started to talk, but the words died on his lips. May the gods give him strength, she was beautiful. Breathtakingly so. In a deep green dress that somehow made her skin glow, her already perfect figure was highlighted to full advantage. He might have seen those scrumptious breasts bare, but somehow the dress plumped them up enough that they suddenly seemed like a mystery.

One that almost had him walking her right back into that room and to the bed.

"Stop gaping," she said and breezed past him.

Niall pursued, eying the way the dress fit a little too snuggly around her firm backside. When she meant to take a right at the end of the hallway, he grabbed her wrist and pulled her left. "Nay, lass. You're with me."

"Ugh, fine," she groaned. "But isn't the great hall in the other direction?"

"Aye." He pulled her into the next chamber. "First, I bathe and change as well."

"Okay," she said carefully, eying him as he sat on the bed and yanked off a boot. "And I'm here *why*?"

"Because I'm honor bound to protect you." He yanked off the other boot. "Which means you dinnae leave my sight."

"You've gotta be kidding me." She looked skyward and spun on her heel. "See ya down there."

With a few quick strides, he made it to the door before her and blocked her path. "You can do one of two things. Sit at the table, have some whisky and avert your eyes like a good lass or..." He couldn't help the involuntary curl to his lips. "Help me bathe like a *really* good lass would."

Her eyes narrowed and she shook her head. "I bet you'd love that, wouldn't you?"

Niall said a few chants under his breath then headed for the tub as he pulled off his tunic. Nicole, meanwhile, started out the door only to stop short. He grinned, removed his plaid then slipped into the water.

"What the hell?" she muttered and tried to walk forward again only to stop once more.

He sunk beneath the water then came up, wiping off his face. "I cast a little spell, lass. You're here until I say otherwise."

"You are such a..." Whatever she was going to say trailed off when she spun and locked eyes on him. Well, really more his chest area.

"Such a what?" he prompted, arms resting on the side of the tub, well-aware that he had managed to tongue-tie her with his nudity.

"Dickhead," she whispered. Her eyes seemed to scan his shoulders, arms and anything else she could manage before she scowled and headed for the table. Better yet, the whisky. Lathering up, he enjoyed the way her hand shook slightly as she filled a mug to the brim then leaned over to sip off the top.

Referring to her unsavory description of him, he said, "Are you interested in the head of my—"

"No, Brute," she cut him off then took another sucking sip so she could lift the cup. "I'm not interested in anything attached to your body."

"All right, *Ungrateful*." Though he meant to leave it at that, he enjoyed riling her up. "Keep telling yourself that."

"You wish." Mug in hand, she walked over to the fire, eyes to the flames as she took several more sips. "Hurry up then."

"Hurrying, love."

"*Love?*" She half snorted, half grunted. "I prefer *Ungrateful* to that."

Niall dipped beneath the water again and rinsed off, a small smile on his face. Using the word *love*, much like getting naked in front of her, was only meant to incite. Loving this lass would be equivalent to burning in hell. There would be no greater torture for a wizard who controlled the element of water.

After surfacing, he stretched, slow and languid, relishing the chance to take a break if even for a moment. A break from worrying about her. A break from protecting her.

It was hard to know if it was the wizard or the man who sensed it first, but the minute Nicole's breath hitched his eyes flew to hers. Back to the fire now, her gaze was locked on him. Not his body this time but his face.

And she wasn't just looking but devouring.

Startled by the stark desire in her eyes and the way his chest tightened then his throat thickened, he clasped the edges of the tub. What the bloody hell *was* this?

Eyes just as startled, she took a step back and whispered, "Get that look off your face."

He arched a brow, about the only gesture he could manage right now he was so caught off guard…so wickedly aroused. It took just about everything he had not to throw her onto the bed and slake his lust. Aye, lust. The sharpest he had ever felt. A harsh feeling that had his groin painfully tight and his stomach muscles burning.

Either it was the look on his face or the way he shifted uncomfortably, but her eyes widened and pupils flared as she took another step back. "Seriously, Brute. You and I aren't happening."

"I agree," he grunted, fighting the rush of need that had his blood boiling. "Entirely."

When was the last time he had lain with a woman? A week or so ago if that? Two of them to boot. So this made no sense. Any woman. Anywhere. At any time. Willing and able. That was his way. Not this…this…his eyes shot to Nicole…her!

She took another sip and another step back. "Still not liking the look on your face."

He didn't like the *feel* of the look on his face. She didn't deserve it. Neither did he. About to tell her that nothing would ever happen between them, he stopped. What was that smell? Smoke? His eyes fell to her skirts.

"Bloody hell," he muttered, swinging out of the tub.

Her eyes went round as saucers when they fell to his groin. "Holy fucking *shit*."

"Ye and yer bloody cursing," he roared as he flew toward her.

"Wha…wha…get away from me!"

She tried to bat him away, but he ducked, grabbed her by the waist and brought her to the floor. Then they rolled because he couldn't get a solid grip on the flailing lass.

"Stop, Nicole," he started but she jammed his chin so strongly, he winced and they kept rolling. For a little thing, she had a hell of a punch. And pinch apparently.

Gritting his teeth, he ground out, "Yer on fire, ye bloody fool!"

"Not for you, Brute!"

"Och." He batted at her skirts as they rolled. "Not lust but *fire*."

Then it was all skirts and tangled limbs as he tried to summon water and douse her flames.

A soft chant followed by laughter met his ears before the flames died and they came to a stop against the wall, half of his body covering hers.

"There's something consistently comical about you two," Rònan said as he leaned against the doorjamb. "And you can thank me later for tempering her fire. Just takes a real man is all."

Niall caught the double meaning in his words.

Rònan might control the element of fire, but he wasn't opposed to controlling something else altogether. At this rate, Niall might just let his cousin have a go at her.

"Oh, man," Nicole grumbled, pushing Niall away as she frowned at her burnt skirts.

"Nothing to worry over," Seònaid said smoothly as she entered.

Niall's door-stopping spell had fizzled the minute he knew Nicole was on fire.

Maybe even a little sooner.

"Niall, get dressed and stop distracting her." Seònaid crouched by Nicole. She ran her hands over the dress and started murmuring chants even as she said, "This is nothing to fret over. See, good as new."

Nicole blinked as the burned edges vanished and the dress became whole again. "Wow, thank you."

"Anytime." Seònaid helped her to her feet. "Are you ready to come down and eat then?"

"Yeah." Nicole ran her fingers through her hair and continued to eye her dress. "Again, thanks. I can't believe you just did that. Very cool."

"No need to ruin a bonnie dress," Seònaid said.

"Nay, just a perfectly good erection, aye Niall?" Rònan joked.

Niall ignored him and set to wrapping his plaid.

"Enough," Seònaid said and shot her brother a look.

 Rònan held his hands in the air in mock surrender. "'Tis never good to be outdone by the enemy never mind an ally." He winked at Niall. "Aye, Cousin?"

"I want out of here." Nicole cast Niall a dirty look. "Total bulldozer for sure."

"Ungrateful wench." He yanked a fresh tunic over his head. "Time and time again."

"Bulldozing Brute," she shot back as she sought out her whisky and polished it off. "Time and time again."

When Seònaid pulled Nicole after her, Niall grumbled, "Good riddance."

"Back at ya, buddy," Nicole muttered before she left.

Niall plunked down on the bed and yanked on his boots. Hell, was he angry.

Rònan filled two mugs and handed one to Niall when he stood. Amusement continued to flicker in the MacLeod's eyes. "She's full of a fire I dinnae know if even I can handle," he conceded.

"She's full of something nobody can handle." Niall downed half the whisky then ran his hand over his chin in frustration as he headed for the door. Though it remained the last thing he wanted to do, he would protect the wayward lass. That meant sticking close to her.

"But she might've been full of *ye* had ye gone about it correctly," Rònan said, falling in beside him.

"I dinnae want to lay with her," he growled, pinning his MacLomain broach at his shoulder.

"But ye dinnae want her laying with any other either."

"She'll do as she likes," Niall groused. "If the gods show me any favor at all, 'twill be with another lad."

Rònan hesitated and Niall felt the weight of his upcoming words.

"Then might I have a go at her?" Rònan shook his head. "I've yet to meet another lass so wild. It stirs my blood."

He and Rònan were close. Closer, mayhap, than he and their cousins, Logan, and Darach. Their personalities were similar and because of that, they related. Not to say they didn't fight. They did. More than the other two ever could. But that was half of what bonded them. Fire and water. Opposite elements. But elements that one way or another were always drawn to each other by necessity.

By an odd need that disallowed the other from overtaking everything in their path.

Logan and Darach were Earth and Air, far more compliant, two elements far enough away from one another that it worked. There was peace.

And far less fun.

After all, Rònan and Niall unabashedly loved the lasses.

So the best thing Niall could do was protect Nicole while she was wooed by someone as powerful as Rònan. It made perfect sense. She would be well cared for and he would no longer have to deal with her crazy ways.

The perfect solution.

Truly.

Niall ignored the nagging defiance flaring up inside him and flung his arm around Rònan's shoulders as they walked. "She's all yours, my friend."

Rònan cocked a brow at him. "Aye?"

"Aye," Niall assured. He tightened his hold, a show of comradeship. "Just watch out. She's got a mean pinch."

"Aye." Rònan chuckled as they headed down the stairs. "I'm looking forward to it."

Hours later, he found himself brooding in front of the fire and somewhat in his cups when Rònan's father, Colin MacLeod sat down next to him. They said nothing at first, just enjoyed the flames on the hearth and the taste of good whisky. Colin had always been his favorite uncle so he knew the MacLeod was biding his time, waiting for Niall to talk first.

While he meant to speak of the upcoming threat in the Highlands and of the wee King, he instead said, "Rònan and Nicole seem to be getting on well."

"Did ye expect any less, lad?" Colin eyed him. "Especially when ye gave my son the go ahead."

"I'd hoped for the best," he lied and took yet another drag of whisky.

"Ye hoped for the worst, ye lying bastard." Colin shook his head and kept eying Niall. "She's too wild for my son."

"Yer son's the wildest of us all," Niall reminded. "Seems the perfect match."

"Nay, my son doesnae need a wild lass but a temperate one that will balance him," Colin said. "One that will whisper soft words of wisdom in his ear as he learns how to lead this clan."

"Aye. Soft, wise words would do him good," Niall agreed, polishing off his drink.

"As strong words might do ye some good," Colin said. "From a wild lass that says what she thinks and has the courage to tell ye things nobody else would."

"The courage to tell me things that nobody else would?" Niall snorted. "Ye make it sound as if I need a telling then."

"Och, but ye do." Colin nodded to a random lass and Niall's mug was replaced with a full one. "More than most, my lad."

Niall guffawed. "More than most?"

"More than most," Colin echoed. "Yer cousins are set to become lairds or already are. Logan of the MacLomains, Rònan of my MacLeods and Darach of the Hamiltons." Colin studied him. "What have ye in yer heart, lad? Have ye a need to find some stability? To start a family?"

No words were more sobering and not for the reasons one might think. "I've a need to protect the wee Bruce from an uncertain future. I've trained my whole life for it. Is that not enough?"

Colin leaned forward, his eyes searching Niall's. "But what of ye and yer desires beyond that? If ye knew right now that everything was well and Robert the Bruce was saved from all harm, what then?"

Niall no longer chugged but sipped at his whisky as he eyed the fire. What would he do with his life if not for the only goal he had lived for? Saving the Bruce. His cousins all had the same goal, but they also had a clan to lead. Him? Nothing but endless lasses, drink and training to be the best warrior Scotland ever produced.

"What do ye want for yerself once yer free of obligations?" Colin said softly.

The sad thing? He had no idea. But he *did* know some things. Important things. The sort he would die for again and again. "To support my cousins and the clans that are mine. The MacLomains, MacLeods, and Hamiltons. To keep protecting ye and those that matter most to me."

"'Tis good this," Colin murmured. "Admirable." His eyes stayed on Niall. "But not enough because they dinnae involve ye seeking a life outside of protecting, outside of all yer honor."

"I couldnae ever stop protecting and my honor is all I have." Niall set aside his drink. "My honor reminds me of who I am."

"Aye, but yer honor also blinds ye." Colin leaned over and clasped his shoulder. "Someday ye'll have to realize that ye've given yer life to everyone else and mayhap 'tis time to take a wee bit for yerself, aye? 'Tis what yer Da wants most for ye."

Niall crossed his arms over his chest. "My Da doesnae care either way."

"Malcolm cares a great deal but is letting ye find yer way."

"Nay, my Da had hoped I might take over the MacLomains instead of Logan." Niall banked old memories. "There was no pride in his eyes when I said I had no desire. That I thought Logan was the right choice."

"Mayhap 'twas because yer Da saw something in ye that even ye dinnae see," Colin murmured.

A wry, half smile came to Niall's lips as he continued to eye the fire. A smile he was long used to wearing. "My Da only ever saw what he wanted me to be, not who I actually am."

"Now see, that's where I think yer wrong," Seònaid said softly as she wrapped her arms around his shoulders from behind and whispered in his ear, "How many times do I have to tell ye, brother, that yer the noblest man I've met and more people see it than ye know."

Niall pulled her around and onto his lap. A much-needed smile came to his lips. They might not be true siblings but she had always been like a blood sister. "And ye've my heart for that, lass." He grinned and tucked her against his chest. "What tears ye away from yer fun to be with we morbid folk?"

"You. Her." Seònaid picked up his mug and sipped. "And Rònan. He's being a regular beastie. When are ye going to put a stop to it?"

When he heard a loud yelp come from behind that could only be Nicole and a roar that could only be Rònan, he kissed the top of Seònaid's head and murmured, "Who am I to deny people fun when there's fun to be had?"

"They're both drunk," she muttered.

"But having fun, aye?"

"Mayhap 'tis time to take a little fun for yerself," Colin said before he stood, kissed them both on their cheek then scanned the hall. "I'm off to find my love."

Niall had no chance to respond before the MacLeod left.

"My parents are too damn lusty even in their old age," Seònaid said, but there was love and approval in her voice.

Niall chuckled. "Yer parents are the youngest people I've ever met even in their fiftieth decade."

"'Tis because they never stop lusting." She pulled back enough to meet his eyes. "But then neither do yours, aye?"

"Och, nay." Niall shook his head when she offered him more whisky. He needed to sober up so he could keep an eye on Nicole. "My parents err on the side of embarrassment they're still so lusty."

Seònaid smiled at him. "Might we be so lucky when we find true love."

"Nay," he admonished. "Love like that is for those who already fought and won their battles."

"Then what of Logan and his lass from the future?" Her eyes met his. "Have they not found love despite the battles that still lay ahead for us?"

Niall shrugged. "Aye, so it seems but Logan's strong and will remain so even if weakened by emotion."

"Weakened by emotion?" Seònaid crawled off his lap and scowled at him. "Yer getting too bloody unfeeling for my taste, Cousin."

Niall caught her hand before she could go too far. Seònaid was his rock. That could never change. "I'm happy that Logan found love. Truly." He inhaled deeply as he met her eyes, never more serious. "Just dinnae expect the same of me, aye?"

She cupped his cheek, voice soft. "I dinnae expect anything from ye, brother, other than that ye'll protect yer own." Then she cupped his other cheek. "But ye need to realize that ye need protecting as much as any other."

Before he could respond, she placed a hand over his heart and continued. "And that might just mean letting go of this for a wee bit, aye?"

"I'll never let go of my need to protect, my vow," he ground out. "Once made it doesnae falter."

"I meant yer heart, lad," she whispered. "Not yer honor."

"Are they not the same?"

"Some might think so." She shook her head and pulled away. "In the end, they've nothing to do with the other."

"But they do."

"But they dinnae." Seònaid took a long swig of whisky, wiped her hand across her mouth delicately and gave Niall a firm look. "Go play, Niall. Ye deserve it more now than ever. Who knows what the morrow will bring."

He nodded once. She nodded once as well, then sauntered off into a slew of men waiting patiently.

"Oh no you *didn't*," Nicole cried from behind him.

When Niall turned, it was to Rònan tossing three skins of whisky in the air. Two of which were caught by adoring women. The third he caught, snarling as he went after Nicole. Everyone whooped as his cousin chased her toward the stairs.

Laughing, she turned and held one firm hand in the air, stumbling to the side as she hiccupped. His cousin stopped short. Like everyone else in her vicinity, she held Rònan captive with the tilt of her hip and the slow lick of her tongue over her lower lip. When Nicole seemed satisfied that she had everybody's attention, she pointed at Rònan and declared, "He thinks he's gonna screw me."

She spanned a pointed finger over the crowd, an unfortunate, loopy look on her face. "Who else is so bold?" Hiccup. "Brazon." Hiccup. "And might I say *fucked* in the head?"

Niall almost picked up his drink again. Almost. If for no other reason than to toast her making a fool of herself.

But he did not.

Mostly because far too many MacLeod men were appreciating her and Rònan was in no condition to protect her because he was equally drunk. So now he watched both carefully not because he was jealous but because he would be damned if anyone hurt them. Not with brawn. Never that. But maybe with words.

So Niall sighed and stood.

"Oh, loooook!" Nicole cried, swinging her faltering finger in his direction. "I see movement."

"As do I, my lass." Rònan, teetering, grabbed a sword off the wall and held it high. "I will defend ye, my fair...fair..." He glanced at Nicole and cracked a grin. "My fair what?"

"Lady, I think," she mouthed, leaning against the wall at the bottom of the stairs.

So now there was a choice to be made. Well, not really a choice at all. He needed to salvage Rònan's dignity as he had just become laird. The only way to do that was to take the attention off his cousin by making a fool out of himself. With luck, that would spare Rònan any potential embarrassment. So Niall bit back his aggravation, grabbed a sword off the wall and pursued Nicole, crying like a madman. "He'll not have ye, lass."

Baffled but apparently not willing to test Niall, she flew up the stairs. If that's what you wanted to call it. More like stumbled and tripped a few times. Rònan tried to pursue but was soon swamped by women. And there was nothing quite as distracting to the MacLeod when in his cups.

"See her to her chamber then, Cousin," Rònan declared. "I will join her shortly."

Nicole spun and contemplated Rònan. "Hmm. Not so sure about that."

"I will," Rònan blustered, a woman now tucked under each arm. "My fair...fair..."

"Lady," Nicole declared with approval then started to teeter.

Niall tossed his blade to Colin and scooped her up before she went over.

"Oh, put me *down*," she complained. "I can walk on my own."

Deciding it was pointless to incite her right now, he ignored both her and the hoots and hollers from the hall...at first.

"No need for the Broun Pincher to take down the MacLomain this time," someone cried.

"Nay, she'll spread her legs willingly enough this go round," another cried.

Niall didn't hesitate, but grabbed a dagger off the wall, turned and whipped it. He could have killed the man but chose not to. Instead, he made sure it whistled close enough to his neck that it pinned his hair to the wall.

There was no need to speak loudly when he addressed the crowd. All had gone silent not only because of the blade but because of the deadly look in Niall's eyes when he scanned the room.

"Ye best be careful what slides off yer tongue when it comes to this lass," he warned. "Ye ken?"

Most nodded. Many yelled, "Aye."

Thankfully, Nicole gave him no fight as he strode up the stairs. The only words she mumbled against his chest were, "I know how to take care of myself. Born and raised in Southie. Not always an easy place."

Niall bypassed her chamber and brought her to his. Even with his threat to the MacLeods, they were rowdy and she was far too vulnerable. By the time he laid her down on his bed, her eyes were closed.

He covered her and was about to pull away when she grabbed his wrist and whispered, "Don't go, Niall. I'm scared."

Chapter Four

NICOLE CRACKED OPEN an eye and groaned. "Oh, crap. Did we *really?*"

It was daylight and she was in Niall's bed. As far as she could tell they were both nude. Of all the men she could have slept with. *Niall? Seriously?* Not only that but it appeared she decided to cuddle with him afterward. She was about to peel her cheek off his shoulder when he lifted something from the side table and handed her a mug. Eyes still closed, he mumbled, "Drink some water. You'll need it."

She *was* thirsty. "I don't get hangovers," she grumbled before taking a deep swallow. "Not that I would know as a general rule because I don't usually drink that much."

"Twice I've met you and both times you've been drunk," he mentioned, taking her cup when she plunked her head back down. She might dislike the guy but he was pretty comfortable and she wasn't feeling all that energized. Not enough to roll away from him that is.

"You try being thrust back in time and learning that wizards and dragon-shifters exist. See how drunk you might get...twice." She closed her eyes, deciding the room was a little too bright. "No matter what, it doesn't say much for you that you took advantage of me in that condition."

"The way I remember it you took advantage of me," he grunted.

"Oh, hell, so we really did." She shifted her legs. "Hmm."

"Hmm what?"

Nicole didn't answer but inhaled, caught by the spicy scent of him. In fact, the more she became aware of his body, the more her senses were kicking in. The steady thrum of his strong heart. The hardness of his muscular body. Then, naturally, images of the way he looked last night flashed in her mind. *Heck*, was he built...in

55

more ways than one. So telling him she figured she would at least feel some remnants of having had sex would feed his ego. And that was *not* an option.

"Nicole?" he said.

"What?"

"You'll want to stop doing that with your knee."

She froze, realizing she had been rubbing it across his groin. A groin that evidently was more than willing to pick up where they left off. Wherever that was. God, how could she totally forget sleeping with him?

"Sorry," she muttered and decided she had better get up.

As it turned out, she wasn't nude but wearing panties. Odd. "Why do I have these on?"

"You would have had the bra on still too, but I didnae see the point," he said. "I dinnae ken the need for such a thing. It looks bloody uncomfortable."

Grabbing the first thing she could find while still sitting, Nicole pulled on his tunic. She glanced over her shoulder at him. "So you screwed me with my panties on?"

Sure, it could be done but had they been in *that* much of a rush? Then again, with their dislike of one another they might have been. Slake the lust and get it over with.

Instead of answering her, he folded his arms beneath his head and studied her. "What's Southie?"

Southie? Ugh, what the hell had she said last night? "You mean *where*." She yawned and padded over to the table where she plunked down and bit into some bread. "South Boston. Why?"

Niall kept eying her, expression neutral. "I was just curious what sort of place bred a lass like you."

She snorted and shook her head. "It's a great place. Home."

"Lots of Irish immigrants," he remarked.

"Sure, I guess." She poured herself more water. "I'm Irish on both sides."

"Both sides?"

"Mom and Dad."

"Ah." He sat up and stretched, his muscles flexing in all sorts of delicious ways. "I never would've guessed."

"Don't be a smartass." She cursed under her breath when she could not pull her eyes from him. It wasn't just his body but his face.

Those full, sensual lips. Those eyes that almost seemed to fluctuate between blue and black. When he got out of bed, her eyes fell to the firm globes of his tight ass. Oh, have mercy. She wanted to squeeze those…

He chuckled and laid the brogue on thick as he grabbed the mug and headed around the bed. "Ye just cannae keep yer eyes off it, aye, lass?"

Nicole didn't let her gaze fall because she knew what she would see if she did. More than that, she knew how much he would enjoy it. "Get over yourself, Brute."

Entirely too comfortable in his own skin, he remained nude and grabbed a piece of bread, winking at her. "I think I like you in my clothes, *Ungrateful*. It puts…"

His lips kept moving, but an all-too-familiar buzzing sound drowned him out. Like it was with Darach, she had trouble following him. And just like his cousin had, Niall seemed to sense something was wrong because his brows lowered and he stopped talking.

Nicole tore her eyes from his lips and focused on downing her water. Anything to keep him from seeing an ounce of fear. Just like last time, whispers started to echo around her. This time, however, it filtered down to one.

A child.

"I can hear them," he whispered. It was definitely a boy and he sounded frightened. *"They willnae leave me be."*

"I can hear them too," she whispered back as she stood.

Niall was right there beside her with his hand on her elbow. She didn't look at him. Instead, she scanned the room for the boy though she knew deep down he wasn't here.

"Where are you?" she whispered.

Nicole sensed the child's hesitation so she said, "I'm your friend."

"As are we all," screeched too many voices.

Covering her ears against the pain, Nicole tried to slide to her knees but Niall swung her up into his arms and sat on the bed. The pain was familiar. Like the earaches she'd gotten when she was younger only a thousand times worse.

While some might cower, she wasn't that sort. No, she screamed at the top of her lungs, "Get out of our heads. Leave the boy alone."

A sharp pain pierced her head then all the voices vanished. The buzzing faded to be replaced with the sound of a gentle wind blowing through the windows and the crackling fire. It was always disconcerting hearing the world again. This time more so.

Not helping any, the door burst open and several people rushed into the room. Colin MacLeod and Rònan had swords drawn. Seònaid and Torra appeared to be chanting in a foreign language.

"Shh, quiet," Niall said to the others as he cupped her head against his chest. "All is well enough."

Though she was tempted to pull away, the comforting thud of his heart was too soothing to resist. Rònan sat beside them and tilted his head until his concerned eyes met hers.

"Are you sure you're well, lass?" he whispered.

"Yeah," she whispered back as the pounding in her head faded. Maybe there was a little bit left but she guessed that had more to do with the hangover she wouldn't admit to.

Rònan squeezed her hand, a flash of anger in his eyes as he continued to whisper. "When you're ready tell me whose bloody arse I need to kick even if 'tis my cousin's, aye?"

"Not your cousin's," she assured softly as she lifted her head. "He's been all right."

She got the sense Rònan wanted to crack a joke but refrained as Seònaid gave her a mug and urged her to drink.

"Thanks," she murmured and took a sip. She flinched and handed it back when she realized it was whisky. "I'm all set with this for now."

"'Twas just to calm your nerves," Seònaid said as she sat beside Niall on the other side. "When you're ready, we need to know what happened."

Torra and Colin stood in front of the fire, their eyes assessing but kind.

Nicole became a little too aware of what she was wearing. Better yet, what Niall was *not* wearing. Clothing.

Speaking to the room in general, she said, "Mind if I get changed first?"

"Nay, of course not," Torra said, shooing everyone out. Rònan tried to stay but she shot him a stern look and though he towered over her, he trailed after his mother.

When Nicole tried to stand, Niall stopped her. Honestly, she was surprised by the concern in his eyes when he said, "Are you truly well, lass?"

Though tempted to tell him that she had been better, it wasn't her style to lean on anybody outside her close network of friends. And even then, she held back. So she pulled away. "Yeah, I'm good. No worries."

Nicole put on her bra before pulling off his tunic. For a split second, she was tempted to keep it on. To remain embraced by the odd sense of comfort it gave her. But wouldn't he just love that. By the time she got dressed, he was fully clothed and looking out the window.

"Tell me what happened before they come back in," he murmured.

"Why?" Nicole gulped down the rest of her water. "We might've slept together, but that doesn't make us a thing, Niall." She shook her head. "So, no."

"I only asked so that you didnae feel overwhelmed." His jaw clenched and his eyes turned her way. "Nothing more."

"I don't get overwhelmed so lose the soft eyes." While she meant to head for the door, instead she leaned against another windowsill and stared out over the loch. "Cassie told you about my issue, didn't she?"

"Issue?"

"Don't play dumb." She kept her eyes glued to the water. "My *issue*."

Niall sighed. "Aye, I know of your *issue*, Nicole."

She just *knew* her friend had blabbed. Damn it. Her eyes shot to him. "So, what, you can't even say the words, *going deaf?*"

Niall leaned sideways against the windowsill and crossed his arms over his chest. "I can but 'tis clearly not easy for you."

Taken aback, her eyes widened. "I'm pretty sure I just said them."

"And I'm pretty sure it wasn't easy."

If nothing else, the guy was a straight shooter. Regardless, she hadn't brought it up so he could revel in thinking he had her all figured out. So she blew him off.

"Why do I bother trying to talk to you," she muttered and headed for the door.

By the time everyone had clustered back into the room and she told them what had happened, Niall was lounging on the bed. He almost acted as if he didn't care. She must have been beyond wasted to spread her legs for that one. Shame on her. Times ten. No, times a thousand.

"It must have been the wee Bruce," Rònan said to his parents.

"Aye." Torra's eyes met her husband's. "Grant has kept in constant contact. All is well at MacLomain Castle."

"Aye." But Colin seemed wary. "I still dinnae ken why the wee lad was sent away from the Mother Oak to begin with. Isn't he safer there? Where Fionn Mac Cumhail's power is the strongest, or is the Celtic god not the one best equipped to fight the *Genii Cucullati?* Better yet, their allies, Brae Stewart and her demi-god chieftain?"

"There is so much that Grant and I dinnae ken right now that we thought it best to keep those who need protecting divided and under our care." Torra's eyes went to Nicole. "I think, mayhap, our plans have changed."

While tempted to brace her forehead in her hands, Nicole kept them in her lap versus crossed over her chest in defense. There was no way she'd shy away from anyone who needed to see strength in her eyes. She wasn't a kid from the underbelly of Southie anymore, but a woman who could handle anything life threw her way. A woman who never once withheld her opinion. "I want to be wherever Robert is. He needs me."

"That's all well and good but not if it means—"

Her eyes shot to Niall. "Was I talking to you?"

"Aye, ye bloody well—"

"Enough," Torra said sharply. "We'll be rallying as many warriors as we can spare and heading for the MacLomains."

"Is that not dangerous? 'Tis across the country," Seònaid started but stopped short when her mother narrowed her eyes. "Aye then. 'Tis a good plan indeed."

When Torra crouched in front of Nicole and took her hands, she sat up a little straighter. Torra's eyes were level and her voice calm. "I sense great strength in you, lass. Never fight it. Always embrace it." She cupped her cheek. "Aye?"

"You bet." Nicole nodded. "I got this."

Torra looked at her long and hard, searching, before she nodded and stood. "All right then. I will see you provisioned. Be in the great hall soon." She stopped before she reached the door and looked over her shoulder. "Do you know how to ride your horse, then?"

She could lie to the woman but knew better. "I'm getting there."

Torra eyed her for another long moment then nodded. "Good."

Then she and Colin left.

What had she gotten herself into? Probably more than she could handle. But it would not be the first time. Ripping off another piece of bread, she scowled at the other three who seemed to be eying her carefully. Wait, make that two of them.

Niall was asleep.

Rònan sat across from Nicole as Seònaid sat on the bed.

Nicole nodded at Niall. "He's a piece of work, eh?"

Seònaid smiled at the brute. "He is who he is and we love him for it."

That statement sent chills up her spine. Had Cassie not said the same thing about Nicole recently?

"Though he's given you to me, he still took good care of you last night, lass," Rònan mentioned, pouring himself not water but whisky. "You should be grateful."

"Huh?" Nicole narrowed her eyes. "He's *given* me to you?"

"Aye, he said I could have you." Rònan took a swig then grabbed some bread as he winked. "And have you, I will."

"Keep dreaming, biker wannabee," she scoffed. "How do you figure he took care of me last night? The way I see it, he took advantage."

Seònaid's brows arched. "Niall made himself look the fool to cover for ye bunch of drunkards."

"Och, nay. We were just having fun." Rònan waved away Seònaid's words and cocked a grin at Nicole. "What is a biker wannabee?"

Nicole rubbed her forehead and muttered. "All the tats and bits of leather that seem to be part of your plaid."

"Tats?"

"Your dragon markings," Seònaid explained. "In her day and age, bikers or men who ride motorcycles, tend to have more of them than most."

"Dragon markings?" Rònan said. "Really?"

"*Tattoos* not dragon markings." Nicole shook her head. "Never mind."

"I like you, Nicole," Seònaid said bluntly, her brogue thickening with passion as she brushed hair away from Niall's face. "But ye should know that the MacLomain saved ye from making a fool out of yerself. More than ye already were, that is."

Nicole frowned. "What are you talking about?"

"Do ye not recall screaming like a banshee that all the men meant to have ye?" Seònaid shrugged and shot her a live-with-your-own-behavior look. "Do ye not remember being so much in yer cups ye could barely stand?"

Nicole flinched as faint memories started to surface. Her and Rònan pouring whisky into each other's mouths. Her dancing on a table blowing kisses to the crowd. Rònan and her grinding with possibly another guy behind her.

Her eyes met Rònan's. "Oh, *shit*. Did I peek under your plaid?"

He offered a wide smile. "'Twas great fun, aye?"

"Oh, *no*." She held her head and groaned. "I'm such an ass."

"'Tis a verra nice arse," Rònan said.

She sat back, eyes wide. "Tell me I didn't moon the crowd. I used to do this thing back in the day—"

"You showed nothing," Seònaid cut in before Rònan could respond. "Mainly because Niall saved you."

"He saved her all right," Rònan grunted. "For his cock that is."

Now it was her turn to say, "Enough." Shaking her head, she pounded down more water, almost wishing it was something stronger. "Obviously I got a little out of control. It won't happen again."

"That would be a bloody shame." Rònan winked and nodded at the bed. "But mayhap ye'll give me a go next time, aye?"

Nicole shook her head. "No more go's for anyone."

Seònaid leaned over and whispered something in Niall's ear. As though he had been shaken, his eyes shot open.

"Sorry to use a spell on ye, lad," she said softly. "But 'tis time for us to journey."

He sat up and did one of those stretches that had a way of magnetizing her eyes.

"What did I miss?" he said.

"Nothing overly important," Seònaid assured then handed Nicole some clothes. "Change into these. They're easier to travel in."

"Will do," Nicole said. When Seònaid left and the men still lingered, she shook her head. "A little privacy please."

Rònan chuckled as he sauntered out. "*Now* she wants privacy."

"Be quick about it, lass," Niall muttered. "We travel soon."

"Sure thing, Brute."

After he left, she *almost* felt bad for calling him that. Kind of. Why had he slept with her after he'd saved her from embarrassing herself even more? He knew she was drunk. It made no sense. Or did it? Maybe he was getting back at her because he was forced to behave like a fool. Yet that didn't feel quite right.

She searched her memory as she pulled on pants and a shirt. Flashes of anything. All she could remember was comfort…safety…lack of judgment. No sex. But that couldn't be the case. This was Niall, after all. He would be the first to judge her no matter how much he might have seemed like a hero. And he would certainly be the first to have a go at her if she was willing. Right? Because all bullshit aside, he was hot and that would have worked for her in a drunken stupor.

She scowled. That didn't say much for her did it?

Hell.

One thing was for sure, she needed to lose any worries or self-doubt because there was a little boy out there who needed her help. A little boy who could hear the monsters in her head. A boy who had the same monsters in his head. So she stood up straighter and did what she always did, met the world with a brave face.

Just like last night, Niall waited patiently outside the door.

"Let's go," she said.

He made a loose gesture, a mild look of exasperation on his face. "After you."

That's right. Every time. But she kept that thought to herself.

For now.

"Aren't you gonna throw on pants?" she said as they headed for the great hall.

"Nay, I rarely wear trousers."

"Why not?"

He shrugged. "They're uncomfortable."

"Uh huh, so it's better to wear a blanket around your waist." She frowned. "Even on a horse?"

"Aye."

Though he said nothing after that, she got the sense he wanted to. So as they walked down the stairs, she glanced at him. "I'll probably regret asking, but what's on your mind, Niall?"

"Do you really want to know?"

"I wouldn't have asked otherwise."

"I doubt that."

"Why?"

"Because I think mayhap you dinnae care either way." His eyes turned to hers. "I think you hope I'll say something that will incite you to once more grow angry with me so that you dinnae have to focus on all that lies ahead."

"Damn." She chuckled, alarmed by how well he already had her figured out. But heck if she would hand it to him that easily. So she played with him. "Guess you have me pegged. Or at least you think you do."

"I know I do," he said when they reached the bottom step.

"Do ya now." She planted her fists on her hips and eyed him. "Then what do you suppose is on my mind right now?"

He leaned down until their noses were inches apart. "I would imagine why you cannae for the life of you remember how good I made you feel last night. Especially when you'll likely hear about the cries of pleasure that came from my chamber."

She narrowed her eyes.

He narrowed his.

"Well, I don't remember a thing," she said. "I'd say that works against you."

"Och, nay. 'Twas in my favor," he growled then had the nerve to wink before he turned away, muttering under his breath, "Such as ye were."

"Brute."

"Ungrateful," he tossed back.

Damn man. Medieval neanderthal. One she couldn't even remember kissing for the first time...because they surely kissed. What had it felt like? No flashes came to mind so not that great she supposed. Regardless, she had a thing about first kisses. They were important.

Really important.

"Come, your horse Vika is waiting for you."

Nicole nodded at Seònaid when she came alongside. "Cool."

The MacLeod woman wrapped elbows and led her through the crowd.

"I'm getting a lot of looks," Nicole said, determined not to be embarrassed.

Seònaid perked a brow at her. "Do you really care?"

"No." But she did. More than she thought she would. "I lived a little last night. Simple as that."

"Aye, I well ken living a little."

"You do?"

"Aye, lass." Seònaid grinned as they made their way down the stairs into the courtyard. "And I'm sure, like you, I've learned something over the years."

"What's that?"

"If I earned the looks, I earned them. If I didnae, I didnae. We must all accept responsibility for our actions."

Nicole wasn't good at well-disguised criticism, but she was in no mood to battle it out. Besides, she really did like Seònaid.

When they entered the stables and she saw Vika poke her head over a stall, Nicole headed her way. Touching the horse again felt like going home. Not to one she necessarily wanted to go to but another entirely. "Hey there, sweetie."

According to Darach, Cassie had been able to speak to her horse telepathically. Nicole wondered if the same thing would happen between her and Vika. She tried not to scowl as she recalled what else he had said. Apparently, wizards could hear her thoughts too. She hoped the heck not, mainly because of Niall. She didn't need that guy inside her head.

Nicole glanced at Seònaid. "Can you and your cousins read my thoughts?"

"On occasion," Seònaid said as she nodded at a stable boy then a horse further down. "If your thoughts are especially strong."

"Super." Nicole sighed. "I'm pretty sure most of mine are."

"Nay." Seònaid shook her head. "Yours are remarkably repressed compared to others."

"Really?"

"Aye." Seònaid asked another stable boy to ready Vika as they headed back out. "But then I tend to think most of what you're thinking comes out of your mouth."

Nicole chuckled. "Isn't that the truth."

"I assume Darach told you about wizards hearing random thoughts then." Seònaid eyed Nicole. "Did he tell you what to expect from a MacLomain wizard who lies with his Broun lass?"

"Nope. Not that I'm Niall's intended woman anyway." Wary, Nicole frowned at Seònaid. "Care to share?"

"You will develop a much stronger mental connection and be able to speak within the mind."

Nicole shook her head. "About the last place I need to be is inside Niall's head."

"Have you sensed his thoughts yet?" Seònaid wore a pensive look. "'Twould be obvious."

"How so?"

"They would be, how to say this, considerably different than yours. It's almost an erotic sensation I'm told." A little smirk crawled onto her face. "And I imagine Niall's thoughts would hold more intensity."

"Sexual intensity?"

"Nay." Seònaid chuckled. "Of another sort I think."

"Ah, you mean his thoughts would be more fired up."

"Fired up?"

"Angry," Nicole enlightened. "Definitely exasperated and maybe even fed up when it comes to me."

Seònaid gave no response but kept a smile in place and shrugged.

"Well, all of that applies to what he actually *says* to me so I doubt I'd know the difference telepathically," Nicole said.

"You would know." Seònaid wore that pensive look again, but she said nothing more as they entered a building full of weapons.

"Oh, *nice.*" Nicole eyed everything with wonder. "Look at all of this."

She had only taken a few steps in when Niall appeared at the door. "I will help you choose a weapon, Nicole."

"Just one?" She frowned at him then looked at Seònaid, who was already heading for another room. "And I'm sure your cousin can help me just as easily."

"Nay, Seònaid is not so much a warrior as she is a shaman of sorts."

"A shaman?"

"A wise one." He started pulling several daggers off a wall. "She has a knack for seeing inside the hearts of men and steering them in the right direction."

"So she's sort of a therapist?" Nicole asked when Seònaid vanished altogether.

"Something like that but with magic attached," he said. "She never needed schooling to do what she does. It comes naturally."

Nicole took the dagger Niall handed her. "I'd like something bigger."

His lip hitched up. "You already had something bigger, lass."

"Shut it." She rolled her eyes at his innuendo and reached for another dagger.

Niall grabbed her wrist, shook his head then nodded at the dagger she already held. "That one suits your size." He grabbed another more compact blade and placed it in her other hand. "And this one."

"I'm not that small," she shot and eyed both weapons with disappointment.

"I'm surprised," he said as he strode to another wall and chose an impressive sword with black leather wrapped around its base.

She tested the weight of the daggers. "Surprised by what?"

His eyes ran the length of her. "That you don't realize how lethal wee things can be."

She couldn't stop a grin. "Did you just compliment me, Brute?"

"If I had 'twould likely be a waste of my time, aye, Ungrateful?"

Nicole eyed him, shocked that she suddenly felt thankful for all his help. Despite how true it might be, she still found the emotion out of context. "Are you inside my head, Niall?"

"Och, 'twould be a bloody dangerous place to be," he muttered as he strode into the other room.

Nicole grabbed a small blade and tucked it in her boot. She cocked her head as she followed him. "Seònaid filled me in on the whole telepathic thing that happens after sex."

"Did she?" Niall kept his eyes averted as he pulled down more weapons. An arsenal really. "Then aye, I can hear your thoughts, lass."

He wasn't being entirely truthful. "Just so you know, I can smell bullshit from a mile away."

Niall strapped on a few weapons, crossed his arms over his chest and faced her. "You dinnae want me in your head so what makes you think I'd be there any more than necessary?"

"I'm still not sure I believe you've even been in my head." She narrowed her eyes. "Tell me exactly what I'm thinking right now."

"We're back to that then?"

"We're back to that."

"Fine." The corner of his lip curled up and he tapped the side of the blade poking over his shoulder. "Besides wishing you could have my sword for yourself…" He glanced down at his plaid. "You're wishing you could remember taking advantage of my other sword." His brow slowly crept up as his eyes rose to hers. "But more than that, you want to remember our first kiss."

Oh, God, he *could* read her thoughts. Bad. Really bad. But she wasn't about to show her discontent.

She shook her head. "Did you just refer to your dick as a sword?"

"Was it not long and hard and—"

"Battle-worthy and memorable?" she interrupted and snorted. "Evidently not."

"'Twas a hell of a battle to be sure," he remarked. "You've a bit o' wildness in you."

Well, *that* sounded about right. "Don't you forget it."

Niall eyed her for a long moment, contemplating something before he set aside his sword and nodded at her daggers. "Show me what Darach taught you and it best be better than your display on the stairs yesterday."

"I was just messing around then." She set one aside then spun fast and low, remaining on the balls of her feet as she thrust at his side. But he moved faster and before she could shift away, he swiped her legs out from beneath her. She ignored the air being knocked out of her lungs and rolled. When he grabbed her ankle, she turned sideways and kicked but not before she slid the dagger out of her boot.

He blocked her foot then dragged her backward, belly down, so quickly she was caught off guard. In a flash, he was on her with both wrists pinned above her head. He squeezed her wrist so tightly she dropped the blade. Although she was getting the hang of anticipating her opponent's moves, she had a long way to go.

"Hell," she mumbled, cheek against the dirt as she panted. Though disappointed in herself, she was all too aware of the feel of him. While he kept most of his weight off of her, he covered her enough that she wasn't going anywhere.

Unless...

There was one weapon she had yet to use. Acting as though she was trying to escape, she pressed her backside up and wiggled it a bit as though struggling.

His breathing switched and his lips came close to her ear. "I know what you're trying to do, lass."

"And I'd say it's working," she murmured, not letting up.

The only problem? Her plan was backfiring. While she might be arousing him, a dull ache had blossomed between her thighs. *Damn.* She seriously didn't want to be turned on by this guy. Yet her heart was hammering and the ache was increasing.

"Ye best be careful about this method when a man has ye pinned." His brogue had thickened right along with something else. "Now how do ye intend to get out of this without being taken against yer will?"

His hot breath fanned down her neck and a shiver rippled through her. "You might be a lot of things, Brute, but a rapist isn't one of them."

"It doesnae matter." He ground against her and she almost groaned. "What matters is the next lad that catches ye in this position. So what is yer next move, Nicole?"

"So no more of the nickname, Ungrateful?"

"Not right now." He pressed down again and the ache became throbs. "Not when I'm feeling *verra* grateful with the way yer moving yer arse."

"I can tell," she murmured, trying to buy time while she came up with a plan. About the only thing her body wanted to do was welcome him. "Stop that."

"Stop what?" he said innocently, his voice a deep rumble against her back as he nibbled at the tender area beneath her ear.

"You're not fighting fair," she accused, trying to think clearly.

"Battling is never about being fair," he said softly and she swore the nibbles turned to soft kisses. "'Tis about winning, dying." His teeth gently clenched her earlobe before he pressed his hips down again and whispered, "Or surrendering."

"There'll be no surrendering to you," she said. Or at least tried. Nothing really came out but a few gasps and a low, unstoppable moan.

"Show me how ye intend to get away." His lips were close to hers. Too close. "Or are ye defeated already?"

Defeated? Heck no. She didn't speak that language. So she cleared her mind and acted fast.

She turned her head as far as she could manage and brushed her lips against his. As she had hoped, he jolted and she flipped. *Don't think, just do*, she preached to herself. Grabbing the back of his head with one hand, she pulled his lips down to hers.

Don't think, just do.

But it was damn difficult as she became far too aware of how perfectly their mouths fit together. How warm, soft yet hard and demanding his kiss suddenly turned. He kissed differently than other guys. Skilled in a whole new way. He varied the pressure of his lips. Gentle and seeking yet confident and persistent.

Don't think, just do.

All she could *think* about were his lips and how tempting it would be to open her mouth and let him in. What was it she was supposed to *do* again?

Win. You're supposed to win.

Right. Now or never, Nicole. So she grabbed a dagger from the pouch attached to his back and held it to the side of his neck.

Niall stilled. His lusty eyes met hers.

"Gotcha," she whispered, struggling for breath.

"Aye, lass. Ye got me," he whispered back before he wrapped his hand into her hair and closed his lips over hers again.

Still holding a shaky blade to his neck, her mouth melted beneath his. Her lips fell apart. She might have a dagger to his throat but when his tongue met hers, she realized he had won this battle by a longshot. He was hungry and she was starved. There was no better way to describe the deep abyss of need she sunk into. Everything but the feel of his tongue and lips fell away. She had no idea if she even held the blade anymore.

So much. Too much. He tasted like liquid fire.

Sinful. Dark. Bright. Sweet. Illicit.

Blood roared in her ears.

Or at least she thought it did.

Suddenly, Niall tore away and ran to the window. Trying to catch her breath, she flew after him and peered out. A beautiful dragon with white, gold, silver and copper scales launched into the air and released another loud roar. Torra MacLeod?

Rònan strode in. There was a look of both fury and anticipation in his eyes as he yanked a blade off of the wall. "Time to fight. Brae Stewart has arrived."

Chapter Five

NOTHING WITHERED A cock faster than war. Or so Niall thought.

As it turned out, he had to cast a spell to lose his erection as he pulled Nicole after him. Warriors already raced out beyond the drawbridge, trying to draw the enemy after them. Rònan had shifted and launched into the air after his mother. Now the dragons reined fire down on an army that was better protected by magic.

If there was one thing he enjoyed above all else, it was battling. Yet this time there was a twinge of discontent accompanying the usual rush. The pure rage he felt streaming off his nemesis had but one goal.

Nicole.

Vika's words entered his mind. *"Ye both need to ride me, lad. 'Tis the only way."*

"Nay, 'tis too much weight," he responded.

Black shadows streaked across the sky as more enemy warriors flooded out of the forest.

Vika broke from the crowd and stopped in front of them. *"'Twill not be for that long. Now!"*

"What's going on with Vika?" Nicole tried to calm the horse as she flung her head and neighed wildly.

He had to give Nicole credit. Most if not all lasses from the twenty-first century would be in hysterics by now. Not worried about a horse. "She wants us to ride her."

"Both of us?"

Vika released a mighty neigh and stomped her foot in response.

"Aye. Both of us." Niall plunked Nicole on Vika then swung up behind her. The horse was large for a female, but this was too much weight.

Bloody hell, the enemy had already infiltrated the courtyard.

"Lean down and hold onto her mane," he growled as Vika bolted and warriors rushed at them. Niall swung his blade and downed one coming in from the right as he whipped a dagger at one coming in from the left.

Vika had more strength than he expected and flew over the drawbridge. All the while, Nicole held on and Niall battled. One of his daggers caught a warrior in the throat while his sword lopped off the hand of another.

In the meantime, Torra had landed in the midst of the warriors beyond the outer portcullis while Rònan swooped and used his wings to bat aside handfuls of men. Their fire might be useless, but the sheer power of their bodies seemed effective.

Cries of pain rent the air and blood slicked the ground as Vika left the drawbridge behind and flew toward the forest. At least at first. Niall was fighting off so many now that it took a few moments before he realized Vika had turned toward the ocean. Now the dragons were in the air, twisting and chasing the dark shadows. The *Genii Cucullati.*

"Niall," Nicole cried in warning. "Who the hell is that?"

His eyes locked on the raven haired beauty standing at the cliff's edge.

Brae Stewart.

Brae's voice entered his mind. *"Aye, that's a good lad. Bring her right to me, Niall."*

"Vika," he said. *"What are ye doing, beastie?"*

The horse ignored him and kept barreling toward the Stewart lass. At least now they were beyond the enemy warriors.

"This can't be good," Nicole said, but there was a much-welcomed calmness to her voice. "That chick is seriously creepy."

"'Tis Brae Stewart, lass." Niall wrapped his arm around her waist and leaned close. "Ye keep tight to Vika's mane and yer thighs clamped, aye?"

"Hell yeah," she murmured and followed his instructions.

"Summon the sea, lad," Vika whispered. *"Pull her to ye like ye never have before."*

"I willnae harm the MacLeods," he replied.

"Do it now," the horse roared. *"Torra can protect her own."*

The horse would not sway from her course and his magic wasn't nearly as strong as Brae's. But did he dare do as the horse requested? Summoning the sea was always risky.

"Think of the wee Bruce and think of Nicole," the horse said. *"Now!"*

He had spent his life working toward protecting Robert...then there was Nicole. "Bloody hell." He held her more securely and murmured, *"Superum mare obtinent et omnia quae sunt, educ nos virtutem.* Gods of sea and all that be, bring forth your power and set us free."

Focusing everything he had into the element of water, Niall flung an arm out. A white film fell over his vision and all became a blur as the ocean roared and inundated. Long funnels of twisting salty water stemmed up and met the sky as ten-foot waves swelled and swelled until they were thirty-foot waves. Brae's head lowered and she flung out her arms, protecting herself as water started to gush over the cliff.

"Oh. My. Friggin'..." Nicole's words faded away as the sea fed the rolling, black clouds and rain came down in a monsoon. Vika, remarkably sure on her feet, continued to fly toward Brae.

Toward the edge of the cliff.

And the power of the horse only seemed to be increasing.

Though Brae threw her magic at them in harsh, unrelenting bursts, they remained unaffected. While he knew the power it took for her to fight the ocean and weather was remarkable, something even greater blocked her.

Tremendous magic.

Hooves thundered over rock as the heavens roared and the sea poured over the castle.

Lightning flashed.

Brae screamed in rage.

"Niall," Nicole said, voice trembling, her words only reaching his ears because she was part of the vortex surrounding them.

"Dinnae be frightened," he said. "A tough lass from Southie isnae afraid of the likes of this, aye?"

"Oh, Christ," she mumbled but he felt the strength she rallied when she heard his dare. "Shut up, Brute."

Despite all the hell they were rushing into and the fact they would likely die, he grinned. "Ungrateful."

"Whatever," she cried as they drew closer and closer to Brae. Nicole squeezed his hand. "Hey, I just wanted you to know…" She hesitated. "That I'm thankful…thank you."

The Stewart lass threw everything, but nothing stopped Vika. Close. Closer.

He squeezed Nicole's hand as well. "I'm thankful too."

Closer.

"Why?"

"That ye care enough to be here. That ye'd fight for a bairn."

Closer.

"Any time," she responded.

"I'm glad you're here for another reason too."

Closer.

"What's that?"

Too close. There was no time.

"Even if that bitch moves, we're sailing over the cliff," Nicole cried and pressed her face against the horse's neck.

So it seemed.

And there was absolutely nothing he could do to stop them.

With a final curse, Brae leapt aside as Vika rushed past and jumped…

Straight over the edge.

Wind and water rushed over them. While he briefly contemplated flinging them off of the horse, he knew it would do no good. So he closed his eyes, wrapped his arms around Nicole and murmured all the comforting words he could think of.

He had done a bloody poor job of protecting her after all.

Then something shifted. The sensation of falling leveled out and almost as if Vika had leapt a fence then landed, she was running again. His eyes shot open as she came to a halt.

They were alongside the loch behind MacLomain Castle. The enemies had vanished and Grant Hamilton and a few others stood in front of them. Grant's arms lowered as the last of his magic faded.

"Niall?" Nicole gasped. "Are we actually alive?"

"Aye, lass," he said, as surprised as her.

"Nicole?"

Nicole's head shot up. "Cassie?"

"Oh my God, Nicole!"

Niall didn't let Nicole budge an inch but spoke into Grant's mind. *"Is it safe?"*

Grant nodded. *"Aye, 'tis safe enough for now."*

When Nicole said, "Let me down, Niall!" he swung off the horse and pulled her after him. Within seconds, she and Cassie were embracing.

Logan walked over and he and Niall embraced, patting each other on the back.

"'Tis bloody good to see ye, Cousin." Logan gripped Niall's shoulders and held him at arm's length. "'Twas no easy thing getting ye here. How fare our MacLeod kin?"

"I've no bloody idea." Niall turned to Grant while keeping an eye on Nicole. Maybe he should have told her that Cassie had gone blind because he knew Darach had not. "I thank ye for your help, Uncle, but what the hell just happened? Are the MacLeod's well?"

"Aye, all is well enough," Grant supplied. "They are safe."

"Cassie?" Nicole had pulled back from her friend and was eying her with concern. "Are you okay, sweetie?"

"Of course I am," Cassie said. "What about you? I was so worried."

Niall tore his eyes away and looked at Vika then Grant. "Who is the horse and dinnae say ye dinnae know."

"I know naught, lad." Grant arched his brows. "What I *do* know is that ye dinnae need to be speaking to me like that."

"Ye know ye do, ye bloody—"

"Come, Cousin," Logan interrupted and nodded toward the castle as he started walking. "Ye've had a time of it. Ye need to rest."

"Cassie," Nicole said, her voice distressed as she peered at her friend and waved a hand in front of her face. "Hell, girl. Can you see me?"

Niall frowned. Though tempted to go to Nicole, he was too aggravated. Not following Logan, he crossed his arms over his chest and kept glaring at Grant. "Ye think to still keep secrets? Do ye have any idea what I just went through?"

"Ye'll be careful how ye speak to my brother, son."

Niall ground his teeth and ignored his father who might have been standing there the whole time for all he cared. Eyes never leaving Grant, he growled, "Do ye then?"

He loved his Uncle Grant with all his heart, but he had never been fond of his evasiveness. That was why Uncle Colin had always been his favorite. He said what he thought and kept no secrets.

That he knew of.

Grant stroked Vika's muzzle and eyed Niall. "Ye'd best listen to yer Da, lad."

"Yes, I'm blind but it's no big deal," Cassie was saying as Nicole grew more and more upset. "I'm okay. Really, hon. I'm more worried about you right now."

"Holy shit." Nicole touched Cassie's cheek, then her shoulders, then her arms, distressed before she pointed all her confusion and rage in his direction. Spinning, she said, "Hey, Brute, did you *know* about this?"

He returned his attention to Grant. "Just tell me, Uncle. Help me better fight the strife ahead."

Nicole strode up and started to poke Niall in the chest, cedar eyes pure gold now. "You knew, didn't you, asshole!"

Niall ignored her and kept his eyes on Grant. "How did we get here? What's going on?"

"I knew enough to get ye here safely," Grant allowed. "That's all that matters."

When Nicole pushed against Niall's chest, a slew of curses pouring out of her mouth, he wrapped an arm around her waist and pulled her against his side. His eyes remained on Grant. "Yer riddles dinnae help my situation."

When Nicole tried to elbow him, he yanked her in front of him and trapped her flailing arms, muttering in her ear, "We will deal with this later, lass."

"Niall, what are you doing to Nicole?" Cassie asked. "Because I swear if you're hurting her."

"I would never hurt her," he returned, flinching when Nicole stomped hard on his foot.

"He isnae hurting her," Grant enlightened as he led Vika up the shore, words thrown over his shoulder. "Everyone needs to head into the castle. 'Tis the safest place for now."

"Aye," Logan said, looping his arm with Cassie's. "Come, lass."

"No," she argued, staring in Niall's general direction. "Nicole, are you okay?"

Something about her tone made Nicole stop struggling. "Yeah, I'm good, sweetie. Right behind you, okay?"

"You sure?"

"Yup." Nicole's voice was the gentlest he had ever heard it. "Definitely."

It seemed Cassie didn't like how gentle Nicole sounded because she stopped Logan and turned back with a frown. "We knew the day was coming when I'd lose my eyesight, Nicole. If you, of all people, start going soft on me then what's the point of staying strong? You were the rock of our group." She ground her jaw before she kept walking. "I'm blind now. Deal with it."

"I'm sorry," Nicole whispered. "I'm sorry," she said a little louder and yanked away from Niall though she didn't pursue Cassie. Instead, she stared after her friend, eyes moist as she clearly struggled with what else to say.

But Cassie had already vanished inside.

"Shit, shit, shit," Nicole muttered to herself as she rubbed the back of her neck. "I totally suck."

Niall might be irritated with Grant, but he figured he ought to try to soothe her. "You dinnae need to be sorry—"

"Shut up, Brute," she cut him off and strode after Cassie.

Anger flared. Bloody ungrateful wench. He strode after her. "If ye tell me to shut anything again I'll—"

She spun, fire in her eyes. "You'll *what*, Niall? Fight me with a dagger only so you can—"

"Och, lass, if ye've a mind to go after my cousin, one of the best warriors in Scotland, then ye'd best do it with a dagger in yer hand," came another voice.

Nicole had no sooner turned when his cousin Machara grabbed her by the scruff of the neck and started dragging her toward the castle.

"Machara," he started.

"Get the hell off me, you bitch," Nicole roared and tried to swing. That did no good. Machara had her in height and weight and was a warrior amongst warriors.

Niall shook his head and groaned when Machara drove Nicole up against the castle wall. "Ye will respect my blood, aye, lass?"

"Watch out, Cousin, she's got a mean," Niall started, but it was too late.

Nicole jabbed Machara's armpit so hard, his cousin fell back. The second she did, Nicole jammed her fist into his cousin's jaw.

Machara stumbled back, a look of both awe and amusement on her face. "Och, ye bloody—"

Niall grabbed Machara's arm before she beat Nicole to within an inch of her life. "Nay, lass. She's with me."

"With ye?" Machara shook her head. "Are ye sure then lad because—"

"Aye, she's with me," he cut in, eying Nicole as she edged closer, eyes wild.

Nicole clenched her jaw as she breathed harshly and rolled her shoulders. But something in either his or Machara's eyes must have translated because she shook her head. "I'm not with anyone."

She shot them a look of disgust then strode into the castle.

Machara pulled away from Niall, readjusted herself then eyed him. "So that's yer lass then, aye?"

"Och, nay, she's the devil's own," he said as they followed Nicole.

"Aye, she has a demon in her to be sure," Machara said as they climbed the tower stairs. She grinned and winked at him over her shoulder. "I like her immensely."

"I figured ye would."

But he was in no mood for pleasantries. While he understood Nicole's anger, he needed answers to his questions. All the truths that he knew were being kept from him.

"What happened while I was away?" he asked. "I noticed Da didnae stay down here long. Running from me as always."

"Malcolm will always support his brother." Machara shrugged. "It seems they both thought it best to walk away from ye."

"'Twould be nice if just once Da stood up to Grant," Niall said as they reached the middle landing. "If he stood up for me."

"Och." Machara flung her arm around his waist as they walked. "They're tight, those two. Always speaking within the mind. Dinnae let it bother ye."

If Seònaid had been here, she would have sat him down and helped him sort through his thoughts. Machara, however, didn't work that way. She only knew how to express herself through battling. So he wasn't all that surprised when she squeezed his waist and strode ahead. "Come on, Cousin. Evil hasnae found us yet. Let's go find a skirt for ye to chase. Might get yer mind off that lass, aye?"

"Aye," he muttered. "I'll meet ye in the great hall."

Machara made a gesture of approval and vanished below stairs.

"Niall," someone whispered.

Cassie? He slowed, trying to figure out where she was.

"Niall." A hand poked out a door further down, waving him forward.

When he entered the room, Cassie was still standing by the door. "What are you doing, lass?"

"I'm not familiar with this room yet, but I made sure whisky was brought here." She held out her arm. "Lead me to somewhere I can sit."

Niall knew the room well. Two mugs and a pitcher had been left on a table. "Aye." He led her to a chair, not moving until she was safely seated.

"'Tis a nice enough room but barren of furniture," he said as he sat across from her. "Rarely used because 'tis near the top of the stairs and runs too cold. It has a small window and—"

He wasn't quite sure how she did it, but Cassie clamped her hand down over the hand he had rested on the table, her voice desperate. "Is Nicole okay? What happened?"

"She's fine," he began.

"You're lying already." She pulled away. "Pour me some whisky then tell me the truth. All of it."

Could he? Should he? Because there was already too much to tell. Too much that Nicole would not want to be shared. But would she be opposed if he only shared it with her friend…someone she cared so much about? He needed to talk to someone. He needed to figure out how to help her. And Cassie was…Cassie. He had liked her from the moment they met. She was honest, caring and overly compassionate.

A good Lady for this castle if ever he met one.

Niall filled their mugs then slid one over until it touched her fingertips. "Where is Nicole now?"

"With Logan." Cassie lifted the mug to her lips. "She's safe. Being cared for."

That could mean a wide variety of things when it came to Nicole. "She isnae good at being contained."

Cassie chuckled and carefully set down the mug. "Never has been." Her eyes turned in his general direction. "But I'm not so worried about her physical state right now as I am her mental."

Niall took a long swig and nodded. A habit to nod he supposed even though she could not see him doing it. "She had a...difficult time last night."

"Tell me," Cassie murmured.

"I've done as you asked." He shook his head. "I havnae coddled her."

When she remained silent, he knew she wanted more.

Though he swore what had happened would always remain with him, seeing the concern on Cassie's face changed his mind. "She has more rage and repressed fear in her than any lass I've ever met," he said softly. "More than any lad for that matter."

"Go on," Cassie said when he hesitated.

"I meant to leave her alone last night, but she was drunk and said she was afraid." He took another gulp of whisky. "That she didnae want to be left alone anymore."

Cassie clenched her fist on the table and swallowed. "Did she tell you why?"

"Aye," he murmured. "'Twas because she was raised in foster care. Parents came and went but never kept her for long. Then problems started with her hearing that made her seem...daft? She didnae tell her foster parents she had trouble hearing and it affected how people treated her. People didnae ken her. They thought her slow. So when she was old enough, she worked hard, made her own way and..."

"And what, Niall?"

"I dinnae see how it matters now," he started.

"It matters," Cassie whispered.

"She went down what some might think a more difficult path," he murmured.

"Say it." Cassie jut out her chin. "I need to hear you say it."

Niall took another swig and contemplated Cassie. Should he or would that betray Nicole's confidence? A confidence that she knew nothing about.

"Niall," Cassie ground out. "You promised me not that long ago that when I went blind you would describe to me my surroundings, did you not?"

"Aye, I did."

"Nicole, Jackie, and Erin *are* my surroundings. They're everything to me. They are my *world* outside of Logan." She leaned forward, her eyes almost meeting his. "I need to know what she told you."

He studied Cassie's face. The pain. The heartache. Above all, the need to protect. He well understood. He had devoted his life not only to protecting the wee Bruce but also his cousins. His family. Love and devotion to kin was everything. Something he respected and stayed loyal to above all else.

Niall set aside his drink and put his hand over Cassie's. "She told me she took off her clothes for money."

Cassie closed her eyes and nodded, voice hoarse and soft. "So she told you that much."

"Aye." He squeezed her hand. "'Tis not such a big thing really."

When Cassie opened her eyes, they were moist and her voice was passionate. "It's big enough, Niall."

How to respond? He said all he could think of. Everything he had said to Nicole last night. "'Twas just her body, nothing else. Nobody had her."

"Every last guy that saw her naked *had* her, you fool. In her mind anyway." Cassie pulled her hand away and shook her head. "I can't believe she told you so much."

"'Twas not all that much," he said, downing the rest of his whisky.

"But it was. More than she's told any guy," Cassie said. "Maybe that explains why she got so irritated with you. She's not used to being so vulnerable."

"Nay." He shook his head. "'Tis just a thing with us."

Cassie ran a finger around the rim of her mug and went unnaturally silent.

Too silent.

"There's more to this, isn't there?" she said softly.

Niall frowned and shook his head. "Nay."

"Niall."

"Aye?"

"What did you do?"

What was it about losing one of the five senses that made a person sharper? Because Cassie somehow *knew.*

"'Twas a rough eve for her," he began.

Cassie pushed aside her mug so harshly that whisky spilled over. "*What* did you do? Because something feels off here."

Niall sighed. He supposed he ought to tell her he truth. "I didnae see why she needed to remember what she told me."

"Niall," she groaned. "Tell me you didn't cast a spell or something."

"What would you have done if someone that didnae like you poured out their heart?" He sighed again. "What would you have done if she was so angry you didnae know what to say or do?"

Cassie braced her forehead in her hands. "You erased her memory somehow, didn't you?"

"Aye, I did." He wished Cassie could see how awful he felt by looking in his eyes. Instead, he hoped it translated when he squeezed her hand. "She has a great deal of anger, lass. What good would it have done her to know how much she shared with me? Especially considering how little she likes me. 'Twould have embarrassed her too much."

"Oh, God, you don't understand," Cassie said. "Your intentions might've been noble, but Nicole will never see it like that. To her mind, you erased a truth she gave you in confidence no matter how drunk she was." She bit her lower lip. "And Nicole doesn't do forgiveness, period. She learned to fight from a young age. She doesn't do hand-outs and, believe it or not, she'd see what you did as one." Cassie sighed. "An epic one, in fact."

"Well, there's no hope for it now." Niall hung his head. "I cannae be compassionate to her impending loss of hearing and I've got to pretend I know nothing of her upbringing. The verra reason she's so bloody difficult now. Because I got the impression that 'twas her younger years that did her the most harm."

"Yeah, for the most part." Cassie looked right at him as though she could see. "I'm not sure how you should go about it, but you need to come clean with her. No more secrets. Because believe it or not, the best way to protect Nicole is to let her into your heart."

Though tempted to pull his hand away, he did not. "My heart?"

"Yeah, *your* heart." Now she squeezed his hand. "An honorable place." Cassie leaned forward. "A place she's not familiar with."

Niall pulled away and refilled his mug. "You give me too much credit, lass." He shook his head. "Considering all I just told you."

"No, actually, I get why you did it." She sipped from her mug. "Though you've hell to pay, you were only trying to spare her feelings. I, for one, think it was pretty great of you."

He eyed her cautiously. "You do?"

A small smile came to her lips. "I do."

"If my lass approves of your actions then so do I," Logan said as he entered. "Because she's wise, she is."

"Am I?" She smiled and held out a hand. Logan took it, kissed the back then stood behind her.

He lowered enough to murmur in her ear. "What are ye up to, love?"

Niall drank and eyed them. What would it be like to have a lass adore him like Cassie did Logan? Did he even want such a thing? It seemed like too much.

Yet…

"So what secrets do ye keep, Cousin?" Logan said, scooping Cassie into his arms before he sat.

Too many already and he didn't like it one damn bit.

Restless, Niall stood. "They're not mine to share, m'laird. We'll visit more later." He kissed the back of Cassie's hand. "For now, I'll leave you two be."

Then he left, ignoring his father as they passed in the hallway. There were men he could please and men he could not. His father had always been one he could not and he was far past trying. Nicole called him a brute? She should get to know his Da.

His conversation with Cassie had left him discontented and out of sorts. He and Nicole might constantly be at odds, but something about Cassie's advice rang true. Yet how would he ever approach the topic with the feisty redhead? Hell if he knew.

So by the time he made it to the great hall his mood was foul.

He might be trying to evade the enemy, but he wasn't entirely opposed to another good battle. The thrill from earlier had worn off. Or was it the fear he'd felt for her life? Hard to know. What he did know was that it would be a good time to find Nicole drunk.

Niall needed her to be boisterous. Defiant. He needed to get outside of his head and she did that for him.

But she was nowhere to be found.

Frustrated, fuming for no real reason, he stalked through the crowd and stopped random people. "Where is the foreigner? Where is the lass with the loud voice?"

Nobody knew.

Where was a good fight when you needed one?

"Nicole?" he roared.

Nothing. Everyone resumed eating and drinking as he made his way toward the fire. When his mind should have been on the trouble ahead, all he could think about was the way she had felt under him earlier.

Their kiss.

That kiss.

So much all at once. Too much. Fast. Furious. She had become his. He had become hers. Not magic but close. Something different. Worth repeating.

Something worth needing.

Bloody hell, he *needed* her.

He wanted to taste her again like he wanted nothing else. Her body delicate but fighting beneath his. Hating but wanting him. Painful but so bloody pleasurable. What was this?

"Nicole," he roared again.

"She's there," someone said.

"Right there," another whispered.

People pointed then turned away. But it was enough.

He found her.

She was sound asleep, curled up on a chair beneath the Viking tapestry. Enough with that. They needed to talk. Now. So he stalked toward her.

Chapter Six

"ARE YE AWAKE?" came a small voice. "Can ye hear me?"

Nicole jolted awake, discombobulated. It took several long moments to figure out where she was and who had spoken. Tucked on Niall's lap, they sat in front of the monstrous hearth in the great hall. He was sound asleep and the place had emptied out. It must be late. Her eyes drifted up to the little boy standing on the landing high above.

He had spoken to her.

His eyes were huge and mournful as he gazed down. His voice was a whisper she should not have been able to hear from this distance. "They willnae stop talking into my mind."

When she tried to move, Niall's arms tightened around her. She peeked at his face. He was still out cold. Even so, there was no getting away. So she gestured at the boy to come down and spoke softly for two reasons. The first? She would rather not wake up the brute. The second? She didn't want to frighten the boy.

"My name is Nicole," she said. "Come sit with me. I won't hurt you." She nodded at Niall. "Neither will he."

"Nicole," the boy said. "I have heard of ye." He made his way down then sat a few chairs over from them, eying his surroundings cautiously before his gaze met hers. "We passed through the oak ford together not long ago. Ye are Cassie's friend."

"I am." She smiled. "And yes, we did pass through the ford at the same time. You're Robert the Bruce, right?"

He nodded. "'Twas scary, aye?"

"It was," she agreed. "You were very brave."

"Aye," he said softly. "I tried to be."

"Me too." It was hard to believe she was talking to the future King of Scotland. Someone who would become infamous. Yet right now he seemed so small and innocent. So vulnerable. "How are you doing, Robert? Are you all right?"

"I am." He nodded before he slowly shook his head. "Or at least that is what I tell my Ma."

"The voices in your head are frightening you, aren't they?"

"Aye," he whispered.

"Did you know I heard them too?"

He nodded. "Do ye hear them right now?"

"No." She kept her eyes with his and her voice gentle. "But I *did* hear you speaking from above when I shouldn't have so that's a good thing."

"'Tis?"

She didn't have a lot of practice dealing with kids so she hoped she was saying the right things. "Yep, because that means I'll probably hear you no matter where you are."

He swallowed. "Where else might I be?"

"Nowhere but here," she started then stopped. He might be young, but she felt he deserved honesty. She wished adults had been more honest with her when she was little. "And hopefully that's where you'll stay. But if for some reason you and I leave here, we're gonna be brave together, right? We're gonna be tough."

"You mean if the evil lass gets me or those shadows," he said, eyes growing wider.

"That's exactly what I mean," she said. "But I don't think they will. You know why?"

He shook his head.

She nodded at Niall. "Because you have mighty warriors like this one protecting you." Then she pointed at herself. "And good friends like me determined to watch over you."

Robert's eyes flickered between her and Niall. "Yer my friend?"

"Absolutely." She nodded then patted Niall's arm. "So is he."

Robert was about to respond when a woman appeared on the landing above, visible relief in her eyes when they locked on him.

"'Tis my Ma," he murmured. "I have to go."

When the woman's eyes met Nicole's, she nodded hello. The woman nodded back.

"Goodnight, Robert," Nicole called after him. "I hope to talk more tomorrow."

"Aye." He offered a little wave and then raced up the stairs.

By the time Nicole's eyes returned to the landing, the woman was gone.

As she stared at the dying embers on the hearth, she again hoped she'd said the right things. While she didn't want to scare Robert, overly coddling him did not strike her as the best course of action considering his circumstances.

"So ye've a kind heart after all," Niall murmured.

"I should've known you were awake," she muttered and met his heavy-lidded eyes.

Something about him like this, drowsy and vulnerable but still alert, struck her as super sexy. Not good. No super sexy Niall for her. But when she tried to sit forward, he kept her locked tight against his chest.

"Stay," he said softly. "I've a need to talk to you, lass."

"You can talk to me just as easily without me on your lap."

"Mayhap." His eyes wandered her face. "But 'tis not such a bad thing having you here."

"I'm not wiggling my ass for you this time," she grumbled. "So stop trying to warm up to me." Her eyes narrowed as worry over Robert was replaced by renewed anger with Niall. "Why didn't you tell me about Cassie?" She frowned. "Why didn't Rònan or Darach? I assume you all knew."

"Because I felt as if you already had enough to deal with," he said. "And I suspect my cousins felt the same. Or mayhap they felt it was Cassie's information to give."

That made sense she supposed. Still, it somehow irked her that Niall kept it from her. It almost felt like a betrayal. How come, though? They weren't close. "Why do I feel so frustrated that you above all kept it from me then? And it wasn't because we had sex. I don't work that way."

Niall shrugged, a strange look on his face when he murmured, "I dinnae know."

Why did he almost seem guilty? "What is it you wanted to talk to me about?"

"If I let you off my lap, will you stay and hear me out?"

That didn't sound good. "Yeah, maybe. It depends on what you're about to say."

"You willnae like it, but I'm of the mind to be honest with you." His eyes searched hers. "I dinnae want the constant strife betwixt us anymore."

"And you being honest is going to put that to rest?" She grew tense. "Something tells me it's gonna have the opposite effect."

"Mayhap." He released her. "But it needs to be said."

"Because you apparently want to be friends now," she said, standing.

"I just dinnae want the strife," he reiterated. "If we're to protect the wee Bruce, we cannae constantly be bickering as we have been."

"Okay." She put her back to the remnants of the fire and crossed her arms over her chest. "Have at it."

He contemplated her for a long moment before he said, "We didnae have sex last night."

Oh, he did *not* just say that. Anger started to bubble up. "Are you serious?"

"Aye." He crossed his arms over his chest as well. "And our first kiss was today."

Ah, so she had *not* forgotten their first kiss. That, at least, was a relief.

"Why the hell did you lie to me?" She shook her head. "You let me think I'd been a total slut. Why would you do that considering all I'm going through right now?"

"Because I was offended that you were so disgusted by the idea that we'd lain together. I have a wee bit o' pride you know." Then he said something she never could have anticipated. "And I didnae know yet if I wanted you for myself."

The same thoughts she'd had about Darach.

Best to stay focused, though. And damn was she pissed. "So first you thought I was a piece of meat you could give away to Rònan." When he looked surprised, she said, "Oh yeah, I heard about that one." She narrowed her eyes. "Then you figured you'd lie about us having sex to what, stake some sort of temporary claim on me?"

"I didnae think you were a piece of meat." Niall ground his jaw. "I would never think that."

"Then what gave you the right to offer me up to another man!"

"'Twas just a means of pushing you away." Niall's tone was low and his eyes level. "But I dinnae feel that way any longer."

Her brows rose. "Oh, you don't do you? Well, I hate to break it to you but your chances with me are slim to none."

The corner of his lips curled up and the look in his eyes was a smidge too knowing. "So there's a slim chance, is there?"

Disarmed by his cool confidence, she shook her head. "Let me rephrase. There's *no* chance."

Yet she wasn't storming out of here like she had every right to do. Instead, her feet were frozen to the floor and her eyes still locked with his.

"Nicole?" It was Cassie. "Is everything okay down there?"

Niall and Nicole kept eying one another. Was everything okay? Not in the least. But when she yelled up to her friend, it was that all was well. Go back to sleep. Then she realized Cassie might need help. When she started forward, Niall came to his feet and stopped her. "She's already gone. She knows how to find her way back to Logan."

Her eyes rose to his. "If we're going to work toward getting along you need to stop blocking my path…in general."

"I'll always block your path if it means protecting you." His eyes dropped to her hand. "But mayhap 'twill be a path we walk together."

He was looking at the Claddagh ring that had mysteriously appeared on her finger. A ring whose clear stone would apparently turn to a gem that matched the eye color of the MacLomain wizard she was meant for.

"I think you hope for too much." She twisted the ring so that the crowned, heart-held stone was facing palm side. "Because I don't do love. Never have. Never will."

"Nor I," he assured, stepping back so she could pass if she wanted to. "But that doesnae mean I havnae grown curious."

"Human nature," she said carefully. "There are two more Brouns coming. There's a good chance one of them is meant for you."

"Aye," he agreed, still standing far too close. "But 'tis not them I'm curious about."

"You should be. They're awesome." Her eyes stayed with his. Why wasn't she stepping away? What kept her from barely breathing? It was an odd and unfamiliar feeling. "They're damn beautiful too."

She got the sense he was as perplexed by his behavior as she was by hers.

"You're damn beautiful," he murmured.

Men had always liked her looks and said as much. Yet there was something different about him saying it. Somehow it weighed better on her in an unexplainable way that she couldn't put her finger on. Then it occurred to her.

He wasn't saying it to get in her pants.

Outside of her friends, it might just be the most genuine compliment anyone had ever given her. Startled by the revelation, she tore her eyes away. Though she wasn't in the least, she said, "I'm tired. Where should I crash?"

"In our chamber," he said. "I'll show you the way."

Her brows flew together as her eyes shot back to his. "*Our* chamber?"

"Aye. 'Tis far too dangerous now to have you out of my sight." Then an edge of humor met his voice. "But worry naught. There are two beds."

"Yet every time I've woken up, I'm in your arms," she muttered and strode for the stairs. "Show me. I'm wiped."

She would never admit it, but everything that had happened at the MacLeod's scared the heck out of her. And Niall had gotten her out of there in one piece. Yet again, he had her back. Where she came from, that meant something. More than he knew.

The chamber was far more spacious than she anticipated and the beds far apart. There were four windows, rounded on top and flat on the bottom. Two on one wall. Two on the other. Nautical tapestries hung around most of the room. But one was different. Where the others were simply ocean landscapes with warm colors, this one was more intense with a single Viking longship sailing its seas.

She stopped in front of it as Niall lit a fire. "He sailed that one, didn't he?"

"*I did,*" whispered through her mind.

Nicole blinked and shook her head.

"Who?" Niall asked.

"The Viking in that huge tapestry downstairs," she said softly.

"*My name is Naðr Véurr Sigdir.*"

"Aye, 'tis the Viking King's ship." Niall came alongside "How did you know that?"

Surprisingly unafraid, she looked at him. "I think he might be inside my head."

"Och, 'tis good that." He didn't doubt her in the least. Warmth filled his eyes. "There is no better ally to have except mayhap Adlin MacLomain himself."

The idea that a ninth-century Viking might be speaking to her telepathically was a lot to swallow. "This is crazy." But she found herself smiling at Niall. "No kidding, seriously?"

"Seriously." Niall met her smile. "Try speaking back to him."

"How?"

"Picture the Viking in the tapestry downstairs and address him directly within your mind."

"That's weird."

"'Tis how you do it."

Always up for a challenge, she nodded and gave it a shot. Picturing the Viking, she spoke within the mind...which was really just *thinking*.

"Hey, nice to meet you Naðr Véurr Sigdir."

"You as well, Nicole," floated through her mind.

"Oh, *damn*." She kept grinning at Niall. "I think he just responded!"

Niall chuckled. "You didnae get nearly as excited when you spoke within the mind to the wee Bruce at the MacLeod's."

"No offense, but this is a *Viking*." Nicole shook her head, downright giddy. "A flippin' Viking."

"I will speak with you again later," the Viking's words floated through her mind. *"Stay brave and stay close to your MacLomain."*

"He's gone," she murmured, still staring in wonder at the tapestry. "Holy hell, this is incredible." Her eyes shot to Niall. "So he was one of the guys who trained you, eh?"

Niall nodded and headed for a small table nestled in the corner. A tray with various foods, a few pitchers, and two mugs lay on it. "Aye, he and his two brothers, Kol, and Raknar."

"Wow," she whispered.

"Are you hungry or thirsty?" Niall filled one of the mugs. "There's water and whisky."

"Water, please." She tore her eyes away from the tapestry. "Not so hungry."

He wore a crooked grin as he filled the other mug then handed it to her. "No whisky then? I figured you'd want that after such a day." He nodded toward the tapestry. "Then that."

"Nah, not right now." But the truth was speaking with Robert had sobered her up in more ways than one. Seeing him had made all of this so much more real. She never actually saw him that day at the ford. It was one thing to know you're supposed to protect a medieval Scottish king. It was another thing entirely to look in his eyes when he was so young. It humanized the concept. Big time.

Niall gestured at a nearby trunk. "You'll find a change of clothes in there."

Nicole nodded then downed half her mug. "I'm not a big fan of sleeping in clothes."

Niall grinned. "Nor I." He gestured between the beds. "Choose whichever you like."

"It doesn't really matter." But she headed for the one closest to the fire. Setting aside the mug, she eyed him over her shoulder. "Think you can keep your eyes off me while I strip down?"

"Nay," he said bluntly. But it seemed he was working on his manners. "Unless you want me to."

"Might be a good idea." Yet she didn't wait for a response as she pulled off her clothes. By the time she crawled into bed and glanced back at him, he was standing there with his mouth hanging open.

"Way to respect a girl's wishes," she said.

"Och, ye've a bloody fine arse," he managed to mutter, a dumbfounded look on his face as his voice grew more guttural. "'Tis a damn hard thing to look away from."

"Speaking of hard things." She gave his billowing plaid a direct look. "You better keep that under wrap because it isn't gonna happen."

If she wasn't mistaken, the Viking King's laughter whispered through her mind.

Niall shrugged and winked as he pulled off his tunic then whipped aside his plaid. "I would never make the wee beastie suffer like that."

"Oh, screw me. *Wee?*" she blurted, eyes pinned where they shouldn't be. There was nothing wee about him. When fire flared to life between her thighs, Nicole rolled over and pulled the blankets up around her neck. "Go to sleep."

Niall chuckled and she heard his bed creak as he crawled in. "If ever ye need a screwing then—"

"Then you'll be the last one I call," she interrupted. "Sleep, Niall."

"Aye." He kept chuckling. "Good night, lass."

"Night," she murmured and closed her eyes. Then opened them. Then closed them again. Over and over for what felt like hours. Every time she closed them images rose up. Dark spirits wrapped around her until they were inside her mind. With an unnatural, erotic allure, they urged her to welcome darkness. Welcome power. Relent.

Be with them. With him.

"I will love ye more than I do her, lass," a deep voice murmured into her mind. *"More than any other."*

The more he whispered, the more she reached out, wanting his touch. Needing it. Then she felt a sense of betraying another. Robert? No, he was only a child.

Niall.

It was always his face rising up when the voice became too persistent. Again and again. Then the murmured voice became a roar.

"Come to me," it demanded. *"Let me show you."*

Nicole bolted up in bed, covered in sweat. Struggling for breath, her eyes flew to Niall's bed. He was there. Sound asleep. It was still dark out and the fire had all but dwindled. Swinging her legs over the side of the bed, she held her head. Was she going insane or were her nightmares somehow real? It was impossible to know.

Either way, she didn't want to be alone. And that was a first. Always a survivor, always a tough girl, she depended on herself. But not right now. Rather than grabbing clothes from the trunk, she scooped Niall's tunic off the floor, pulled it on and crawled into bed with him. Out like a light, he didn't move. So she cuddled close, tucked her hands against his side, inhaled the scent of his skin and closed her eyes.

Then nothing touched her.

And she slept.

Soundly. Sweetly. She slept.

The sound of thunder rolled through her dreams. Soft rain started to fall harder. But there was no darkness here. Only passion. Tenderness. Then wild need. Something she had never felt before.

A weapon-roughened hand skimmed the side of her waist then cupped her butt, squeezing before it drifted up her spine. One vertebra at a time, it explored, making her feel delicate and feminine. The sensations rippling through her were new and different.

Lost in the dream, she whispered Niall's name. She knew she did. But it sounded far away. Fingers tentative but eager, she traced the contours of his heated flesh. Ridges, muscles, up his abdomen until she ran her hands through the light smattering of hair on his chest. She exhaled with desire as she trailed a finger over the pathway of his collarbone then up his strong neck.

A deep masculine groan vibrated from within his chest, rumbling through her body until it pooled between her legs. Desperate to ease the ache, she spread her legs and pulled him closer. Burning skin came against her as a blazing tongue met hers.

Something about that.

Something about his kiss made her eyes shoot open.

The dream snapped shut.

When she froze, Niall pulled back. Breath ragged, he stared down at her. She stared up at him. Light flooded the chamber and he was over her. Ready. Just like she was. The heavy weight of his erection rested against her stomach.

Nicole closed her eyes and released a harsh breath. This wasn't what she wanted when she crawled into bed with him. No, she needed comfort. A man who would keep her safe. Was she beyond aroused? Yes. Did she want sex? Yes. Wicked. But not like this. Not right now.

She barely managed a weak whisper, one that didn't sound convincing in the least. "Stop."

As she had done, he released a harsh breath and rolled off of her, words husky. "I'm sorry, lass. I didnae even know ye were there until…"

When his words trailed off, she put a hand to her forehead. "It's okay. I shouldn't have crawled into bed with you to begin with."

"Nay, 'tis good ye did," he started but stopped when a rap came at the door.

"Nicole?" Cassie said softly. "Are you awake?"

"Yeah. Give me a minute." Nicole swung out of bed. "Is everything okay?"

"Yes," Cassie responded. "It's just late and I was hoping to hang with you a bit."

"Me too. Be right there." She glanced at Niall. "Throw on some clothes, eh?"

"She cannae see me," he murmured but was already out of bed and wrapping his plaid.

Her gaze stayed on his ass until it was covered. How could it not? He was a masterpiece. Before he could catch her ogling, she grabbed her clothes off the floor.

"Nay." He opened the trunk. "There are fresh clothes in here, lass."

"Thanks. Toss 'em over."

"Trousers or a dress."

"Pants." She slid them on after he handed them to her.

A cocky grin split his face. "You can keep wearing my tunic if you like."

She rolled her eyes. "It goes to my knees."

"'Tis a bloody shame." His eyes drifted down her legs with appreciation. "Makes me wish I was shorter."

"I'll bet." She yanked off the tunic and pulled on the one he handed her. "Stop gawking, Niall."

He kept grinning after he had an eyeful of her breasts. "You ask too much."

"Common decency is all," she murmured, smiling as she turned away.

"Common decency?" She heard the smile in his voice. "'Tis nothing I make a habit of."

Nicole worked her feet into boots while chugging the last of her water. When she opened the door, Cassie was standing right there. A well of emotion tried to surface as she looked into her friend's blank eyes. No. Wrong words. Not blank but adrift and unfocused. But damn if she would let Cassie know her thoughts. She had been clear yesterday about not wanting to be coddled and Nicole understood that more than most.

"Hey, hon, sorry for the delay." Nicole wrapped elbows with her and headed for the stairs. "So what's up?"

Cassie steered her past the stairs and down a hallway. "I was hoping for some time alone."

"Sure thing." Nicole kept smiling so that it translated to her voice.

They were just about to turn onto a wall walk when Cassie stopped and said over her shoulder, "Alone means alone, Niall."

"I cannae leave her alone even for—"

"I know you're honor-bound to protect her," Cassie said. "But Logan has at least five men out here. We'll be okay. Promise."

"Aye, lass." Nicole heard the discontent in his response. "I will remain here in the hallway then."

"Perfect, thanks," Cassie said as they continued out. The air was cool. Almost as if autumn was right around the corner.

Nicole sighed. "Sorry, having a bodyguard is a new thing."

"Hell of a bodyguard." Cassie smiled as they stopped at the rampart. "Incomparable in my opinion."

"Who, Niall?"

"Heck yeah, Niall." Cassie leaned sideways against the wall, her eyes sort of drifting as she smiled. "He's one hell of a fighter."

"Better than Logan?"

Cassie's smile took on a feminine softness. "Nobody can fight like Logan."

"I believe it. He looks fierce." Nicole grinned and took her hand. "He's damn hot too."

"I know." Cassie turned her face into the wind and closed her eyes. A moment later she turned her head and seemed to look directly at Nicole. "I'm worried about you."

Nicole breathed deeply. "Am I allowed to say I'm worried about you too or are you gonna bite my head off again?"

"I just need you to be who you've always been, Nicole," Cassie said softly. "I need that solid, sometimes bitchy, crass, for real voice around me. Not someone who feels sorry for me..." Her voice grew even softer, "Or someone playing it safe so it keeps the spotlight off them."

"Come again?" Nicole said without thinking. But that was her. Think it. Say it. Much like Cassie did but worse. "Never mind." She squeezed her friend's hand. "You're right. I was being weird yesterday and that's not me. Especially with you. Sorry about that."

"I know you love me and that you're worried. Me going blind scares the crap out of you, doesn't it?" Cassie said. "Because you're afraid you, Jackie and Erin are next."

Nicole again struggled for breath. She didn't give a shit about going deaf. It was coming. Maybe. But watching her friends struggle with their disabilities? That was hard. She wanted to give her ability to see to Cassie. Anything to take that new slightly aloof look off of her face.

That wasn't the Cassie she knew.

No, that Cassie was gone forever.

Stolen from her. Stolen from them all.

"I'm super happy," Cassie said, almost as if she could hear Nicole's thoughts. "Happier than I ever was when I could see."

"Really? You're happy?" Nicole studied Cassie's face. It was hard to seek the truth when she could no longer lock eyes with her friend. "Even with all the crap on the horizon?"

"Yeah." Cassie bit her lower lip and her eyes moistened. "You have no idea. Logan is..."

When she trailed off, Nicole wrapped both hands around Cassie's. "He treats you well."

"God, yes." Cassie smiled. "I love the heck out of him."

"Cool." Nicole couldn't help but smile. "I hope so because it would've been easier for you to face blindness back home. Modern day."

"Maybe," Cassie said. "But I doubt it." She redirected the conversation. "So what's going on with you and Niall? He's something, huh?"

"He's a pain in my ass," Nicole admitted, smiling unintentionally. "One of these days I'll get in a solid punch that takes him down."

Cassie laughed and light entered her eyes. "Now that would be worth *seeing* but," she kept grinning and shook her head, "I'd be good with just *hearing* it."

"It'd be hard not to hear." Nicole laughed as well. "It'd be like an earthquake hit."

"Right." Cassie snorted, but there was a mischievous glimmer to her eyes. "All those muscles must weigh a ton."

"Too many muscles in my opinion," Nicole granted. "He could stand to work out a little less...or battle. Or whatever."

"Hmm, I dunno." Cassie seemed to contemplate. "He's sorta built like the guy from *Scorpion King*."

"Oh, he's smokin' hot."

"Yup." Cassie fanned herself. "Wicked hot."

"He's almost as hot as they come," Nicole relented, trying to push Niall from her mind. Trying to pretend she didn't think he was *as hot* as they came.

"Almost?"

"Almost," Nicole said and left it at that.

This was a thing she, Cassie, Jackie and Erin did. They had formed a book/movie/music club years ago to create a bond. Something they could talk about once they faced their upcoming disabilities. A common thread that kept them connected to the real world.

But now it seemed the real world was medieval Scotland.

"Niall cares about you," Cassie said, her voice going soft again.

So they had arrived at the real reason they were out here.

Nicole pulled her hands away and leaned against the battlement, eyes to the loch. "Niall doesn't know me."

"But he wants to."

"No man really wants to know me, Cassie." She shook her head. "And I don't blame them."

"You've always said that and I've always told you that you're out of your mind." Cassie turned her head toward the loch as well. "Niall's not like the other guys you've met."

"Obviously."

"Trust me, Nicole, he's not," Cassie murmured. "He's as caring and lost as you are."

"I'm not lost, sweetie." Nicole pressed her teeth together in frustration then loosened her jaw. Cassie didn't need her to be difficult. "After all, I'm here, right?"

"Yeah." Cassie crossed her arms over her chest. "And that's good because somehow you're more 'here' than you ever were at home. I might not be able to see, but I can feel it in you. Like a beast somehow being calmed. You're fighting going deaf, but it's no longer dragging you down." She shook her head. "Something in you is...lifting? Changing."

Nicole inhaled a shallow, ragged breath. Because they were such close friends, she offered a partial truth. "It's not easy traveling back in time and learning everything I've learned. It's nuts." She frowned. "But yeah, I'm good. Better than I thought I'd be."

"Because of Niall," Cassie prompted.

"No." But she realized Cassie was dead on. "Okay, maybe a little." She half sighed, half growled. "He's been...around."

"Around?"

"Clearly you made sure we shared a chamber so yeah, around," she said.

"I did," Cassie acknowledged. "So did Niall. He takes protecting you very seriously."

"I'm definitely catching that." Yet no sarcasm met her words. The surprising truth was that she was grateful. More than she figured she would be.

Cassie was about to respond when Niall stepped out onto the wall walk. "Come, lasses." He had never looked more serious. "The wee Bruce is in trouble."

Chapter Seven

DISGRUNTLED, LOGAN PACED in front of the great hall's fire as Niall sat between Grant and Malcolm. Marjorie, Countess of Carrick, held her son Robert against her as he covered his ears and wailed mournfully. Nicole and Cassie hovered nearby, as helpless as everyone else.

"He cannae stay here," Grant said softly. "We've got to get him somewhere that the voices cannae hurt him."

"But where?" Malcolm frowned. "Mayhap the Mother Oak?"

"It couldnae hurt to try I suppose." Grant sighed. "I will send word to Darach and Rònan. If we are to travel then all the warriors raised to protect the Bruce should be with us."

"And me," Machara declared, joining them. "I was there training right along with them."

"Aye." Niall nodded. "Ye were, lass."

Machara arched a disgruntled brow at Logan when his eyes narrowed on her. "Have ye an issue with that, m'laird?"

"Nay." He shrugged. "I just thought mayhap ye'd want to help Cassie oversee the castle. And 'twould ease my mind to know ye were watching over her as well."

"Och, ye bloody arse." Machara's eyes narrowed too. "Ye've tied my hands together good and tight with that request, aye?"

Logan was about to respond when Nicole released a painful groan. Niall was heading her way before anyone moved.

"What's wrong with her?" he bit out sharply at Marjorie, not caring in the least that he addressed royalty.

When Nicole slumped back with her hands over her ears, he scooped her up.

"She simply held Robert's hand." Marjorie shook her head, equally distressed as she held her son against her chest. "She said she might be able to ease some of his pain."

This was similar to what had happened to Nicole at MacLeod Castle but far worse based on her trembling body and the pain twisting her face.

"Bloody hell," he whispered and stroked her hair as he tried to soothe her. His eyes flew to Grant. "We need to get them out of here. *Now.*"

"Aye." Grant's eyes went to Malcolm. "Ye'll be coming as well, aye?"

Malcolm nodded. "Aye."

Logan looked at Conall, his second-in-command who had just come in the door. "Make ready a hundred of our best warriors. We leave soon."

"Och, so ye'll take Conall will ye," Machara muttered. When Conall saw her striding his way, he scooted out the door. "That's right, run ye bloody bastard. I'll see that ye rally the right warriors before ye make off with our Laird."

"'Tis all right," Niall murmured in Nicole's ear when she started shaking more violently. "The pain will be gone soon."

But would it be? He had no idea. All he knew was he did not want her suffering. His chest tightened and breathing became more difficult. Hell, battling and certain death around every corner didn't feel nearly as bad as this.

With Nicole tucked safely in his arms, he strode for the door.

"Nicole, sweetie, are you okay?" Cassie said from behind, panic in her voice. Though he knew he should stop so she could say goodbye to Nicole, Niall's anxiety and anger were building. He needed to get her out of here.

"'Tis all right, lass," Logan murmured. That was the last thing Niall heard before he exited. By the time he made it to the courtyard, the horse was ready. It looked like they would be riding Vika again. Machara was cursing up a storm as she sent some warriors away and called others over to join their band.

Conall shook his head and handed Niall all his favorite weapons, cursing under his breath at Machara with equal fervor. "Blasted, lass. Last time she went and I was left behind."

Even if Niall weren't sick with worry over Nicole, he would not engage Conall about Machara any more than he would talk to Marchara about her issues with Logan. The two had an ongoing battle that far outweighed the friction she and Logan shared.

Conall held Nicole as Niall swung up then he handed her over. Niall nodded his thanks then turned Vika toward Grant and Malcolm. He wasn't overly thrilled his father would be joining them but knew he was a powerful wizard and warrior in his own right.

Niall took the satchels handed to him and attached them to the horse as the Countess stormed after Logan, shaking her head. He had Robert in his arms. His voice was both curt and compassionate. "'Tis best that ye stay here, Countess. I cannae in good conscience have yer life put at risk as well."

"My son's life is worth more than mine," she argued. "Let me come. Let me protect him."

"Ye've other children that need ye." Logan's eyes met hers and softened. "Countess, ye know I willnae let harm come to yer wee bairn. We are sworn to protect him."

Niall's attention was torn from them when Cassie rushed over. A stable boy guided her, clearly fearful whether he should be doing as much. But Cassie was in a state and there was no stopping her.

"Where's Nicole?" she said, upset as she reached out her hand.

"Here," Nicole groaned. If he didn't have such a secure arm around her waist, he knew she would be draped across the horse.

Niall leaned over and guided Cassie's hand to Nicole's. "She isnae well, but I swear I'll see her to safety. I'll find a way to ease her pain."

He had never meant anything so much.

"I know you will." Cassie felt around until she managed to cup Nicole's cheek. "I wish I could go, sweetie. Like I said, you're in the best hands possible."

"Right, all the muscles will save me," Nicole whispered then released another groan.

"That's right." Cassie stood on her tip-toes and kissed Nicole's cheek. "Love you, my friend. Go kick some ass now, okay?"

Nicole was in too much pain to respond. Niall took Cassie's hand and squeezed it. "I'll take good care of her."

Cassie nodded, tears in her eyes before she redirected her attention to the stable boy. "Please take me to the Laird."

Meanwhile, Logan had evidently convinced Marjorie to let them take Robert because the boy was already astride Grant's horse. Though her eyes were moist, the Countess stood tall, her stance strong.

"'Tis a short distance to the oak but ye'd best have the horse at a run," Malcolm said, coming alongside. "The enemy is far too unpredictable."

"Aye." Niall nodded and kept trying to comfort Nicole the best he could. "I will follow Logan's lead."

Their eyes met and he wondered for a moment if his father would have something to say about his intentional slight. But Malcolm only nodded. "Vika is strong. She will get yer lass there safely."

"Aye." Niall turned Vika away. Anything to keep from talking to his father. Their conversations, no matter how brief, never seemed to end well.

"Oh, *hell*," Nicole gasped and clamped her hands over her ears.

Little Robert wasn't faring much better as he cried softly.

"I thank ye for joining us." Logan steered his horse around the warriors, voice loud. "Ye might not see an enemy, but that doesnae mean they willnae be here. Keep yer weapons at the ready and race for the oak. Laird Grant will see us to the Mother Oak from there."

The men nodded, fearless as the portcullises were raised. Half the warriors led, the other half fell in behind them as they raced over the drawbridges and onto the field. Though he could see nothing of Brae Stewart and her minions, Nicole let out an alarming wail and wrapped her hands into Vika's mane. Little Robert was flat out screaming.

Soon enough they discovered why.

Not only the *Genii Cucullati* spirits appeared but something far more ominous. Dwarfing the black shadows, it shifted and fluctuated until it began to take form. Without prompting, Vika raced harder than she had before. Grant and Malcolm started chanting, as did Niall and Logan. The warriors kept close to the monstrous shadow, but there was nothing solid for their blades to fight.

"If I go to him he'll let everyone go," Nicole groaned. "Even Robert."

Niall frowned. "Go to who?" His eyes stayed on the inky cloud. "*It?*"

"Yeah," she gasped. "He'll make Robert's pain go away too."

"Nay." Niall held her tighter. "You're not going anywhere."

Vika seemed to agree because she continued racing toward the tree.

Magic crashed against magic as they fought the strange entity. The nameless thing. Was that Brae's demi-god laird? It had to be. Logan roared with rage when the spirit gods ripped away several warriors in an instant, their screams an echo on the wind.

Yet their shapeless nemesis remained without form, without identity as it pressed against their magic.

Nothing Logan did with Mother Earth affected the thing any more than Niall summoning water. Even when Darach appeared and flew across the field using wind, it had no effect. However, when Rònan appeared on the horizon, his massive winged body closing in fast, the entity seemed to take notice.

"Oh, no." Nicole shook her head and struggled against Niall. "It's gonna hurt Rònan. You've gotta let me go!"

"Stop!" He clamped one arm around her, all the while throwing magic. "My cousin will be all right."

"No." She tried to flail against him, but he had her locked tight. "He's gonna get slaughtered. You have to trust me!"

He spoke telepathically to Grant, Malcolm, and his cousins. *"Nicole says the beast is going after Rònan."*

It took a split second before he realized Grant's intention when he swung his horse around, came alongside and swung Robert onto Nicole's lap. Powerful magic swirled in his eyes when they met Niall's. "Get them out of here now!"

Niall nodded and Vika kept going. Nothing was harder than watching what happened next. Despite all Grant and the others threw at it, the enemy was indeed going after Rònan. Though he felt the tension in Nicole's body, he knew she remained silent for Robert's sake.

The dragon and the behemoth black cloud crashed into one another mid-air. Better yet, it seemed to envelop his cousin. Somewhere deep inside, he heard the mental roar of his Aunt Torra's dragon as her son was swallowed by the beast. Pure anguish rent him as he felt not only her pain but Rònan's swiftly followed by the remainder of his family.

"Bloody hell," he whispered. It took bone-deep honor not to stop the horse and rush to Rònan's aid. To somehow save him. But he had spent his life preparing for this moment. He had devoted his life to protecting Robert the Bruce and the future of Scotland.

So he focused on the tree and let everything else go.

It might seem like they were going to run right into the trunk, but magic of another sort roared up around him. The portal that only those with MacLomain blood could use opened as wind rushed around them. Then the tree vanished and a suctioning sensation seemed to yank them forward. The next thing he knew, Vika stopped and everything quieted.

They had arrived at the Mother Oak.

A massive tree that grew up the side of a mountain and spread its top into the mouth of a cave, it was unlike any other. He swung down and pulled Robert and Nicole after him. Holding the wee Bruce, he kept a steadying hand on Nicole as they acclimated.

"How are ye, lad?" he murmured to the bairn.

Trying to hide his sniffles and red eyes, Robert said, "The pain is gone." His eyes rounded. "So are the voices in my head."

"Aye, 'tis good." He kissed the top of the boy's head then turned his attention to Nicole. She had one hand protectively on Robert's shoulder and the other cupping her forehead as she leaned against Vika. "How are you, lass?"

Her eyes flashed fire as they met his but softened when she looked at Robert. "The pain's gone. So are the voices." She gently squeezed the Bruce's shoulder. "See, I told you we'd face this together. Are you sure you're all right?"

Robert nodded and offered a wobbly smile.

She smiled in return. "I'm going to sit down for a sec, okay?"

"Aye." His little brows pulled together. "Can I sit with ye then?"

"Of course you can." She took a few steps and sunk down onto a thick branch before holding out her arms. "Come here, you."

Niall was about to bring him over, but Robert shook his head. "Nay, Mister. If she can walk then so can I."

"Call me, Niall." He smiled and set the boy down.

Robert, little shoulders thrust back, walked over and plunked down on her lap. Moments later, the air around them started vibrating. More were coming. Of all people, Machara and Conall first.

"Ye bloody fool," Machara spat at Conall. "How dare ye push me here? There was fighting to be had and kin to be protected!"

"Ye would've been next ye ungrateful—"

"Conall. Machara. Enough," Niall cut in and nodded toward Robert. "Save yer bickering for later, aye?"

They scowled at each other before they separated. Soon enough, more warriors started pouring into the tree through the portal. Niall did his best to remain patient as his eyes scanned everyone. Machara plunked down next to Nicole and Conall joined him.

As Niall was first-in-command and Conall his second they had long ago struck up a friendship. Too often they had saved one another's lives. He had respect for the man that almost rivaled what he felt for his cousins. Voice low, he said, "What happened?"

A heavy frown settled on Conall's face. "Half our ranks lost last I saw."

Niall felt like he had been punched in the gut. Those were some of their fiercest warriors and longtime friends.

Upset, he growled, "Why did ye come through before them? Ye should've been the last lad standing."

Uneasy, Conall's eyes flickered to Machara. "One of those shadow creatures had at her. When I tried to push the lass into the tree, she fought me."

If it had been anyone else he might have thought Conall was looking for the easy way out but he knew better. His friend would lay down his life for their clan, especially for their Laird. "Then I thank ye for saving her."

"She's ungrateful," Conall muttered.

"Dinnae get me started on ungrateful lasses." He set his jaw and prepared for the worst. "What of my immediate kin?" His eyes met Conall's. "Rònan?"

Conall at least had the decency to look him in the eyes as he shook his head, emotion evident in his voice. "'Twas not good, friend."

Those words weren't just a punch in the gut but a knife down his middle. But he had seen Rònan get out of tight situations before. He prayed he would again. "Did ye see him die then?"

Conall hesitated and clearly did not want to continue as he said, "The last I saw he had been consumed. When the monster released him, there was naught but ashes left in its wake."

Though Niall knew she couldn't hear them, when his eyes went to Nicole, her gaze locked with his. She must have seen the anguish he thought well-hidden because though she thrust out her jaw in defiance, moisture welled in her eyes.

The air vibrated and more warriors rushed in followed by Grant, Malcolm, Logan, and Darach.

No Rònan.

Malcolm's eyes searched out Niall and for a moment he thought he saw relief flicker in them. But there was no way to know before they turned to the fifty or so warriors left. "Ye did good lads. Follow me and we'll set up camp below."

Logan's eyes narrowed with anger on Machara. "I told ye to stay and protect Cassie."

"I told her to follow afterward," Grant said. "Seònaid and my daughter, Lair will protect yer lass. They're stronger in magic and fight nearly as well as Machara."

Logan frowned but said nothing.

Grant's eyes went to Machara. "Take the wee Bruce with ye so that ye might show him the Defiance again, aye?"

Machara eyed her kin. She knew they needed to talk without the Bruce around so she nodded and looked at Robert. "I know we saw it not that long ago, but would ye like to come and see one of the first portals ever created in Scotland by the great wizard, Adlin MacLomain?"

A small smile blossomed on his face. "Aye."

So they were off, leaving him, Nicole and his immediate family behind.

The minute they were gone, Nicole strode toward Niall, renewed anger in her eyes. "Rònan's dead, isn't he? All because your stubborn ass wouldn't listen to me!"

"Enough!" Grant roared, stopping her dead in her tracks. Niall didn't much blame her. Not once had he heard his uncle raise his voice against a lass...against anyone besides the enemy for that matter.

Logan and Darach remained silent. Darach hung his head while Logan seemed sad and aloof as he clenched his fists by his side. Vika trotted to the far side of the cave and kept an anxious eye on them all.

"Everyone sit," Grant said, his voice far softer. "Now."

Nicole sunk down on a branch next to Darach and held her head in her hands, whispering, "I could've stopped this. I could have saved him."

"I heard the enemy in your head, lass." Grant shook his head. "Ye could have stopped nothing." Then, despite the anger and grief he struggled with, he crouched in front of her and tilted up her chin until their eyes met. "Evil makes bargains but never sees them through. 'Tis half its allure. But their terms are never real. Never met. You cannae offer yourself up so that others might be saved."

"I could've at least tried." Her eyes narrowed on Niall. "But the choice was taken from me."

"Niall followed my orders," Grant said. "And followed his own honorable heart by protecting you and the wee Bruce when all he wanted to do was save Rònan. Dinnae fault him for such a thing. 'Tis nothing but misplaced blame. Blame you should only have for the evil that we now face."

Nicole frowned and remained silent.

Grant stood and walked further into the tree, eyes to the setting sun. He remained silent for a few long minutes. Nobody spoke. There was too much heartache. Too much sorrow. When Grant at last turned, his uncle's words were surprisingly strong. "I no longer feel Rònan's essence, but that doesnae mean he's gone. The enemy is part of a Celtic Otherworld that I dinnae have the power to access. There is a verra good chance he has been taken there."

"Why, when 'twould make more sense to kill him?" Darach said. "'Twould be one less thing for the enemy to deal with. A dragon-shifter no less."

"A dragon-shifter." Grant arched a brow at his son. "Now that would be a powerful beastie to have at his disposal, would it not?"

Niall felt a spark of hope. "But Conall said there was nothing but ashes left behind."

"Were there naught but ashes left behind when the *Genii Cucullati* transported Brae Stewart out of this cave not that long ago? And is she not verra much alive and well?"

"Aye, she is," Niall said. "But I felt the bone-deep loss of Rònan as did his parents."

"As did I," Grant said. "Yet might it not feel that way when our kin is ripped from this world into another? Not death exactly but a shifting betwixt realities or dimensions."

"That sounds sucky as hell but better than death I suppose," Nicole said. Yet the moisture had vanished from her eyes. Instead, there was a glimmer of hope. "Damn, if that's the case then they snagged the wrong guy. Rònan will be pissed."

"Aye," Logan agreed, his eyes on Grant. "Do you really think he's alive, Uncle?"

"Aye, I do. I have to," Grant whispered, eyes turned back to the sunset. "We all have to."

Niall understood his reasoning. Rònan would never give up on any of them if there were the slightest chance they still lived. So they couldn't give up on him either. "How do we find him then?"

Grant shook his head and turned, eyes meeting Niall's. "You dinnae try to seek him, lad. 'Tis for me and mine to locate him. You and your cousins will stay here and protect the Bruce and Nicole until I contact you again."

By 'me and mine' Niall knew he meant the Next Generation excluding Logan, of course. Grant intended to seek out the help from his lot and their Broun witches.

Grant's eyes turned to Nicole and he said remarkably surprising words. "You will stay here until the Celtic god Fionn Mac Cumhail says 'tis safe to leave." He gave her a knowing look. "'Twill likely be when my Viking ancestors come to help you."

Chapter Eight

NICOLE WATCHED AS Grant vanished into thin air and almost wished she could do the same. Sure, she was tough. She had learned to wear a brave face a long time ago. But this? This was beyond anything she had grown a thick skin for.

As if he sensed her distress, Darach wrapped an arm around her shoulders and worked at a grin. "Not quite what you thought it'd be, now is it?"

"Hell, no," she murmured and couldn't even manage a grin. "If I had known all this back in New Hampshire, I would've called a taxi and booted it."

"Och, nay." He squeezed her shoulders. "Had you known all this, Niall would've never had the chance to drag you here. You would've been here already."

Was that true? She would like to think so but damned if she knew. Then again, now that she had met little Robert the Bruce, she knew he was right. There would have been no need for Niall to drag her.

Niall.

Just when she started to soften toward him, he got her riled up all over again. She might understand what Grant told her in regards to Niall, but for whatever reason, it didn't lessen her aggravation. The target of her sour thoughts now stood in front of them, arms crossed over his chest and a scowl in place as his eyes flickered between her and Darach.

"Come, Darach," Logan said, evidently sensing a renewed battle on the horizon. "Let's go check on the wee King and make sure there's game roasting."

Darach cocked a brow at her. "Are you well enough, then?"

Niall's eyes narrowed on Darach. "She's well enough, Cousin. Off with ye now, aye?"

"Are you, Nicole?" Darach repeated, not intimidated in the least by Niall.

If Darach did one thing for her, he made her feel like her twenty-first century self again. A strong woman that could handle life. So she gave him the best grin she could muster. "Yeah, I'm fine. Thanks."

Darach kissed her temple then winked at Niall. "I best let the MacLomain have his way then."

"He's not having his way with anyone," she shot, frowning.

"Aye, then." Darach shook his head as he left with Logan.

Bracing her hands on the branch, she narrowed her eyes at Niall. "Stop looking at me like that."

"Like what?"

"Like you've got some sorta claim on me," she said. "Because you don't."

"Nor do I want one."

"Yet you said just last night you were interested in me."

"I said I was curious."

"Same thing."

He shrugged. "I changed my mind."

She shrugged. "You would."

"Would you rather I didn't?"

"Hell, no." She started to head after Darach and Logan, but Niall grabbed her wrist and pulled her in another direction.

"Excuse me," she started but he nodded at a small rock ledge.

"Climb," he said as he grabbed a satchel.

She frowned. "No."

"Just go. I need to head that way and I willnae let you out of my sight."

Trying to stall him, she nodded at the horse. "What about Vika?"

"Logan summoned grass and I made sure there's water," he replied. "She will be fine."

Nicole navigated around him and patted Vika. The horse ignored her and chomped on grass.

"Come, Nicole or I'll throw you over my shoulder again."

"*Or* I could follow the crowd," she pointed out.

Niall made a gesture at the ledge. "Come."

Though tempted to be defiant, she knew darn well he had become a strange sort of safety net in this absurd reality she'd been thrust into. "Fine."

Navigating the rock easily enough, she climbed up onto a ledge. It was long and broad. An area that didn't quite reach the top of the mountain. Multiple rock formations arced and sliced toward the sky around them.

"This is where the Baby Oak originally grew," he said. When she looked at him, he continued. "The oak that's now outside MacLomain Castle."

"Really?" She looked around in awe.

"Aye." He pulled her until they entered a small cave much different than the one they had just been in. A piece of the mountain cut away from the rest. Open at the top, it hosted a free-standing wall with an exit and entrance. Water cascaded down the inner wall, shimmering in the orange rays of a dying sun.

"Whoa," she whispered. This place almost looked man-made. Like one of those set-ups the rich and famous paid big bucks to have created outside of their homes.

"There's a pond at the top of this mountain that feeds into a waterfall on the other side." He nodded at the sheet of water running down the rock. "This is run-off."

"That makes no sense." She ran her hand through the cold water. "What feeds the pond at the top?"

"I dinnae know." Niall shrugged and pulled off his tunic. "Nothing about this mountain has ever made sense, including how the Mother Oak ended up here."

"Maybe just a lot of rain then?" she asked, trying to figure out the magical world she had been dumped into. Nicole kept her eyes *off* his impressive body and *on* the mystical cave.

"It rains a lot in Scotland but not that much." There was no wink to go along with him tossing aside his plaid. Instead, she got the feeling that he remained as irritated with her as she was with him.

"So the waterfall just keeps on falling," she murmured, her traitorous eyes drifting back to him as he scooped water over his head. God, he was a good looking man. So, so, much man. She took in his broad shoulders. The way they tapered down to slim hips and, she cleared her throat, there was that ass again. So firm she bet it felt like steel.

"Aye," he said, before scooping some water into his mouth and turning.

His eyes remained closed as he ducked his head back beneath the water then ran his hands through his hair. Nicole inhaled sharply, leaned back against the wall and eyed him with avid appreciation. So many long muscles and in all the right places.

Then there was the main muscle.

Even flaccid, he had her licking her lips.

"But mayhap you're not so interested in the waterfall after all," he murmured.

Their eyes locked.

"I am," she assured because it seemed like the right response. The only response. "Nothing more."

"Then dinnae worry over the mystical mountain, lass." A slow grin came to his lips. "Bathe. You might not get another chance anytime soon."

"Hmm." She narrowed her eyes. "Maybe after you leave."

Where did her anger with him go? Because she needed it back. She needed that wall between her and everything that might happen. No, everything that *was* happening. So she picked a fight. "Besides, you'd be the last one I'd get naked for right now."

"Who *would* you get naked for then?"

He didn't seem all that aggravated anymore either. Probably because he had caught her checking him out.

"I dunno." She crossed her arms over her chest. "Maybe Darach."

Instead of getting jealous, he chuckled and turned back to the water, his brogue thickening. "Ye dinnae desire the Hamilton so stop yer games."

"You seemed to think so down at the oak," she shot back, frustrated for no good reason.

"Och, nay." Niall kept splashing water over himself. "'Twas Darach's desire for you that got me going."

Really?

"There's nothing between us," she said without thinking.

"There's something," he murmured.

Maybe she should take advantage of bathing while she could. After all there was no deodorant in the thirteenth century. Which made her wonder as she pulled off her shirt. "How do you guys not stink without modern day stuff?"

"Modern day stuff?"

"Yeah, like deodorant." She wrinkled her nose and yanked off her boots. "You should reek considering how active you are." When his eyes drifted to her, she shrugged. "Seriously, you guys are slinging blades all the time, right?"

"We might not be of the twenty-first century, but we know how to bathe, lass." His eyes made a slow roam over her as she worked at pulling off her pants. She might have stripped for a living for a few years, but for some reason his steady gaze made her feel like a novice. So she glared. "Eyes off me, Brute. This isn't for you."

"Bloody hell right. The Devil's own," he murmured and resumed splashing water over his face.

"What'd you say?" she retaliated, more than content to be arguing with him as she sauntered over and put her hand against the stream of water before pulling it back. Damn cold.

"I can warm it for you."

Nicole hitched her jaw and eyed him…before her gaze dropped. Oh, hell, he was getting aroused. "I can handle cold water."

Could she ever. Most of her childhood was made up of it. At least in the foster homes she resided in. They might have received money from the government, but they didn't always use it for the utility bills.

"Aye, I dinnae doubt you can handle the cold water." He placed his hand against the wall. Water ran over it as he said, "From this water might there heed, a bit of warmth for a lass in need. *Inde aquarum non exaudiam aliquantulus puella indiget Flamma.*"

Nicole did her best to show no response when the water warmed. Like a soothing bath sort of warm. She was a grown adult and well past her childhood. She had warm enough water in her little apartment in Southie. But this…well *this* was luxury.

A luxury she fully intended to take advantage of.

"Thanks," she said, halfway meaning it as she pressed up against the waterfall. It felt *so* good as it poured over her body. As much as it could considering it wasn't gushing water. She leaned her head back, closed her eyes and smiled.

This felt *awesome*.

Magic at its finest.

Who cared if it was Niall's magic.

Niall.

When her eyes shot open, he was no longer there.

She spun. There he was. A foot away if that. Watching her. When he spoke his voice was low and husky, his brogue so thick she could barely understand him. But she understood the look in his eyes. The blatant need. One that said far more than his eager arousal.

Somewhere in the back of her mind she knew what was happening. They were both beyond saddened and stressed over losing Rònan. They needed a diversion. Release. An escape from all the tension.

"Do ye desire another?" he said. His eyes were flaring not blue but almost black with passion.

A dark, eager need.

It was strange and frightening…but arousing.

To answer one way meant that he would step away. Because he would. That was just who he was. To answer another way would invite something else altogether. Something she wasn't sure she was ready for.

But something she wanted.

Craved.

Her nipples tightened and she swallowed as their eyes held. Answer him, Nicole. Give him what he wants. Yet something flared in her. She wasn't good at giving men what they wanted.

Still, she whispered, "I don't desire another at the moment." And because she refused to let him think he had her all figured out. "Not even Darach."

Niall cupped her chin firmly and made sure her gaze stayed with his. "Then ye desire me?"

Her lips throbbed and she shook her head. Letting Niall know she wanted him was a bad idea. Yet at some point she went from shaking her head to nodding.

The stream of water behind her thinned as he came closer but not too close. His eyes went blue. A dark blue made of sex and sin and desire you almost wished you didn't want. His thick lashes lowered and tried to hide his true intentions. "Tell me, Nicole."

She forgot what she was thinking.

She forgot how she was supposed to respond.

"I don't desire you," she whispered, desperate to break free from a spell she secretly hoped was inescapable.

"You lie." Niall pressed the pad of his thumb against her lower lip and dragged it down as he came so close that there were a scant few inches between them. When he spoke, it was barely a whisper. "I want ye something fierce, lass." His finger dragged off her lip. "Here." Then it scaled her cheekbone, the touch almost rough. "Right now."

"No," she moaned as his lips whispered over hers.

"Yes," she groaned as they trailed down her neck.

"Aye or nay," he murmured, falling to his knees.

"Oh, shit," she whispered as he grabbed her hipbones, used his elbows to spread her legs then blew her mind.

"Hell, hell, oh, *hell*," she whimpered, her head falling back against the rock. Warm water kept pouring thinly behind her as she tried to focus.

She groaned again, grateful he held her up as he did things with his mouth that would put most men to shame. Already, far too many muscles were loosening and tightening and—she bit her lower lip hard—he was rocking her world far too quickly.

Too much.

Too fast.

Wrapping her hand into his hair, she had no choice but to give in.

"Niall!" she cried.

An orgasm ripped through her so sharply, even the sound of wind whistling through the cave and the waterfall faded away. He seized her hips tighter and licked his way up her torso, murmuring, "No Darach or anyone else." He whipped her around so quickly she barely had time to put her hands against the wall as his whisper came close to her ear. "Just me."

Burning up, she almost wanted the water cold again. So much fire. Too many loose, weak limbs. But only warm water poured past her as his heated flesh pressed against hers. His lips remained close to her ear.

"Tell me what ye want, because I'll not take it from ye." One strong hand spanned her stomach and the other clamped over her hand braced against the wall. His arousal pressed against her backside, as determined as his words. "Tell me."

What did she want? Him? Yes. But more. Somehow more.

"Niall," she whispered.

"Nicole," he whispered back, voice strained. "Gods, lass."

Then he turned her head just enough that his lips closed over hers. Desperate, needing something far beyond the remnants of the climax still quivering through her, she kissed him. It wasn't just a meeting of the lips, but an explosion as their tongues swung together.

Seeking.

Challenging.

Desperate.

She knew what was coming. She knew what he asked of her. But when she widened her legs just enough and he pressed forward, she whimpered into his mouth. Not because it was bad but because it felt so damn good.

Too good.

He continued kissing her as he eased into her. It was profound. Different. A mutual gasping for breath as they inch by inch moved closer. Became one. Or so it almost felt as their lips sought, their tongues tangled and their breath mingled. Unrelenting, his thrusts remained gentle until he filled her completely. All the while, he kissed her, tasted her, made her feel wanted in a way she had never experienced before.

When their lips separated, it was only so that he could murmur, "Nicole," against the corner of her lips. Breath harsh, she seized the side of his head with one hand and pressed her cheek to his. This was a moment she could relive again and again. One that made her feel cherished. Beautiful. Fulfilled?

"Och," he murmured as if he could hear her thoughts. "Ye are so bloody beautiful in ways ye dinnae ken."

Though tempted to ask if he was inside her head, she was far too focused on him being inside her body. And that feeling had her cupping the back of his neck when she sensed he would shift away.

"No," she whispered, too much pleasure already shooting through her. "Stay."

Niall said nothing but dropped his head beside hers, words clearly a struggle. "Aye, lass."

There was no hesitation. Just impatient need when he braced her hands against the wall and moved. Not away. Not at all. Only closer. When he started thrusting, she didn't recognize the sounds coming from her mouth.

Animalistic at first.

Then mewling.

Then something else altogether.

Something made of not only her voice but his.

Water ran over her arms, breasts and torso, warming and caressing her skin.

"So bloody good," he groaned before he muttered, "Closer."

The word was barely out of his mouth before he spun her, lifted her and thrust inside her once more. His eyes were savage with lust as her back met the wall and water sluiced over her shoulders, then down her body. Smoothed by centuries of water, the rock wasn't rough as his thrusts increased.

Arms and legs wrapped around him, she gasped against the side of his neck as he moved. Something wild had been unleashed in them. Something that made her dig her heels into his ass and her nails into his back. She even nipped his damp skin she was so desperate.

Crazed.

The scathing passion between them grew so intense that it almost felt like lustful anger. A sexual challenge. Near raving lunacy. Explosive energy.

"Ye'll not bring me down with a pinch this time," he ground out as his thrusts only intensified.

"Maybe not with a pinch," she panted.

About the last thing she wanted him to do was stop but she was unable to cease clawing at him. Arousal like this brought out a whole new beast in her. One she was meeting for the first time. It seemed he was meeting a whole new monster too as a deep rumble started in his chest.

Then there were growls.

Hers.

His.

Water heated. Steam rose. Fog drifted.

Furious passion screamed up and staggered cries of pleasure mixed with flat out cursing. Almost at the exact moment her body let go, he squeezed her backside, thrust deep and released a strangled roar.

Everything after that was pure, untouchable oblivion. Daggers of searing ecstasy shot through her over and over. There seemed to be no source of origin but a full-body experience. An event that involved not only her flesh but her soul.

Deep.

Thick.

Consuming.

A transcendence of epic proportions.

It was impossible to know how long she drifted, caught in a whirlpool of near incoherency. What was this? Sure, it was one hell of a multi-orgasm. But somehow it was more. Better.

Addictive.

When she at last came down from her high, she realized he was kneeling. His forehead rested against the rock next to her and he had the back of his forearm braced above her head. From the sounds of it, he was as winded as her.

Head leaned back against the rock, she chuckled softly. "Looks like more than just a pinch can bring you to the ground."

Niall's lips again came close to her ear, his words low and hoarse. "Ye can bring me to my knees in such a way anytime ye like, lass."

She almost said the same but bit her tongue. It seemed like, what? Commitment? Or not. He didn't strike her as the type to want that sort of thing. The whole 'me not Darach' comment was just him going all alpha on her. Nothing more. No, she remained silent because she didn't just want to be a booty call. Did she? Maybe she had gone down that road here and there with guys in the past but not anymore.

Almost afraid to look and trying to be discreet about it, she sort of stretched and lifted her hand. The Claddagh ring remained unchanged. *Phew.* At least that was her initial response. Then she felt a little something else. A nugget of surprising disappointment. Uh oh. Not good. Not when it came to a guy like Niall. Or a girl like her for that matter.

She was about to lower her hand when she spied some red.

"Oh, damn," she muttered. "Blood."

"Aye." He squeezed her backside and she jolted. Zig-zags of fresh pleasure shot through her. There was a chuckle in his voice as he stood and set her down. "Ye've got some bite to ye, lass. In more ways than one."

Nicole flinched when he stepped away and put his back to the water. A total of ten scratches lined his shoulder blades. Five on one side. Five on the other. "Well, I've never done that before. Holy shit."

Not seemingly bothered by it in the least, a cocky grin curled his lips. "Battle wounds well earned."

Nicole rolled her eyes and leaned back against the rock. While tempted to say, "Hell yeah they were," she figured he didn't need the ego boost. Even if he *had* earned it. So she shrugged and offered her own cocky grin. "Consider yourself lucky. Crème of the crop here, baby."

"Crème of the crop?"

"Best of the best."

His brows perked and for a second she thought he was going to make a smartass comment. But something stopped him. Instead, she swore he whispered, "Aye," before he headed for his satchel.

Why was he so compliant?

"No witty comeback?" she challenged, then joined him.

Niall handed her a dress and started wrapping his plaid. "Were you hoping for one?"

She shrugged and frowned at the satchel. "No pants in there?"

"Nay." He ran a hand through his wet hair and she sensed that he was struggling with something.

"What's up?" Nicole pulled on the dress and eyed him. "You seem off all of a sudden."

Not bothering to answer her question, he pulled on a tunic then started to tie up her dress. "We need to rejoin the others."

"Obviously." She batted his hands away and continued tying. "I don't like being ignored. Especially after what we just did."

"'Twas just sex." He rubbed the mark on his neck from her teeth and somewhat relented. "Good sex."

Her brows shot up. "Wow, I pegged you for a few things, Niall but not a total douche."

She yanked on her boots and conveniently set aside the fact that she tended to treat guys like he was treating her right now.

"Was it more than that to you then, lass?" he said softly as he pulled on his boots as well.

"No," she shot. Damned if she would say otherwise now. But it hurt and that irritated her to no end. "Like you said. Just sex."

Once she was ready, she didn't bother looking at him but strode back in the direction they came. Before she got too far, he grabbed her upper arm and spun her back. "'Twas a good exchange betwixt us. I dinnae ken your anger now."

"Exchange?" She kept frowning. "That's a hell of a thing to call what we just did."

"I made you feel good. You made me feel good. Is that not an exchange?"

"I guess," she muttered and tried to yank her arm away.

"Answer my question, Nicole." She was going nowhere fast as he held her shoulders firmly and searched her eyes. "Why are you so upset?"

"I'm not," she spat. "But if you don't let me go that'll change."

"Mayhap I asked the wrong question before." She couldn't quite pinpoint the look on his face as he continued. "Were you hoping that I wanted this to be more than just sex?"

Now he was cutting too close to something she had no desire to scrutinize. So she narrowed her eyes and played it safe. "Are you getting sappy on me, Niall?"

"Sappy?"

"Overly emotional with your feelings toward me."

Something close to alarm flashed in his eyes before he scowled and brushed past her. "I dinnae get sappy over lasses."

At least he had let go. "Yeah, same here when it comes to guys. Total turn-off."

The truth was the only type of sappy she had dealt with were guys going all mushy when they learned she had issues with her hearing. It was pathetic. If she wasn't going to be soft about her affliction, then they shouldn't be either. Yet one way or another, all the guys she had dated ended up treating her differently when they found out.

And she did not want to be treated differently.

So she kept looking for the guy who understood her. Who would realize that she was strong and be strong alongside her. She didn't want or need to be coddled.

"Can you climb well enough?" Niall asked as she followed him back down into the oak's cave.

"Yeah, why?"

"There's a wee bit o' a climb ahead." He checked on Vika and Nicole patted her.

"Feel better now, lass?"

Nicole frowned and eyed Niall. He hadn't said that. And it certainly had not been little Robert. Tentative, she responded within the mind. *"Who is this?"*

" 'Tis me. Vika."

"Oh, damn," she said aloud by mistake. Nicole had started to give up hope that Vika would speak telepathically to her.

"What?" Niall asked.

"I think I'll keep you my little secret for now," she said to Vika as she rubbed her muzzle. *"Nice to meet ya by the way."*

"Ye as well," Vika said.

"Nothing," Nicole responded to Niall's question. "Just stubbed my toe."

Niall tossed her an odd look and shook his head. "It typically takes hitting the toe on something for that to happen, aye?"

Nicole made a loose gesture over her shoulder. "Back when we were screwing around." She gave him a pointed look. "It got pretty rough there."

"Aye." Apparently that was enough of an explanation because he nodded and gestured for her to follow him.

"You have everything you need?" she asked Vika.

"Aye, lass. Dinnae worry over me."

Nicole rubbed her muzzle one last time and followed Niall down a narrow hallway before they arrived on a ledge.

"Holy fuc….fudge," she murmured, staring at the massive cave they entered. Mist swirled down from above until it vanished below. A massive, twisting stalactite wrapped from the ceiling to the ground.

A ground that was *way* down there.

"Fudge?" he asked.

"Huh?" She tore her eyes from their surroundings.

"You just said fudge."

"Oh." She shrugged. "I'm trying to work on my swearing because of Robert. It's not cool to do around kids." Nicole sighed. "And I tend to have a filthy mouth on occasion."

"Aye." Niall's eyes dropped to her lips and it seemed he understood the twenty-first century saying this time. His words were very soft, but she heard them. "'Twould have no time to be filthy if put to good use."

"Keep dreaming, buddy." Yet she found herself imagining the possibilities. Before he could catch on that she wasn't opposed to his innuendo, she said, "I spent a lot of time growing up on the streets. I guess that's where I learned to curse."

"Why were you on the streets so much?"

She was so busy trying to evade talk of oral satisfaction that she had introduced something she never meant to. Her upbringing. "Just tends to happen when you're raised in the city." Peering over the edge, she changed the subject. "Please tell me this isn't what you were talking about when you mentioned climbing."

But she knew it was because everyone else was down there.

"Aye." He eyed her feet. "But now I dinnae know with your sore toe and all."

He was trying to call her bluff. So she went with it. "You're a wizard. Can't you snap your fingers or something and get us down there?"

"Nay." He offered her a devilish grin seconds before she realized his intentions.

But by then it was too late.

Chapter Nine

NIALL GRINNED AS Nicole muttered, "You suck," approximately twenty-seven times on the climb down. She was a wee enough thing so it wasn't especially treacherous save for the few times she wiggled in defiance. But then there was the bonus of her perfect arse doing all the wiggling. By the time they made it to the bottom, she had started to mix in some especially creative alternatives to her typical array of curses.

"I can't believe you flung me over your shoulder and climbed down, you ass...sertive person," she growled as he lowered her. Nicole shoved him away. "Darn dangerous."

Niall chuckled as she strode, limp-free, toward his kin. He called after her, "'Tis good that your toe doesnae seem to be bothering you anymore."

"It was a stubbed toe, Brute." She shook her head. "Everybody knows the pain doesn't last long."

He knew damn well she had been lying and he knew why. Vika had spoken to her within the mind. What he hadn't been able to figure out yet was why Nicole didn't just say as much. But if there was one thing he had learned about her it was that she was more guarded than most. And fiercely protective of her privacy.

A sense of privacy she still had no idea she shared with him.

The sense that he should tell her the truth only grew stronger and stronger. He might find Nicole to be one of the most exasperating lasses he had ever met, but she was also, by far, the most exciting. There was so much about her that drew him closer. Not just her rebellious nature but the layers beneath that were slowly but surely being revealed.

Her concern over Robert.

Her unwavering devotion to her friends.

The endless courage that existed at the root of her.

"So ye couldnae manage the climb on your own, aye lass?" Machara taunted Nicole as they joined everyone around a fire. Tucked beneath a plaid, the Bruce slept.

"More like your meathead cousin can't keep his hands off me," Nicole retorted and plunked down on a log beside Darach. He wondered if she did that on purpose to make him jealous.

Niall sat across from them, stretched out his legs and nodded his thanks when Logan tossed him a skin of whisky. Eyes still on Nicole, he said, "All you have to do is say no, and I'll keep my hands where they belong, lass."

It wasn't quite saying they had enjoyed each other's bodies, but it wasn't quite saying they had not either.

Malcolm's eyes narrowed on Niall. "'Tis best you both keep your hands where they belong on this mountain and well you know it, Son."

As if he could have walked away after she said yes. He had never wanted to be inside a lass so much...*needed* a lass so much. It had been an unthinkably powerful experience made up of not only extreme lust but something far more.

Something that could be life-altering if he were not careful.

"That sounds serious," Nicole said in response to his father's statement. But her eyes didn't narrow on Malcolm. No, they narrowed on Niall. "What does he mean?"

Darach's eyes were narrowed on Niall as well.

Logan simply had a 'you're on your own with this one' look on his face.

Machara chuckled. "Och, have ye not heard of the mystical fertility powers of this mountain, lass?"

Nicole's eyes widened and swung her way. "Come again?"

"'Twas only said to be because of the Baby Oak," Niall assured.

"Yet Alan and Catriona Stewart conceived their twins, Brae and Cullen on this mountain before the Baby Oak was born," Darach said.

"Oh, shi...ship," Nicole stuttered, eyes growing wider even as she navigated around swearing.

Malcolm sighed and frowned at Niall, clearly getting the answer he sought based on her reaction. "Some say it was the power of

Torra embracing her dragon for the first time here that turned that acorn into a tree but others have long speculated that the mountain helped."

"Aye. Nobody else got around to testing the theory after that." Machara winked at Niall then arched a brow at Malcolm. "Until your lad was conceived."

Nicole's eyes went to Niall and she whispered, "You were conceived here?" Then her eyes slowly swung to Malcolm and it seemed she wasn't concerned in the least that she addressed his father. "You ended up with Leslie's sister, Cadence. A woman from the twenty-first century." She swallowed and kept going. "Was she on birth control?"

"Nay," Malcolm said and Nicole slumped with visible relief.

"Wasn't that because—" Machara started.

When Malcolm shook his head sharply, her words trailed off.

"'Twas because it was her decision not to be," his Da said.

Niall almost took the escape his father seemingly offered after drawing him out to begin with but truly didn't believe what they said about the mountain. So he looked at Nicole and told her the truth. "My Ma was told by doctors that she couldnae conceive so there was no reason for birth control."

Nicole blinked several times as she processed the information. "Yet she did on this mountain."

Darach being Darach tried to ease her evident discomfort. "Are doctors not often wrong about such things? Miracles happen."

"Oh, you're a miracle all right," Nicole said softly, eyes narrowing even further on Niall. "It'll be a fuc...fudgelike, God-da-dang great, miracle if I don't frigging kill you—"

"Fudge-like?" Machara interrupted.

"She's trying not to swear in front of the Bruce," Niall muttered and took a hearty swig from his skin.

Nicole started to swig from the one Darach handed her but stopped, cheeks turning red as her anger grew. Och, the bloody lass was already worried about being pregnant. Niall set aside his skin and frowned.

If she was not going to drink neither would he.

Obviously she was on birth control and they had nothing to worry about. He had yet to impregnate a woman and he had lain with his fair share. Even so, something took root in him at the notion. At the idea that he and she might have…

"*What* is that look on your face, Niall MacLomain," Nicole said, voice rising as she stood.

"Until Fionn Mac Cumhail makes himself known, I'll not have the wee Bruce awoken," Malcolm warned.

Darach stood and pulled Nicole after him. "Come, lass. Let's talk, aye?"

She muttered a whole stream of half swear, half made up words and reluctantly let him lead her away. It took just about everything Niall had not to stop them…to tell Darach to get his bloody hands off her.

"The lass doesnae need this extra strife right now, Son," Malcolm said softly. "Ye werenae wise to lay with her here."

Logan looked between them before his eyes landed on Malcolm. "Ye know as well as I, Uncle, that when the time is right with our lasses, the time is right. It cannae be helped."

"Mayhap not," Malcolm said. "But 'tis always truth we give our lasses before such things. 'Tis unfair otherwise."

"If I believed in the fertility rumors about this bloody mountain, I would have," Niall defended. "But I dinnae so willnae apologize."

"Nor should ye if ye truly believe such," Machara agreed, trying to detour the conversation as only she knew how as she looked at Conall. "But dinnae ye get to thinking I want yer cock anywhere near me."

"If I wanted it near ye, it would already be there," Conall muttered under his breath.

"Och, ye've had me so often in yer thoughts ye dinnae know the difference anymore," she scoffed.

As she likely intended, all eyes swung her way.

"It sounds as if ye've given this far too much thought yerself, Cousin," Niall said.

Conall kept muttering under his breath as he pulled the game that had been roasting off the flames.

Machara was about to respond when something shifted in the cave. Cool, then warm wind blew around them before a glow flashed then vanished. A tall, golden warrior strode forward.

Fionn Mac Cumhail.

All stood and bowed, but he shook his head. "Nay, enough with that." His eyes scanned them. "Are we not all equals, then?"

Equal to a god? Not likely. But none argued as Fionn sat on a log, a frown on his face. "We've a grave problem."

Fionn had just finished saying that he compelled Darach to join them when his cousin and Nicole returned. Though she was clearly still upset with him, Nicole said nothing as she and Darach sat next to Niall. When Fionn introduced himself to her, Nicole managed a weak hello. Niall didn't blame her. It wasn't every day you met a Celtic god.

Though he did not mean to in the least, Niall took her hand and squeezed. And though she definitely did not mean to in the least, she didn't pull away.

"While I would like to say you are safe here," Fionn began, his eyes locking on Nicole. "You are not." Then his eyes went to the sleeping future king. "Nor is he. At least not right now."

Nobody said a word as the god considered them. "As your enemy and her ill-begotten partner play their games from the Celtic Otherworld, we need to play ours where there is more power to be had. A place where there is more strength to catch our nemesis unaware."

His eyes traveled from Logan to Darach before they once more landed on Niall. "You will welcome help from your Viking ancestors."

Nicole tensed. "The Viking King."

"Aye." Fionn nodded with a tepid but warm enough curl to his lips. "He is waiting for you, lassie." His eyes swept over the rest. "All of you."

"Where?" she said.

"Eat. Rest." Fionn stood. "But not long." He looked at Niall. "You will know when 'tis time to go."

"Are we safe?" Nicole said. Leave it to her to question a god.

But Fionn didn't seem put off as his eyes met hers. "I would not have it otherwise."

Then he was gone.

Quicker than he came.

Nicole blinked a few times in disbelief. "This is good."

As always, she seemed to take everything in stride. All things considered, what sort of twenty-first century lass so easily accepted

131

that a man had just vanished before her eyes? But then not only had she seen Grant do it but Nicole was different.

Far more resilient than most.

All remained silent for the most part as Conall handed them meat and they ate. Niall let Machara finish his whisky then filled it with water for him and Nicole to share.

While there was a certain comfort in knowing they stood a fighting chance against Brae Stewart, he also felt uneasy. The Viking King, Naðr, had made contact with Nicole at MacLomain Castle and now they would be going to him? Did that mean back to the ninth century or would the Viking be coming to them? Whether it had been said or not, he felt solely responsible for Nicole and Robert so deep down he trusted no one.

Not a Viking ancestor or even a god.

And curse his eyes but they kept going to his father. What was he thinking? It was unusual for Malcolm to remain silent. Typically, he would have carried on about the fertile mountain and his son's poor timing.

But no.

Even as they finished their meals and set to slumber, his Da did not look in his direction. Why? Was he so disappointed in Niall that it was impossible to even look at him? Yet the more that line of thinking festered the more he was glad Malcolm ignored him.

Only when they laid their plaids and set to rest did his father glance his way. Likely because Niall refused to let Nicole lay beside Darach. Enough was enough. She might not be his lass but he would be damned if she rested near anyone but him. Nicole, naturally, muttered about him being a jackass the whole time but kept it at a whisper likely because she didn't want Robert to wake and hear her.

In the end, she was beside him but turned away.

But she was beside him.

Though tempted, he didn't wrap his arms around her but stayed close. He kept telling himself it was because he meant to keep her safe, but there was more to it than that. Something he scowled at even as everyone else slumbered and he eyed her red hair resting against her slim neck. He wanted to run his finger up the slender column until he again cupped the fine bones of her cheek. To feel that softness again. He licked his lips. To taste the smooth satin of her skin and hear her moans. The pleas that said *don't* even as they said *do*.

Almost as if she sensed his thoughts, she turned.

He stilled as she tucked herself against him and nuzzled her nose up beneath his chin. She inhaled then exhaled softly before her breathing evened. Careful but desperate, he wrapped his arm around her and pulled her close. All he could think about were their moments together earlier. How she was worried that he was getting sappy.

She had no idea how sappy he almost became.

Niall breathed in her sweet hair, scented by the mountain. Scented by their lovemaking. He took Cassie's advice as if sent from the gods. He did not want to scare her away.

He did not want to lose her.

Did he?

Nay.

But how could he keep her without losing himself? Because a lass like Nicole meant to steal away his soul and make it her own. She was fierce and a warrior in her own right. A lass who fought with her heart when he was used to fighting with weapons.

Yet there was an ease to her.

One that he felt bone-deep. One that made his worries vanish when they should remain firmly in his mind. One that made the world and all its distress fade away as they curled into one another. He typically didn't sleep long. Ever. It was an age-old habit born of training to protect the Bruce.

But she made him sleep.

Soundly.

Peacefully.

A peace that was ripped from him when the sound of crashing water filled his eardrums. Loud. Fast. Here. When he bolted upright, Nicole stirred. She sat up as his eyes swept over the cave.

All was quiet.

"What's going on?" she murmured, groggy as she looked around.

"Darach, Logan, 'tis time." He stood. "We need to go."

Like him, his cousins slept on the edge of awareness and were up immediately as were the remaining warriors. All he could think about now was Rònan. Why had they not asked the god about him?

But somehow he knew Fionn kept things exactly how he intended them.

Which irritated the bloody hell out of him.

But also made him hopeful.

Had the god done such with purpose? Was his cousin still alive? Cursing under his breath, Niall realized how untrustworthy his mind had truly become. How deluded all their minds had become.

He glared first at his father. "You thought not to ask after my cousin?"

Malcolm seemed discontented but said nothing as he stood, his gaze sweeping over everything.

Nicole rubbed her eyes as she tried to acclimate. "Again, what's going on?"

"Something. A vision of sorts." He nodded at the wall they had climbed down earlier. "We need to go that way."

So they all headed toward the rock wall. When Nicole paused at the makeshift ladder, he said, "I will carry you again, lass."

That got her going.

Nobody said a word as they climbed. Malcolm carried Robert the Bruce. Nicole fared well, likely because Niall stayed behind her, a constant reminder that he would carry her if need be.

When everyone reached the top, Niall allowed his senses to take over. "This way."

None questioned but followed as he led them through the Mother Oak's cave toward the exit to the ledge he and Nicole had been on before.

"What about Vika?" Nicole asked.

"I dinnae know, lass." He frowned. "We can only hope that Fionn sees fit to send her after us."

"Forget that." She stopped next to the horse. "If she stays, I stay."

"Nay." Darach took her wrist and pulled her after him. "'Tis far too dangerous."

When she pulled against him, Darach shook his head and warned, "Dinnae think I willnae throw you over my shoulder like Niall did." He nodded at Niall. "If my cousin says 'tis time to go, then 'tis time."

He'd never more grateful to anyone when Darach decided to handle the stubborn lass this time. His nerves were on edge. Raw.

Her stubbornness would send him spiraling out of control. He couldn't handle that right now. Too much was at stake. And he was even more grateful when she followed rather than ending up on his cousin's shoulder. But then he knew Vika had helped convince her to leave as well.

Niall led them over the rock ledge to a steep incline that lead down into the abyss of the mountain. His father's eyes met his. "Are ye sure, Son?"

"Aye." He nodded. "Now."

Malcolm eyed him for a long moment before he nodded as well and ushered the others down. By the time they reached the backside of the waterfall, his sense of urgency had grown. Whatever was coming was almost here.

Time was running out.

"I don't like this," Nicole started as he grabbed her hand and yanked her after him.

"Niall." Her voice sounded not panicky but firm as he murmured a chant and the waterfall shifted so that they could pass through easily. "What's happening?"

If he knew, he would tell her. His eyes fell to the lake at the heart of the waterfall as they exited. The pull he had felt in his dream rose.

One made of water.

Urgency.

Escape.

He pulled Nicole close and shook his head. This made no sense. What was he looking for? Waves lapped. A moon shone overhead. There was nothing here.

Yet the need grew stronger.

"He's coming," Nicole whispered.

Niall didn't need to ask. She referred to the Viking King.

Regrettably, he was not the only one coming.

"We've got problems," Machara muttered seconds before a host of enemy warriors roared out of the forest onto the shore. Malcolm kept Robert with him as Niall handed Nicole a dagger and withdrew his sword. Meanwhile, his cousins and fellow warriors had their weapons drawn, eyes not only on the approaching clansmen but on their surroundings. Looking anywhere Brae and her dark shadow monster might be.

Logan started chanting and the ground shook, throwing the warriors off balance. Niall summoned the waterfall's spray to gush against them. Darach called on the wind to slow them down even more. Yet soon enough they were clashing blades. Again, Niall found it difficult to relish a good battle when he had not only Nicole but the Bruce under his charge.

Like him, Nicole took up position in front of Malcolm and the wee King. Niall had to give her credit. She'd paid attention and learned how to use her blade. One warrior already had a gash across his arm. Fueled by pain, he ducked and came at her.

"Och, nay," Niall muttered as he drove one man through with his sword while whipping his dagger at the one rushing her. It was a clean hit in the side of his neck and the warrior fell to his knees in front of her. With a wild look in her eyes and several creative words, Nicole gave him a solid kick to the face and he went down for good.

Despite their dire situation, Niall chuckled as he fought two more men. Yet the chuckle died as he realized how many warriors were pouring out of the forest. Literally an army. His eyes shot to his father and he roared, "Get Robert and Nicole out of here."

"Aye." Malcolm nodded at the lake. "Soon enough."

Wind not of Darach's making had started to whip up over the water, and a thick fog curled over the lake masking everything. Even so, Niall and his cousins had no choice but to remain focused on fighting. Logan was methodical as ever as he downed man after man. Darach fought with two swords, moving faster and faster as he ducked, spun and sliced.

Niall growled in renewed frustration when by habit he sought out Rònan. They had always battled alongside one another and he felt the loss of his brother-in-arms deeply.

When Nicole screeched, his eyes flew her way. A warrior had managed to take her down and was seconds away from running his dagger across her throat. Niall roared with rage, unable to get to her as he fought off three more warriors.

Machara had nearly reached her when Nicole drove her knee up into the man's groin. Taking advantage of his weakened condition, she grabbed his dagger and sliced it across his throat.

Machara, a wide grin on his face, arrived just in time to pull the dead warrior off his lass. Eyes wide, Nicole was shaking but able to stand as she nodded thanks to his cousin. Niall's adrenaline was still pumping and he managed to take down all three warriors with one mighty swipe of his blade.

By the time he reached Nicole, three things happened at once.

He saw the blossoming blood on her shoulder.

The dark monster enemy cloud appeared.

But so did a Viking longship.

Chapter Ten

NICOLE HONESTLY DID not know what to focus on first. The Viking ship or the concern and fury in Niall's eyes when he saw her wound. More than that, the savage way he started fighting as he kept anyone from getting too close to her. He was brutal. Ruthless.

Impressive.

Yet eventually, like any normal twenty-first century woman would do, her eyes swung back to the massive ship. Better yet, all the rugged men climbing down from it. Holy *hell*. Where had they come from? This was nothing but a lake. Or so she assumed. No matter what, they were here and a totally different breed from the Scottish warriors.

Nope, these guys were definitely Vikings.

Long haired, bearded, tattooed Vikings.

Her eyes went to the man leading the way. Huge, with black hair and a fierce expression, she knew exactly who he was. The Viking King, Naðr Véurr Sigdir. He nodded at her before his blade crashed into an oncoming warrior's.

His voice entered her mind. *"You need to get your people on the ship now."*

Nicole immediately relayed the message to Malcolm, who must have told the others because they started for the ship even as they fought. She didn't get far before a Viking scooped her up.

"I can walk," she said, ignoring the sting in her shoulder.

"But I can walk faster." The handsome Viking with bedroom eyes winked at her. "Kol's the name. I'm the King's brother."

"Nicole," she murmured before he handed her off to another and she was swung up into the ship. When she saw that Robert was already safely on board with Malcolm, she rushed to the side and tried to peer through the fog. Where was Niall? She was probably better off without him but still. She couldn't just leave him behind.

Wind roared as the black shadow overhead fluctuated and twisted, trying to get closer to the ship. Only then did she see the behemoth Viking sitting on the dragon prow with his arms raised in the air. Head back, he appeared to be chanting...and somehow keeping the monster at bay as men started to climb aboard.

Logan arrived first followed by Kol and Naðr. By the time Darach, Machara and Conall boarded and the ship appeared to be pulling out, panic had set in.

"Darach." She grabbed his arm. "Where's Niall?"

"He wanted to make sure our warriors made it back to the safety of the mountain. He'll be along," he assured. "Niall tends to fight for as long as possible."

"He'll be along," she mouthed and shook her head as the last Vikings boarded and started to row. "I think the hell not."

She had just managed to swing her leg over the edge to head back down the ladder when Naðr pulled her back into the ship. "You're not going anywhere, woman."

Before she could respond, he swung over and vanished. By this time, the oars were really starting to move them and the sail was being raised. The black shadow kept rushing at the ship but whatever the guy on the prow was doing seemed to be working. Nicole was just about to head after Naðr when he returned.

Her eyes flickered from him to the ladder. When Niall didn't appear, she shook her head and started in that direction. No sooner did she reach the side before he swung over and sat on the edge, sword still clashing with someone behind him.

Kol captained the ship and roared for the men to row harder. Niall made one more driving thrust before he muttered, "To hell with ye then."

By the time he jumped into the ship, he was soaked and speckled with blood. The look in his eyes when they swung her way was indescribable. Angry. Relieved. Concerned. He pulled her back against him, wrapped an arm around her waist and kept his sword in front of her. Nicole realized he was defending her until they were clear of the black shadow.

Thick, soupy fog poured over the ship as waves crashed against the hull. It was nothing short of spooky as the whiteness scooping around her became so dense that she could barely see Niall's sword. The air chilled and the scent of sea salt filled her nostrils. Too much time went by as they stood there waiting. Expecting. Ready.

"We arenae in Scotland anymore," Niall eventually murmured and slowly lowered his blade. "'Tis safe enough for now."

"Not in Scotland anymore," she whispered. Her eyes widened as the fog started to dissipate and revealed not a lake but an ocean. By the time the last wisps of condensation cleared, white-tipped jagged mountains etched the horizon.

"Welcome to ninth-century Scandinavia, lass," Niall said softly.

A loud roar of approval arose in response to their surroundings, rumbling along the ship like thunder. Darach and Logan were embracing Kol and Naðr as everyone offered a hearty greeting.

Instead of doing the same, Niall turned her and eyed her shoulder. "Bloody hell." His concerned eyes met hers. "Are you well?"

"I'm fine," she assured as he scooped her up then sat her down on a bench by the mast.

He crouched, a heavy scowl on his face as he tried to inspect her wound. "We need to get this cleaned and wrapped before it festers."

"It's just a scratch," she said. Or at least she thought so. It had been a slice, not a thrust.

"Let me see." When he started to pull down the corner of her dress, she stopped him.

"Hell, Niall. Do you see how many men are on this boat? You can't just strip me."

"I dinnae care how many—"

"Let me take a look," came a deep rumble before another man crouched next to Niall.

Nicole almost pulled away he was so ferocious looking. With tattoos wrapped over his bare head and two skinny braids hanging from his goatee, he was even fiercer than the Viking King. She narrowed her eyes as it occurred to her who he was. "You were just up on that prow, weren't you?"

"I was." His voice was surprisingly gentle considering his size. "My name is Kjar." He gestured at her shoulder. "I can take care of that for you."

Niall nodded and sat next to her. "Aye, 'twould be most appreciated, friend."

"How are you gonna—" she started but froze when Kjar put a gentle hand on her shoulder. Niall's arm slid around her waist as an alarming heat encompassed the wound. When a pinch of pain stabbed her, Niall's arm tightened. Yet the pinch faded fast and left only mild warmth in its wake. She peeked beneath her dress after Kjar pulled his hand away.

"Oh, wow," she exclaimed. "The wound is totally healed."

Kjar grunted and nodded, apparently more concerned about other things. "You've been touched by the Celtic gods." Kjar's eyes shot to Niall. "A dark god."

Nicole frowned. "Excuse me?"

Disgruntled, Kjar stood and gestured at Niall. "Come, we must speak with Naðr and your cousins immediately."

"Hello? Anybody listening to me?" she said as they ignored her and headed for the Viking King. Nonetheless, she called after Kjar. "Thanks by the way."

Nicole sighed as she eyed the men and tried to keep her fear at bay. A dark god had touched her? Yet deep down she wasn't all that shocked after the nightmare at MacLomain Castle and the voice in her head when Rònan died. No, vanished. Because she refused to believe he was dead.

"It seems we're changing course," Kol commented as he sat down beside her. He glanced at her shoulder. "Are you better now, Nicole?"

"Yeah, thanks." She eyed him. "Care to share how Kjar managed it?"

He handed her a skin. "Demi-gods have a way with healing."

"Demi-god!" Nicole almost took a swig but lowered it when she remembered that she might have been duped into pregnancy. "Are you shi...sharing the truth?"

Kol looked at her oddly either because she didn't drink or because of her stuttered words.

"Yes, Kjar is half god." He cocked his head. "Why do you not drink?"

"Is it water?"

"No. It is ale." He nodded. "Good ale."

"Oh, I could really go for some good ale right about now," she murmured but continued to try to give it back to him.

"Loki's balls, then drink, woman. You earned it."

"Och, she cannae, lad. 'Tis verra likely she's carrying a wee one," Machara said, plunking down on Kol's other side. She offered a somewhat flirtatious grin. "How fare ye, old friend?"

Kol grinned. "Married." The grin grew wider. "And happy."

"Ye *married*?" Machara's brows shot up. "I didnae think the day would ever come."

"Nobody thought the day would ever come." Kol chuckled before his eyes swung back to Nicole. "Were you hoping to be with child, then?"

Of all the blasted conversations to be having with a ninth-century Viking.

Damn Niall.

"Hell, no," she said but felt a strange little flutter in her stomach as her eyes found her brute of a MacLomain. Ugh, when had she started thinking of him as *her* MacLomain? Time to lose that thought.

"Then your worries are over," Kol assured. "Because you're not with child."

"How do you know?"

"His dragon blood," Machara kicked in and winked. "Allows them to sense things like that. They can hear it and smell it. It's the same with arousal."

"Oh, super," she muttered in regards to the arousal comment. She felt both relief and something else at the confirmation that she wasn't pregnant. What that something else was she had no idea.

"Och, lass," Machara said softly. "Judging by that look on yer face mayhap ye werenae so opposed to the thought of a wee bairn." Her sly eyes went to Niall. "Or mayhap 'twas the thought of sharing a wee one with my cousin."

"*Definitely* not," she shot back and took a hearty swig of ale. Warm and flat, it was *nothing* like the icy brew back home. But it warmed her belly instantly so she took another deep swallow.

If possible, Niall's scowl was fiercer than before as he headed back in her direction.

She shook her head and pointed at her belly when he leaned against the mast. "Nobody in here to worry about." Then she gestured at Kol. "So says the dragon blood apparently." She handed him the skin. "So have at it."

Honestly, it had been sort of sweet when he stopped drinking last night. She didn't know many guys who would do that.

"I need a moment alone with Nicole," Niall grumbled.

Kol and Machara made quick work of vanishing as Niall took a hearty swig then sat down next to her.

"I thought you'd be happy that your thoughtless actions didn't get us in trouble," she said and took the skin back.

"My thoughtless actions?" he growled.

"Yeah, the whole having sex thing when you knew I could've become pregnant."

"I told you and everybody else that I dinnae believe such about the bloody mountain." He took the skin back after she swigged and murmured, "Besides, 'twould not have been such trouble."

She frowned. "Now see that's what I thought that look was on your face last night and told Darach as much."

"Aye, lass, when ye should have been speaking with me not him."

"I wasn't given much choice at the time." Nicole narrowed her eyes. "And in case you haven't noticed, you and I don't communicate all that well."

"'Twas verra good communication on the mountain, aye?" He narrowed his eyes as well. "Or so said your screams of—"

"I'm not talking about sex and you damn well know it."

"Sex and communicating isnae our primary concern anymore, lass." Niall handed her the skin. "'Tis more at stake now than ever before."

The look on his face was daunting. Different. He was worried about her in a whole new way. "What is it?"

Nicole wondered if he meant to wrap his hand around hers as his brogue thickened with his emotions. "'Tis what Kjar sensed when he healed you."

"Yeah, a dark god. He said as much."

"Aye, one who has wrapped his soul with yours." He pulled her hand onto his lap almost as if he could better protect her that way. "'Tis how he is able to speak within your mind."

She again thought of the nightmares she'd had at MacLomain Castle. "And in my dreams."

"Aye," he said. A tick started in his jaw as his eyes stayed with hers. "You are in far more danger than previously thought."

If there was one thing she could consistently credit Niall with it was brutal honesty. Though tempted to take a hearty swig, she took a small sip and handed the skin back. Even if she wasn't pregnant, drinking too much didn't seem like such a bright idea.

"I'm not scared," she lied and made sure she kept the fear from her eyes. "I can take care of myself. I'm more worried about Robert right now."

The rock of the ship and the lap of the waves seemed to fade away as he searched her eyes. There was something new in the way he looked at her.

"Ye might keep your fear well-hidden, but I see it, lass," he whispered and touched her cheek. "Ye dinnae need to hide it from me."

For a moment, she was tempted to lean into his touch and relent. To share not just her current fears but those that had been deeply ingrained for a very long time. To share even more than she had with her friends. Yet even as she teetered close to giving in, her sense of self-preservation won out. She tore her eyes from his and pulled away. "I'm not hiding anything, Brute."

Niall sighed and wrapped a heavy fur cloak around her shoulders when Naðr handed it over. Even she could admit it was pretty intimidating when the Viking King crouched in front of her. He had a way of looking into the soul that put her on guard.

"It is good to finally meet you in person, Nicole." He squeezed her hand. "How are you feeling?"

"Uptight," she answered frankly. "Can you blame me?"

He shook his head. "No." Then he nodded over his shoulder. "Soon you will board a smaller ship that will take you to our dragon lair. As I'm sure you understand, I cannot bring you to my fortress and put my kin at risk. Not only do my people need to be safeguarded but we have children born of dragon blood and they must be kept clear of this new evil. They are more vulnerable than most to creatures born of the Otherworld, even if it's Celtic and not Norse."

His tone turned especially serious. "Kol and Kjar will stay with you and the MacLomains until I hear from Grant. As I would, my brethren will protect you with their lives."

"Heck, you've already saved my life." She shook her head. "Keep Kjar and Kol with you." She glanced at Niall then his cousins. "I'm in good hands. You should totally protect your family."

Naðr squeezed her hand again then stood. "The MacLomains are my kin as well, woman." He offered a small smile that she knew he hoped was comforting. "Which means you and the future King of Scotland are mine to care for too."

"You should at least keep the demi-god with you, right?"

"Kjar stays with you."

Nicole had no chance to argue any further before another ship appeared alongside theirs. After that, everything happened quickly. Nicole, Robert, and the MacLomains boarded the new boat along with Kol, Kjar and a handful of warriors. Then they were off. She watched as the large Viking ship drifted away.

"You can always speak to me within the mind," Naðr assured telepathically.

She bit back a smile. *"Good to know. Thanks again for all your help."*

Jagged cliffs were already rising up on one side of the ship as they started to navigate around tons of rocks.

When Robert joined her, eyes wide, she took his hand and smiled. "Beautiful, isn't it?"

He nodded and looked at her shoulder. "Yer a mighty warrior, Missus."

"Remember, call me Nicole." She lifted him onto the bench next to the center mast and held him in place so that he could see better. "After all, you're my friend, right?"

Robert nodded, eyes wider and wider as they navigated closer. "I've never traveled through time before."

"Pretty fun, isn't it?"

He nodded again, a shaky smile blossoming on his face. "Aye, but I feel really far away from Ma now."

"You might be but," she patted his chest, "She's always right there inside your heart so she's really not that far away at all."

His eyes glistened for a moment before he thrust back his shoulders, nodded and eyed the cave they were entering. "Aye, she is always with me, Nicole."

She smiled, marveling at how smoothly the ship docked alongside a wooden pier built into the torch lit rock wall. Three people waited for them. A gorgeous woman with brown hair, a small boy and a teenage boy. When they finally made it onto the dock, Kol pulled the woman into his arms and kissed her soundly before making introductions.

"This is my wife, Amber," he said, adoration in both his voice and eyes as he looked at her. Then he lifted the little boy and held him on his hip. "And this is my son, Tait."

A perfect mixture of his parents, Tait was bound to be a lady killer when he got older.

Tait nodded at them then narrowed his eyes on Robert. "Tait 'the fierce'!" he declared.

Kol kept grinning and nodded at the teenager. "And that's my nephew, Heidrek, son to Raknar."

As tall as Niall, but a few inches shorter than Kol, it was clear Heidrek wasn't done growing. God help all the Norse girls when he was. Hair shaved on either side, his pale blond hair was tied back. Still gangly but already broad in the shoulders, his light blue eyes locked on Nicole with interest.

"Her name is Nicole," Darach said as he pulled Heidrek in for a hug and ruffled his hair. "And she's way too old for you, lad."

Heidrek shoved away, scowling as he ran a hand through his hair in embarrassment.

"Awesome to see you guys again," Amber said to the MacLomains, hugging them before she grinned and pulled Nicole after her. "Even *more* awesome to meet someone from my own century."

Tait, meanwhile, held a wooden sword to Robert's chest. "Go forth at your own peril!"

Robert puffed up and looked down his nose at the little Viking. "Ye better bloody well get that blade off me."

Tait didn't budge an inch. "Loki's balls, you make no sense with that accent, enemy!"

"Kol," Amber warned over her shoulder. "He's too young for that."

"Enough with the cursing, son." Kol's words faded away as he tried to break up the children.

Amber chuckled and shook her head as she led Nicole up the long dock and further into the cave. "His turn to deal with our little guy. Mom needs a break."

"I'll bet." She eyed Amber up and down. "So you're from the twenty-first century?"

"Yup. 2015."

"No kidding." Nicole grinned. "Me too."

"Yeah, I've heard a bit about your tale," Amber said as they entered a huge cave with endless stalactites and stalagmites. A fire burned brightly at its center. "But I'd love to hear all the details."

"I'd like to hear your story too," Nicole said as they sat on a rock next to each other and Amber handed her a skin. "Obviously you're American. Where were you born?"

"New Hampshire but I traveled here from Winter Harbor, Maine." She gave Nicole a knowing look. "Pretty sure you've been up that way recently."

"No shi...sure have." Nicole shook her head. "That's where Cassie and I began this whole escapade. With help from a guy named Sean O'Conner."

"I know Sean well." A warm twinkle entered Amber's eyes. "How's that sexy fisherman doing anyway?"

"Still sexy as ever," Nicole assured and eyed Amber. "So how well did you know him?"

"Well enough." Amber proceeded to fill her in on parts of her and her sisters' adventures that involved traveling back in time to be with Kol and his brothers. It was fascinating. Yet soon enough the enigmatic woman turned the conversation back to Nicole.

"So you ended up in the Scottish Highlands, eh? And you're meant to be with one of those Scotsmen." Amber's eyes traveled over Logan and Darach. "Not those two." They landed on Niall. "But him."

The guys sat on the opposite side of the fire, catching up with Kol, Kjar, and Heidrek as the little boys fought with wooden swords. Machara and Conall had gone to catch fish for dinner.

"I'm not meant to be with anyone, *especially* Niall," Nicole said in response to Amber's assumption. She ought to just leave it alone but no. "Why would you think that?"

"Besides the way you're constantly looking at each other?" Amber grinned. "I know Logan's already hooked up and Darach's not your type. That just leaves Niall." The look she slanted at Nicole was telling. "And Niall's just the sort of challenge a woman like you needs."

"The same could've been said about Rònan." Nicole sighed as she thought about him. "And I haven't been looking at Niall in the least since we came in here."

But she knew she had been. Too much.

For safety reasons that is.

"I heard about Rònan." Amber squeezed her hand, a troubled look on her face. "He's about as tough as they come so I know he'll be okay. Dragon shifters are survivors to say the least."

Nicole nodded but remained worried. "He's a great guy. I hope to hell he's not dead."

"Kol and his brothers don't sense that he is," Amber said gently. "But they *do* feel he's lost. And in a bad way."

Though about to comment, Nicole bit her tongue. Nothing she said would come out right and she wasn't sure she wanted to hear anything that might douse all hope. Call her a cautious optimist right now.

Amber and Nicole kept chatting for a while before Machara and Conall came back with fish and they started cooking. When Amber went to Kol, Heidrek wasted no time joining Nicole. Maybe it was a Viking thing but he possessed more self-assurance than most kids his age.

"You are very beautiful," he led out.

Not above being paid a compliment, she grinned. "Thanks."

Heidrek nodded, his eyes glued to her face. "Are you spoken for?"

Nicole almost laughed but stopped. He might seem confident, but there was no reason to test that theory. She remembered all too well how vulnerable being a teenager could be. Especially being a teenager who kept that vulnerability tucked away deep inside.

"Actually, no. I'm not spoken for yet," she replied.

"Would you like to be?"

"Aye, lad," Niall said, joining them. It seemed the brute knew how to be tactful after all. "But because of that ring she wears it can only be with a MacLomain."

Though clearly frustrated by Niall's interruption, there was genuine affection in Heidrek's eyes when he addressed the Scotsman. "I take it you wish to be her MacLomain."

Niall shocked her with his response.

"I wish to be her friend and see where that takes us."

Heidrek considered Niall before his eyes quickly returned to her face. "And do you feel the same way about Niall?"

"I don't know," she began, sort of baffled by the conversation. "Maybe." Easy goes it. "To the first part anyway."

"You should know that I am next in line to be king and could provide well for you, woman." Heidrek's gaze never wavered from her face.

"Wow, you see something and you go for it, eh?" She offered a crooked grin. "You realize I have at least a decade on you, right?"

When Heidrek frowned in confusion, Niall chuckled. "Like Darach said. She's too old for you."

"Her age means nothing to me," Heidrek said. "She is very beautiful and I have heard she is fierce in battle. Those are two things I admire above all else in a woman."

Niall shrugged and relented. "She *is* fierce in battle."

Nicole eyed him. "Bet your ass-assigning me the correct description, I am."

Niall chuckled. "There are all sorts of other descriptions I could assign you as well."

"So you think her fierce." Heidrek kept staring at her. "Do you not think her beautiful as well, Niall?"

Niall made a project of eying her up and down, obviously enjoying himself. "Aye, she's bonnie enough."

"Well, I would make you my queen if you would have me," Heidrek said to Nicole. "Regardless what that ring you wear is supposed to mean."

"I appreciate that, Heidrek." Nicole made sure she kept just the right tone. "But the truth is I'm hoping to return home when all of this is over."

"Ah."

When she heard the deflation in his voice, she nudged his shoulder playfully. "Hey, you're hot as heck and heir to the throne. Girls are gonna be beating down your door if they aren't already."

Confusion knit Heidrek's brows.

"Och, laddie, you've a Ma and two aunts from the future. Have you not caught on to their way of speech yet?" Niall filled in the blanks. "She thinks you're handsome and that you'll have plenty of lassies wanting you." Before Heidrek could respond, Niall finished bluntly with, "And she's too bloody old for you." Then he winked. "But not for me."

"If you change your mind, my offer remains," Heidrek said firmly as he stood. Nicole's eyes widened when he knelt on one knee, kissed the back of her hand and used his eyes in a way that would likely win over the heart of every girl he ever came across. "I would be honored to call you my own."

Then with a flourish, he strode away.

"Damn," she murmured and slid a look Niall's way. "You might be able to learn something from the kid, Brute."

"He's a good lad." Niall looked after Heidrek fondly then eyed her as he took a swig. "And 'tis safe to say I've learned everything I need to when it comes to dealing with a lass like you."

The way he rolled his tongue in his cheek filled in all the blanks.

"Get over yourself," she muttered but grinned a little before she sipped. It continued to amaze her how she could go from despising the man one second to getting a kick out of him the next.

Niall winked before he retrieved some fish for them and showed her how to eat it. Though it wasn't as tasty as what she ate at Weathervane Seafoods, it wasn't half bad. You just had to ignore that it had a head and eyeballs.

Thankfully, the remainder of the evening focused less on all the crap they were getting ready to face and more on friends reconnecting. She found the Vikings very interesting, especially Kjar. He had a great sense of humor and was about the last person she would've ever guessed was a demi-god. In truth, he seemed the least mystical of them all with his biker looks and hearty attitude. Apparently he was happily married to a powerful seer who remained behind to help protect the fortress. They had three little girls between the ages of two and four who kept his face animated as he shared stories of their endless conquests...ones that clearly included winning his heart.

After hours of battling, Robert and Tait had long fallen asleep, swords still in hand as they curled up together under a fur. Amber and Kol were in and out of the conversation, so in love and lust she wondered if they ever came up for air. Logan had nodded off but not before sharing several stories about Cassie. They might not have been together long, but it was clear in the way he spoke of her and how his gaze drifted to the fire too often, that he really missed her.

Now Darach sat on one side of her and Niall on the other as they lounged and enjoyed the dwindling fire. Backs against a rock, they had several furs over them as Nicole yawned and looked around. "Where'd Machara and Conall go?"

"Hopefully slaking their long overdue lust," Niall mumbled.

"'Twould make life more peaceful, aye?" Darach said.

"Aye," Niall agreed before he cocked a grin at his cousin. "Or mayhap 'twould only make matters worse."

"Why's that?" she asked.

Niall shrugged. "'Tis hard to imagine Machara tied down to one lad and Conall would want as much."

"So 'twould be a bloody good fight if she strayed," Darach continued.

"Because she would," Niall said.

"Aye."

"You don't know that," Nicole defended. "Maybe she's finally getting what she's always wanted."

Niall and Darach glanced at each other and shook their heads before their gazes returned to the fire.

"I dinnae think 'tis likely," Niall murmured.

"Nay," Darach agreed.

Niall snorted. "Unless he has a magical cock that is."

"Stop." Nicole shook her head and sipped from her skin. She had managed to make it last all night. "I'm all set with magical cocks."

Yet she chuckled.

So did Darach.

Then Niall.

Not full out laughter just low key shared amusement as they all likely visualized Conall trying to lock down Machara long term with his magical cock.

"Everyone should rest," Kjar declared at last and gestured at Niall. "You and your woman will take Naðr's cave."

"I'm good with crashing right here," she argued as Niall pulled her up. She glanced at Darach. "C'mon, you can sleep in Naðr's cave too."

"Nay, lass." Darach's eyes flickered between them and he shook his head. "I'm fine right here."

"Whatever," she muttered as Niall pulled her after him down a long, twisting hallway.

She stopped at the cave entrance and shook her head. It was mind-blowing. Huge and sweeping, wall-bracketed torches lined the curved walls. Gentle waves lapped against the shore of an inlet well-protected by rugged cliffs. A mammoth, full moon sat low in the sky, glittering orange and white over the ocean. What really got her attention though was the monstrous bed against the far wall. Torches burned on either side, giving it a throne-like look.

"Och, lass," Niall said softly as he pulled off his tunic and gave her a hungry look. "I think mayhap this is the second time ye dinnae look *ungrateful* in the least."

Chapter Eleven

NIALL PURPOSEFULLY DID not look at Nicole as he yanked off his boots, whipped aside his plaid and strode into the water. "Come, lass. If there's one thing you need to learn about being a warrior 'tis that you should always bathe after battling."

"Here we go again with this," she said.

"Aye." He turned and eyed her once he was waist deep. "The salt is healing. You need to wash."

"Kjar already healed me." Yet her eyes stayed on his chest as she started working at the ties of her dress. "But you're right. Not cool to sleep with blood on us."

Niall dipped beneath the water but didn't stay there long. He meant to keep drawing her in then he meant to take her again. And again.

"You've got that look in your eyes," she complained even as she worked faster at her ties while simultaneously trying to peel off her boots.

"I dinnae ken this look ye speak of," he said, thickening his accent because he liked the affect it had on her.

"Uh huh," she muttered and made a sloppy mess out of getting her clothes off before she strode into the water.

He had already warmed it so instead of sloshing in the arctic chill of the Norwegian Sea she instead enjoyed a temperature closer to the Caribbean's.

"Oooh," she exclaimed. Her nipples tightened to mouth-watering points as her flesh met both the warm water and icy air.

Though tempted to yank her into his arms, he instead lowered into the water and floated. The waves were rough, but he quelled them just enough. Not so much that she could find balance, of course. No, he intended to *be* her balance one way or another.

When she got deep enough, he held out his hand. "Dip beneath then let me show you something."

"C'mon, don't be that obvious," she said as she ignored his hand and sunk before surfacing.

He curled his fingers. "It's not what you think."

Nicole hesitated but not as long as he figured she would before her hand slid into his. Niall pulled her close, put his hands on her waist and strode a few steps until she was between two juts of rock. Then he pushed her back against the cave wall until she grabbed the rock on either side.

"Have ye got a hold, lass?" he murmured, sorely tempted to take her right now.

When she wrapped her arms over either side and gasped, "Yes," he pulled away.

Niall made his way to the next indentation and wrapped his arms over either side as well before his eyes went to hers. "So you've got a good hold, aye?"

She flung her head a little when wet hair flopped in her eye. "Yeah, why?"

"You'll see. Hold on tight." Niall murmured a chant. "From the gods of the ocean I thank ye, might your waves once more be. *Oceanus a diis gratias agite undas iterum vestri erunt.*"

Nicole yelped with pleasure when the waves swelled to what they should be and the ocean frothed and swayed beyond their alcoves.

"Wow," she exclaimed, eyes almost child-like as she swayed gently and laughed. "It kinda feels like a Jacuzzi with one helluva view."

The moon all but swallowed the sky and the waves ebbed and flowed. Truly magnificent. But not nearly as enchanting as her face as she let go and embraced something else entirely.

Pure fun.

Pure enjoyment.

He laughed and nodded at the alcoves that kept them safe. "Do you want to know where we are?"

"I know where we are." She laughed as well. "Naðr's lair."

"Aye, 'tis true." He nodded at the alcoves they were in. The one beside hers then the two next to his. "But there is a story behind these."

She kept smiling as she splashed her feet. "Okay, I'm listening."

"'Tis said that when in dragon form the Viking King slashed his mighty claw here for his Queen, Megan," Niall said. "So that she might find enjoyment and escape as you are now."

Her eyes widened as she really looked at the five deep indentations or gashes in the rock.

"Holy hell," she whispered then bit her lower lip. "I mean...darn, this is incredible."

Nicole's eyes shot to his. "He must be massive! But then he's pretty huge in human form."

"Aye." Niall put his hand over hers but kept his eyes on the ocean. "Naðr and his brothers are amongst the greatest men you will ever meet." Because he couldn't help himself, he tossed a grin her way. "Outside of me and my cousins that is."

"All of you," she murmured and shifted her eyes to the ocean, "Are something else."

She did not pull her hand away.

He smiled and turned his gaze to the sea. They stayed that way for a while as she enjoyed the water. As she enjoyed not being so guarded.

When she eventually spoke, her words were soft. "Your dad didn't stick around long tonight. Where'd he go?"

"I dinnae know." Niall shrugged and kept his eyes on the waves. "To sleep I suppose."

"You guys don't get along so well, eh?"

Normally and with anyone else, he would steer the conversation away but something about being here with her made him speak what was in his heart. "We did...years ago."

"What happened?"

"Time," he murmured. "It passed and he didnae like what I made of it."

"Why?"

Niall hesitated, that old familiar tension seeping into his body.

"You don't have to tell me if you don't want to," she murmured.

The problem? He *did* want to tell her. Everything. And that alarmed him. Even so, he kept talking. "'Twas simple really. Da wanted me to become Laird of the MacLomains but I said nay."

"Did the clan want you to become laird?"

"Aye." Niall shrugged again, almost as if his father was in front of him and he was once more explaining his reasons. "But 'twas not for me. I grew up at MacLomain Castle. I grew up alongside Logan. I recognized that he was meant to lead. Not I."

Nicole remained silent for several long moments before she murmured, "Were you afraid to lead?"

"Och, nay. Not for a moment." His eyes went to hers. "While the clan might have thought me a good fit and my Da wanted it, 'twas never my passion. I love my cousin and saw greatness in him."

"So you didn't think you were great enough?"

"Aye," he said, his eyes suddenly pleading with hers as they had with his father years ago. "But my greatness exists in protecting my Laird. In recognizing that our clan is better off with Logan as chieftain and me as his first-in-command."

Nicole's eyes searched his and he got the feeling that she could see the truth behind his words, the passion and devotion behind them. "Would you have done anything different if you'd become the Laird or do you stand behind everything Logan has done?"

Nobody had ever asked him that.

Nobody had ever wondered if he doubted his decision.

"Not for a moment," he said softly and honestly. "Logan has done well by our clan and I'm verra proud to serve under him."

"That's great," she whispered and wrapped her hand with his. "Have you ever told your dad that?"

"There isnae any point." He shook his head. "Da sees things one way. I see them another."

"Yeah, I get that I suppose." Her eyes kept with his. "But whether or not you want to hear it, it sounds like your father cares about you."

Not likely. "How so?"

"Because he wanted you to succeed. I don't know him very well but in your day and age or more importantly in his eyes, that meant you taking the lead. One he'd had before you." She shrugged. "It sounds to me like he just wanted the best for you and didn't respond quite how you'd hoped when you didn't live the life he had carved out for you."

"You think he wanted the best for me?"

"Definitely." She squeezed his hand. "Hey, parents can suck but look at the bright side…he cared. Who knows, maybe he saw you not wanting to become chieftain as abandoning something that he had worked hard to build for you...to give over to you. Maybe in some weird way he saw it as you rejecting him."

Too many long nights he had spoken with his cousins about this very subject but not one of them had phrased it like she just had.

"I didnae reject, Malcolm." He turned his troubled gaze to the ocean. "I would never reject my Da."

Nicole remained silent for a time as he mulled over her words. When she spoke, the octave of her voice had changed. "Where's your mom? I haven't heard much about her."

"She's been at Hamilton Castle." A comforting smile came to his face as he thought of her. "My Ma is a good lass. We're close."

"That must be nice," Nicole said so softly he nearly missed it.

Torn from deep thoughts, his eyes returned to her. He was on the verge of telling her what she had told him that first night but stopped. Instead, he said, "What was your upbringing like?"

Maybe, just maybe, she would give him the truth and the secrets he held would fade away.

"Cozy enough." But there was a hitch to her voice. "Mom and Dad were both born and raised in Southie, but they did good by me." She shrugged and didn't meet his eyes. "I've got no complaints."

So she was determined to build her lies. In an odd way, he understood. "Why so much time spent on the streets where you learned to curse then?"

"Because they worked hard," she retaliated a little too quickly. "I had to make my way to and from school. That meant walking because hell if I'd take the bus. Bunch of scuz-nuts."

He didn't like that he lied to her any more than she lied to him, but he kept at it regardless. "So outside of walking to school, life was good at home? You loved your parents?"

"Yeah," she murmured and he cringed as her strong thoughts bombarded his mind. *I liked the idea of them anyways.*

Because they had lain together and he was a wizard, her thoughts were far more open to him. That meant he literally had to close off his mind if he wanted to give her privacy. Which he really didn't.

Not right now.

"You're lying," he said softly.

She pulled her hand away. "No, I'm not."

He knew he should stop talking and let it go, but he realized that an opening had been provided. "Did Cassie not tell you what to expect after sleeping with a MacLomain wizard?"

When Nicole lurched forward, Niall chanted and the waters calmed. But not before she got snagged by a wave. He moved fast and caught her around the waist. Then he kept walking. Even though she scrambled, she couldn't do much as he braced his feet on the rocky bottom and kept her out beyond where she could touch the bottom.

"Stop, Nicole," he grunted when she tried everything.

An elbow jab.

A kickback of the feet.

As a last resort, a wiggle of her perfect arse against his groin.

He wrapped an arm across her chest and waist and locked tight. "Stop, Nicole."

She stilled but remained tense. Worse than that, all the thoughts she had been so good at repressing started to slam into him as she ground out, "You better not be in my head, Brute."

Though he wanted to take her anger and pain and make it his own, he knew he would get further if he pushed her away. So he shut off his mind, a sensation that he knew would rock her to her core.

What shocked him was how lonely he felt the moment he did.

"Nicole," he whispered. "I'm not in your head, lass. You have my word."

"I know." Her body slowly relaxed. "I don't know how I know, but I do."

He released a harsh breath as he severed their connection. Though he had known it was there and had been aroused by it, he had no idea how deeply she'd wrapped herself inside of him. Much like she curled against him when they slept. The comfort she had subconsciously sought wound deep and true. Deep into a place that had him scooping her up and striding for the bed.

The want he had for her not only physically but emotionally was profound.

Too much.

Too fast.

"Put me down," she said but only halfway struggled. "Now, Niall. Put me down!"

"Aye." He tossed her on the bed then came down after her. Hands wrapped around her wrists, he dragged her up the bed until he came over her entirely. "Now you're down, lass."

Niall released her hands, clasped her cheeks and kissed her hard. So hard and so thorough, he lost himself. Lips open and receptive, she managed to groan his name into his mouth as her legs spread. Her nails dug into his shoulders and he relished the idea that she might reopen his wounds.

All of them.

Inside and out.

"Niall," she gasped against his lips when he grabbed her arse and took her with him as he rolled onto his back. Hands clamped firmly on her upper thighs, he closed his eyes and struggled for breath. The bloody lass ripped the life from him and there was still so much straining betwixt them.

Lies.

A need for honesty.

"Open your eyes, Niall," she demanded and pounded on his chest. "Open your fuc..fantastically gorgeous eyes."

Niall welcomed her anger and released her thighs. Clenching his fists, he rested his hands by his side as she came close. When he opened his eyes, hers were narrowed.

"My eyes are open, lass," he whispered. "I can see ye."

They both knew he was not talking about his vision but something far deeper. When she shifted and slowly sunk on to him in the best way possible, he clenched his teeth. All the while her eyes stayed locked with his and her lips inches away.

"You think you have me all figured out," she whispered as she filled herself and licked her lips in a way that made him groan. "But you don't."

His eyes remained open.

It was impossible to close them.

Not with the rabid determination that combusted between them. She loved his body like she fought it. Hard and fast and furious. There was nothing slow about the way his lass moved. As she had with a dagger in her hand, she had something to prove.

And bless the bloody gods, right now she was proving it to him.

No lass had ever moved her hips quite like Nicole did now. It almost took more than he had not to flip her over and move faster.

To show her just how quickly a man could take her when he meant it with all his heart.

Heart.

His heart.

Niall shook off the sentimental feeling as he kept his gaze locked with hers. As she ran her nails down his chest and ate him alive with her eyes. His lass might have been born in the twenty-first century, but she was every inch a medieval warrior in more ways than one.

But he was a warrior too.

And he wanted to conquer.

So as her pace increased along with her moans, he kept his hands down and willed his arousal to wait…to satisfy. He growled and groaned, but he refused to let go as she reached her peak and locked up over him. Saliva pooled on his tongue as her eyes rolled back and her body rippled and quivered. He'd never seen anything so beautiful…so raw. It took everything he had to hold back.

Yet there were bonuses to sacrificing.

To letting the lass win her battle.

She needed it and somehow he understood that because he needed it too.

He allowed a small, easy smile to curl his lips when she shuddered and sank down against him. Unable to stop, he breathed in the salty scent of her soft hair and flexed his hips ever-so-slightly to remind her it wasn't over.

"Hell," she whispered.

But he was in no rush. There was a certain satisfaction in feeling her body tremble against his. In feeling her climax ripple on and stroke him into a lush need that only became sweeter because he knew it was far from over.

He rolled her slowly until she was beneath him then thrust once sharply. Like a bow with a notched arrow, she cried out, arched and released again. Now she wasn't defiant and fighting him but open…

Honest.

Again he let her ride it out.

Eventually, her eyes cracked open a fraction and she whispered, "Don't look at me like that, Brute. Just take care of yourself."

"Aye, lass," he whispered and stroked her damp cheek. "I will."

When he moved, it wasn't harsh and demanding but slow, easy...different. He had never lain with a lass and wanted to watch her every reaction. He had never lain with one and wanted to hear every little sound she made, feel every reaction of her body when he touched her.

It was new and strange and he liked it.

So he took the time to feel her heated, silky skin. The way it tightened at the base of her neck when she swallowed then moaned. How the bones of her chest led to the firm plumpness of her breasts. He dragged his hand down her slender waist, interested in the dip that allowed his thumb to brush over her bellybutton.

Her legs slowly rose and she shook her head, eyes still barely open as she whispered, "What're you doing? Don't do that."

He skimmed his hand over the smooth curvature of her hip then scraped his fingers lightly over her arse when her leg lifted. Hungry for something he didn't understand, he devoured her lips when she tried to talk again. What other word was there for it? Nothing felt so intense as the need to taste her denial and passion not from below but from right here.

This time, there was no talking around his kisses. He wasn't giving her a chance to speak. Whatever was happening between them sped up and slowed down all at once. Like a violent waterfall crashing then finding peace in a still lake.

If he started moving again, he didn't know when. This was too all-consuming and unique. He wrapped one arm around her waist and dug his hand into her hair as he let go. Of what he would never know. Not physical but mental release.

Something soul deep.

Something his and hers.

Theirs.

Kisses turned into strokes of the tongue until nothing but their bodies moving together cut through. They were no longer desperate to take control but to drown in whatever they were creating. This thing that had them stroking and caressing instead of forcing and taking.

When their moans came, they mingled.

"Niall," she gasped.

"Nicole," he groaned.

Again and again they said one another's names as they drenched themselves in a passion that only grew stronger. He moved. She moved. They moved. He never wanted it to stop. Was this bliss? Eternity?

"Oh, God," she gasped, legs wrapped around him and hands clasping either side of his neck. "What are you doing to me?"

Damned if he knew and hell if he cared.

Sweat slicked, they ground and swayed against each other, their eagerness growing as they no longer tried to get closer but sank into whatever had ignited between them. Desperate to touch every inch of her but keep their lips close, their harsh breath intermingled as their lips pressed then grazed then pressed again.

Their hips moved against each other's as they struggled to somehow merge. The sensations were too strong now. The need too great. Body tight against hers, they thrust and drove each other closer. So much. Too bloody much.

When fire tore up his spine, he roared and gripped the bed, concerned that he might hurt her. Nicole again clenched the sides of his neck, pressed her cheek against him, arched and cried out. He had no idea if the sounds he heard came from her or him as sharp pleasure screamed through him and he let go.

Long, hard and with no end in sight, he let go.

It was the most freeing moment of his life in ways he did not understand.

Aye, sexually, but so much more.

So, *so*, much more.

"*For me too,*" she whispered into his mind as he jerked against her, far gone.

It was a long while before either of them were able to move, let alone speak. But he still heard those whispered words in his mind. A response to his own thoughts. Words he apparently couldn't block if he wanted to. Ones she never intended for him to hear.

For me too.

Words that had literally just changed his life.

Chapter Twelve

NIALL HAD LONG dozed off yet she still hadn't pulled away.

She could.

She *should*.

But no, Nicole remained draped over him, tucked beneath furs he had at some point pulled over them. The crash of waves echoed through the cave and torches burned. Yet for the first time in far too long she focused less on what she could hear and more on what she was feeling.

So much feeling.

The lingering pulses between her thighs that should be long gone. The smell of his skin, taxed but salty and spicy at the same time. She kept trailing her fingers down his bicep and forearm, fascinated by how the muscles wove together before they culminated in his strong hand.

His other hand remained clamped possessively on her butt.

What were they doing? What *was* this? She was still pissed that she lied to him earlier about having parents. Why not just tell him the truth? Deep down she knew why. Telling him would let him into her inner circle and nobody was allowed there except her closest friends. Letting a man so close was not going to happen. Nobody got inside her heart like that and the idea that Niall just *might* have made her feel shifty. Edgy. Angry.

But excited and eager.

Those last two emotions almost made her flee. Out of this cave. Back to Amber. Back to Darach. Anyone who could point a finger at Niall and say, "Back the heck off!" if she wanted them to. Because she did. Or so she tried to convince herself. Yet instead of running she snuggled closer…as close as she could get.

"Go if ye need to, lass," he whispered. "I willnae hold ye back." Niall was awake.

How did he know she wanted to run? Was he in her head again? Cheek still pressed against his chest, she said nothing. Better to let him think she was snoozing.

"I know you're awake," he murmured, stroking her shoulder so gently she barely felt the touch.

Not the type to evade, she murmured back, "I'll leave when I'm ready to."

"I'd rather you stay."

Nicole was about to bite back with a remark about how damn lucky he would be if she did, but frowned and said nothing. The truth was she didn't want him to move...them to move. The comfort and safety she felt in his arms was...what? Something she was unwilling to let go of. Even if she refused to admit it.

"I'm still here, aren't I," she whispered, frustrated that she felt the need to say it. But *not* saying it was impossible.

Now he stroked her hair. Just a light touch. As if he wasn't claiming her but wanted to offer simple comfort. "Aye, you are."

Again, her traitorous eyes went to the ring on her finger. Still the same. Good. What a relief. Right?

"Nicole?" Niall said softly and wrapped his hand over hers.

"What?" she mumbled. A surge of irritation blew through her when he brushed his finger over the stone at the heart of the ring, stealing it on and off from her sight.

Niall being Niall didn't hold back. "Are you hoping this stone will match my eyes?"

"No," she said too quickly. She kept staring at the ring, lost in a variety of emotions.

As he seemed to like to do, he surprised her when he pulled her ring to his lips, kissed it and murmured, "'Tis a telling ring this. One that I find myself needing an answer from."

"No," she repeated, on auto-drive now as she yanked away, sat up and frowned at the ring. She shook her head and stood, repeating, "No," as she pulled his tunic over her head.

"I didnae mean anything by it," he said gently.

"Hell if you didn't," she muttered and plunked down in a chair by the fire. "You're obviously interested in me again."

"Aye, I am." Niall kept lounging casually on the bed, all his splendid nudity laid out for her to admire. "But truth be told, I think mayhap I've been interested in you from the start."

Nicole frowned. "I'm a waste of your time, Niall." Her eyes met his. "You might think there's hope for us, but there's not."

She didn't much like the softening in his gaze as he considered her.

"I disagree," he said. "But I willnae push you, lass. Either you want me or you dinnae."

"Well, I don't." She gestured at the bed. "Outside of the obvious that is."

Niall leaned over and pulled a skin out of a satchel then tossed it to her. "There's water in that if you're thirsty."

Was she ever. Nicole nodded thanks and took several long gulps before she noticed the way he was looking at her. As if he had something to share but was not sure where to start. "What?"

Niall stared at her for a long moment before he sighed. "I dinnae want the lies betwixt us anymore."

Nicole didn't like the sound of that. "What lies?"

"The first night you arrived at MacLeod Castle," he started. "The night you were in your cups."

"What about it?" she said cautiously. "I thought you already came clean about that night."

"Partly." His eyes stayed with hers. "But there was more." He cleared his throat. "Quite a bit more." He held up another skin. "Mayhap you'd like a wee bit o' whisky first?"

Damn. He thought to soften the blow with booze. "No whisky. Seems like that's where all my troubles begin." She was almost afraid to ask, but was all about ripping the bandaid off fast. "Out with it."

Niall took a swig. Way to go liquid courage. "You shared a lot about your life that didn't exactly match up with what you were saying earlier about your parents."

"I did *not*," she whispered and shook her head. Despite how intoxicated, she wouldn't share that information with anyone outside of her friends. "You're full of crap."

"You told me about going from foster home to foster home. About the difficult years when you first started having trouble with your hearing and how misunderstood you were," he said, voice low and even.

Oh, no. Why the hell? She must have had one heck of a look on her face because he grew concerned and started to stand.

Nicole put up a hand and shook her head. "Stop right there."

"Why would I have *ever* told *you* all that?" she murmured, well aware she wasn't denying it. "Of all people."

"You said that you'd been scared your whole life and I made you feel safe," he said softly. "That you trusted me to keep your secrets."

"And did you?" she shot back, growing angrier as his revelation sunk in.

When he remained silent, she narrowed her eyes. "*Did* you?"

"Aye, for the most part," he began, a flicker of guilt in his eyes.

"God damn it, Niall!" She stood, fists clenched. "Who'd you tell and how much did you share?"

Niall stood and wrapped his plaid around his waist, a heavy frown on his face. "I only spoke with Cassie so that I could better ken how best to handle all you told me."

"Cassie?" A flash of hurt went through her when she realized her friend had kept this from her.

"She cares for ye, lass," he said. "As do I."

"Well get over it," she retaliated. "Because you seriously don't stand a chance with me now." Before he could respond, she said, "What else did I share with you? Tell me everything."

As if she had not already blurted enough.

Disgruntled, Niall let his plaid hang low on his waist and took another hearty swig of whisky. "That you were truly frightened of going deaf, that you had taken off your clothes for money and that you lost your virginity far too young."

"Wh..what?" she stuttered. *Nobody* knew that last one, not even her friends. She had always figured it was a minor detail and nobody's business.

Clearly she had thought it was Niall's.

This made no sense. None at all. "Why would I tell you so much?" she whispered more to herself than to him. "And heck, you'd think I'd remember just a little bit of it."

"*Well,*" he started then sort of trailed off before his expression once more grew guilty. "I might've made sure that you didn't."

"Made sure," she said slowly. Nicole blinked several times, staring at him, before the truth at last dawned on her. He might look like a hot-as-hell Highlander, but he was also a *wizard*. Her eyes went wide and anger bubbled straight to the surface. "Did you somehow erase my memory?"

He flinched and rubbed the side of his neck. "I didnae think ye'd want me to—"

"Holy crap, you did. You ass-as I live and breathe total jerk!" Furious, Nicole didn't think but acted and whipped the skin at him.

Niall evaded the projectile. "Ye had enough going on and I didnae think—"

"You sure as hell didn't!" Now she was just throwing anything she could find which unfortunately for him were rocks.

But he was quick and dodged them. "Och, lass, 'twas not as bad as all that. Was it not better to forget how much you shared with me? At least at the time."

"How much I shared with you?" Whip. Whip. Then it occurred to her what he had likely done and she grew more upset. "I never told you any of that, did I? You read my frigging mind!"

"Nay, I would never do that." She heard the anger he tried to repress as he dodged to the left before a rock clipped him on the shoulder. "*Never.*"

"I don't believe you." Whip. "You knew I was vulnerable and drunk so made yourself at home in my mind." Whip. "Total douchebag thing to do, Brute."

"Nay, I didnae invade your thoughts," he growled, evading another rock as he stalked toward her. "And there's only one way to prove it."

He had nearly reached her when a firm voice resounded from the entrance. "What hails here? Take one more step, Highlander and you will find my dagger in your back."

Niall didn't stop at Heidrek's threat any more than Nicole stopped whipping rocks. He had nearly reached her when he must have sensed something because he spun fast and caught a dagger inches before it hit him. Meanwhile, a small rock pinged off the back of his head. Enraged, Niall started toward Heidrek.

Everyone save Amber and the children had appeared at the commotion. Heidrek, caught in his own folly, took a few steps back at the rage on Niall's face.

The teenager froze at Kol's low words.

"A Viking does not attack his kin without the King's ruling. And he certainly never stabs his kin in the back but looks him in the eye. 'Tis cowardly to do otherwise," Kol warned Heidrek with disapproval. "You will reap what you sowed here, Nephew."

Heidrek had a split second to nod before Niall drove him back against a wall and held the dagger to his throat. Still shaking with fury, Nicole headed in his direction but Machara grabbed her arm and shook her head.

"Do ye truly think I would hurt Nicole?" Niall said, his tone dark as he came nose to nose with Heidrek. "Ye've seen me several times throughout yer young years. Have I ever once laid a hand on a lass?"

"No." Though he trembled, Heidrek's eyes remained with Niall's. "But then I have never seen you care so much for a woman either. And I have seen too much passion lead to bad things. I have seen men beat their women over it. As I have seen women try to do the same to their men."

"See, there ya go," Nicole said. "He was just trying to protect me."

"I know what he was trying to do," Niall growled, blade still to Heidrek's neck. "'Twas how he went about doing it that was wrong."

"Aye," Malcolm agreed as he leaned against the entrance with his arms crossed over his chest. "'Twas ill that and according to your Viking customs, my place to take ye down if my son shows ye mercy, Heidrek."

Nicole was surprised by the smattering of thoughts that raced through her mind. Ones she realized were not hers but Niall's. How shocked he was that his father had said that. How he had no clue what to make of it. Then her words to him earlier about how his father might have felt he was being rejected when Niall didn't become laird.

She was startled by how profoundly her advice had affected him.

"I am sorry," Heidrek said, not struggling against Niall. "I was wrong. Have I your forgiveness?" He swallowed. "If not, I hope you make it quick so that I might be taken by Loki because Odin would not have me."

"No, he would not," Kjar agreed. "There would be no feasting in Valhalla for you."

Now that her haze of anger was fading, Nicole understood what they were doing. Showing the kid tough love. Probably a good thing. Even in her neck of the woods, you didn't stab a man in the back.

"Give me yer word now that ye'll never do the likes of that to yer kin again, aye?" Niall said to Heidrek.

"You have my word," Heidrek said. "Never again."

Niall eyed him for another long moment before he nodded, embraced him and clapped him on the back. When he stepped away, Heidrek turned to Malcolm. "Have I your forgiveness as well, Malcolm, father to Niall."

Malcolm eyed him long and hard as well before he nodded. "Ye do. Dinnae do such again."

He said more, but that old familiar buzzing sound drowned out his words. Nicole closed her eyes and tried not to panic as she braced for pain. Instead, Vika's words floated through her mind. *"Where are ye, lass?"*

She was about to respond when strong hands clamped her upper arms. Her eyes shot open. It was Kjar. He put a finger to his lips and shook his head. Then he mouthed, "Say nothing."

"Lass, can ye hear me?" her horse said. *"Where are ye? I'm afraid."*

Niall put a comforting hand against her lower back even though she saw the worry churning in his eyes. Despite the anger she had felt, knowing he was there kept fear at bay as her gaze returned to Kjar. She didn't dare say anything let alone think it. Because though it sounded just like her, it was obviously not Vika speaking.

Though they did it slowly so that they didn't alarm her, she was well aware of the MacLomains, Kol and even Heidrek forming a protective circle around her.

"Respond to her," Kjar mouthed. "Tell her you have fled South. That she is safe and you will send for her soon."

Good thing he did *not* have a brogue or he might have been damn tricky to understand. Doing her best to keep her mind blank, she repeated his words. No sooner did she 'say' what was asked of her did the buzzing start to fade and as always, everything seemed loud. The spit of torches. The crashing waves.

Kjar spoke softly as if he sensed her transition. "The demi-god has left your mind."

Nicole had no clue she was shaking until Niall pulled her into his arms. She rested her cheek against his chest and struggled to breathe evenly. "I should go back. If he has Rònan, I can free him."

"Nay," Niall murmured and stroked her hair. "Ye need always remember what Grant said. The evil beastie speaks naught but lies. Dinnae forget that."

"You will not be safe here much longer," Kjar said. "Though the Celtic demi-god might have been led astray, his connection to Nicole only grows."

"How do we stop that?" Niall said.

"Can I stop it?" came a small voice from the entrance.

Robert.

Nicole pulled away from Niall and headed for him. The idea of the little boy getting involved in this cut deep. "You don't. Not ever. I've got this." Before he could utter a word, she crouched and hugged him. "You stay clear of the bad guys no matter what. Do you understand?"

"But if I can help," he started.

She cupped his cheeks and met his eyes. "The best way for you to help is to listen to those protecting you. And I just happen to be one of them. I'm asking you as one of my best friends to always stay with the MacLomains even if I go away. *Especially* if I go away."

When his eyes grew moist, Nicole hitched her jaw and nudged his chin up. "None of that, little guy. Now's the time for you to be strong and *listen* to those who care about you. How else are you gonna become a great king someday if you don't listen to those you trust most?" She tried to be a little less stern. "Do you trust me?"

Robert blinked away tears and nodded. "I do, Nicole. Verra much so."

"Good," she said firmly and smiled. "That's what I like to hear." She winked. "When I'm hearing straight that is."

The Bruce gave a little grin as well.

Convinced that he would be okay, she nodded at the entrance. "Why don't you go lie down with Tait again?"

"Och, nay," Robert scoffed, putting his shoulders back. "'Tis time for that poor excuse of a warrior to rise up to battle once more."

Before she knew it, the Bruce spun on his heel and strode in the opposite direction, set to go to war with a wooden sword. Only when she stood and turned back did she realize she had an audience. Everyone had been watching their exchange closely. When she saw the look of pride on Niall's face, she scowled and mumbled to the crowd, "Stop snooping already."

"I think ye need to get around to marrying Niall so I can call ye my cousin, lass." Machara chuckled. "What good times we'll have together in battle!"

"I don't need to marry the big oaf to have fun fighting alongside you, sweetie." Nicole winked. "I'm doing just fine fighting single."

"Aye, ye are." Machara grinned. "And 'twill only be more distracting to the enemy if ye do so wearing my cousin's tunic such as ye are."

"Aw, hell," Nicole muttered as she eyed her outfit and fingered her well-tousled hair. When Niall offered a smug grin, she narrowed her eyes. "I'm not done being mad at you, Brute."

Logan and Darach chuckled but were smart enough to remain silent. Machara, however, had no such qualms. "Aye, ye two will always be battling because ye like the making up part too much."

"Ha ha." Nicole could dish it as well as she could take it so she perked a brow at Machara. "Speaking of battling and making up. You must've worn Conall out good seeing how he's not here, eh?"

"Och, nay, he's right..." Machara's words died on her lips as she looked around. "Where the bloody hell did he go?"

Alarm flickered on everyone's face as a loud roar echoed through the cave. Kol was gone in a flash with everybody racing after him. Nicole skidded to a halt, dumb-founded, when she reached the main cave.

Complete chaos reigned.

And Brae Stewart was at the heart of it.

"How the heck is she here?" Nicole cried as Niall handed her a dagger and took up a stance in front of her.

"I can protect myself," she started but snapped her mouth shut when he shot a look over his shoulder she had never seen before. One that said she seriously didn't want to mess with him right now.

Meanwhile, Brae had Conall by the throat and was doing something to him with magic that had him screaming in pain. The MacLomains and Vikings alike proceeded with caution. Kol, however, was all about protecting his wife and son because he roared and shifted into a dragon.

Everyone started throwing magic at Brae, but to no avail. She was well-protected by something powerful and remained untouchable as she flung aside Conall and strode for Robert. Kol tried to attack her, but his massive wings buffeted against something unseen.

"Oh, shit," Nicole whispered. When Tait roared, "Robert the Bruce is mine!" then shifted into a little dragon to defend him, she knew they were out of time.

There was only one thing left to do.

She darted around Niall and raced toward Robert and Tait, ignoring the sting of her bare feet on sharp rocks. Brae was moments away from flinging her hands out at the little dragon when Nicole cried, "Take me. I'll lead you to the other rings!"

Roars of defiant rage came from behind. Darach, Logan, Machara. But none was so loud as Niall's. She came to a screeching halt in front of Tait and Robert, not concerned that there was a child dragon at her back that was nearly as tall as her. One that might not realize that he shouldn't slaughter her to get to the enemy.

Brae's clever eyes met Nicole's. "Now, *see*, that's a good lass. This was all my Laird truly wanted…at least for now."

She might be terrified, but Nicole wasted no time walking straight up to Brae Stewart. "Let's go, then."

"Aye, lass."

The last thing Nicole heard within the black whirlwind that suddenly whipped around her was Robert's wail. "Naaaayyyyy!"

Pain ripped through her as darkness swamped everything and the ground fell out from beneath her. There was no way to know if she screamed or if it was the deafening sound of magic as she fell. Almost like she was falling into the pits of hell. Then she landed. Not hard but bone-jarringly enough that she yelped.

All went very, very silent after that.

Splayed across the ground, she remained quiet as she tried to acclimate. First, she wiggled her toes and fingers and moved all her body parts. Everything seemed intact if not a little banged up. Instead of sitting, she played dead and blinked, waiting patiently for her eyes to adjust to the dim light.

Slowly but surely, she was able to see her surroundings. She was in some sort of small glen surrounded on all sides by tall, jagged, lonely mountains. A dry riverbed cut through dead grass and a cold wind whistled. It almost sounded like the distant wails of tortured souls. Barren, twisted trees completed the spooky package.

Playing it safe, she remained still for a long time and made sure she was alone before she carefully sat up. When she did, she saw someone else lying beside a nearby tree. Squinting, she gasped. Was that Rònan? *Please* let it be him.

"Rònan?" she said, but it only came out as a weak whisper so she cleared her throat and tried again. "Rònan?"

No response. Nothing. But the clearer her vision became, the more convinced she was that it was him. His tattoos almost seemed to glow. So she crawled toward him and kept at it. "Rònan, you gotta wake up. C'mon!"

"Oh shit, no," she murmured when she got close enough. He was covered in blood, chained to a tree and had clearly been beaten up. A ripped plaid covered half his body and one eye was so swollen it was nothing but a slit. Sitting against the trunk, she pulled his head onto her lap and felt for a pulse.

He was alive.

Nicole blinked away tears of relief and brushed his limp hair away from his face. What was left anyway. It looked like half of it had been singed off. Hell, what had he been put through?

Though angered by his poor treatment, she kept it out of her voice and whispered, "It's okay. I'm here. You're not alone."

She adjusted the plaid around him the best she could then kept stroking his hair. Anything to lend comfort. Hours must have passed before he grabbed her hand and pulled her palm against his cheek.

"Rònan?" Her heart leapt with hope. "Can you hear me?"

"Aye," he croaked, his good eye opening just a sliver. "Ye smelled my burn and came, lass. How did ye find me?"

What was he talking about? Then she realized that he had a fever. Unless his skin was naturally this hot. Hard to know with a dragon-shifter. "I was brought here by Brae Stewart, Rònan. Do you know where we are?"

"Ye've been like some sort of angel in all this darkness. So verra beautiful." His eyes seemed to drift. "All that glorious white hair."

Though confused, Nicole went with it. Anything to keep him calm. "Glad I was there for you, hon." While desperate for answers, he was definitely out of it so she let it go. "Why don't you try to rest some more?"

"Will ye stay with me, lass?"

"Of course."

"Aye, then," he whispered and his eye slid shut.

Nicole leaned her head back against the tree and sighed. Why was she here? What was going on? Were Robert and Tait safe? She felt so helpless. There was no way to know how long she stared at the creepy landscape before her eyes drifted shut. She obviously dozed off because she nearly jumped out of her skin when Rònan's deep voice jolted her awake.

"Nicole?"

"Yeah." She blinked. "I'm here."

Rònan grunted, sat up and held his head. "Bloody hell, where are we?"

"Damned if I know," she said, trying her best to remain calm.

He frowned at the metal link around his ankle then shook the chain, tracing its origin to the tree it was wrapped around. "Och," he muttered, yanking at the thing.

"Stop." She grabbed his arm. "Just relax, get your bearings then we'll go from there."

Rònan kept frowning and murmured chants to free himself, but it did no good. She didn't think it would.

"Brae Stewart brought me here so I'm pretty sure that chain's locked up tight with ungodly magic," Nicole informed. "So chill the heck out, okay? It's been a long day."

"Bloody hell," Rònan repeated and eyed the tree before truly taking in their surroundings and mixing it up Nicole-style. "Bloody *fucking* hell."

She might be at the pit of the world, but a chuckle worked its way to the surface. "Gotta stop swearing, my friend. You're set to protect a little boy that doesn't need to hear it."

Rònan plunked down beside her and leaned back against the tree. "I dinnae see how it much matters now."

Nicole averted her eyes when everything fell out. "Fix your damn plaid, Rònan."

"Och," he grunted. "'Tis nothing ye havenae seen before."

"Oh, right." She peeked at him. "Did I really look beneath your kilt then?"

He nodded. "'Tis hard to imagine ye dinnae remember what ye saw. 'Tis quite impressive." A small grin came to his lips despite their circumstances but fell away as he eyed her. "Even if ye could, ye wouldnae want to remember, aye?"

"I dunno." She shrugged, suddenly uncomfortable. Not because of possibly having seen his goods but for another reason entirely. "Just keep your plaid where it belongs."

"Aye, lass." He frowned as he fingered what hair he had left. "The bastards will suffer for this."

"It's not too bad." Nicole shrugged and attempted a grin. "Sort of a *Mad Max* look."

"Mad Max?"

"Just a movie. Don't worry about it."

Rònan sighed and nodded again as he continued to take in their surroundings. "Enough about burned hair and impressive cocks. Tell me what happened since last I saw you."

So she told him. Carefully and slowly and without too much detail. After all, there was no way to know who was listening. When finished, she licked her lips, thirsty.

Rònan mulled over her words for several minutes before he squeezed her hand. "Like my brethren, I am so proud to have you amongst the MacLomains, Nicole. You are a true warrior and hero."

"Stop it." She pulled her hand away. "Anybody would do the same when it comes to protecting a kid."

"Nay, you're wrong," he said softly and took her hand again. "Most would like to think they would, but true bravery isnae so easily found. Not the kind you possess."

"Then you underestimate people," she said. The truth was she would have shunned her own words even a few weeks ago but not now having met the MacLomains, MacLeods, and even some Hamiltons. "I'm surprised to hear you say as much because you've been surrounded by courageous people your whole life."

"True," he conceded. "But they've been people born and raised in an era where they had no choice. Not like you who was born in the twenty-first century. And even then I wonder how many would sacrifice themselves for someone who wasnae their kin as you have done."

"Probably tons." She shrugged. "It's no big deal, okay? So let it go."

"If that's what you prefer." But Rònan was as blunt as her if not a smidge more direct, pouring on his accent likely because he felt like it. "So tell me, how goes lying with my cousin? Have ye lost yer heart, then?"

"To Niall? God, no." Nicole pulled her hand away again and snorted.

"Well, I wasnae referring to Logan because he's taken and Darach could only handle the likes of ye for so long." He tugged at her way oversized tunic. "Nay, yer a perfect fit for Niall if ever I saw one."

"I don't *fit* with anyone." She batted his hand away, cursing that she still wore Niall's shirt. "Least of all your brutish cousin."

Rònan grinned and a twinkle lit his good eye. "So ye *have* lost yer heart!"

"How the hell did you get that outta what I just said?" She shook her head. "I think you're still suffering from a fever."

He brushed his knuckle playfully against her cheek. "Because ye blushed." Then he winked. "And the minute I spoke of him ye smelled of arousal."

"Jesus, Rònan." She tried to shove him away, but he wrapped an arm around her shoulders and kept her close.

"Sorry, I cannae help my dragon senses." Rònan kept grinning. "While I'll admit to wanting you for myself, what you feel makes me verra happy. Niall isnae only my cousin but my closest friend."

Nicole rolled her eyes and gave up. "So what if I like sleeping with him. It doesn't spell love so you need to give up hoping."

"Och, dragon-shifters dinnae *hope* but *know*."

"I don't love him," she mumbled.

"I do."

"You're supposed to."

Rònan eyed her. "And you're not?"

"No, not if I don't want to."

"He once said something like that to me about lasses." Rònan leaned his head back against the tree.

Nicole couldn't help it. She took the bait. "What do you mean?"

"That he would never be forced into love like his parents were," Rònan said.

She frowned. "But I thought his parents totally fell for each other and weren't forced."

"They were. They did," Rònan said softly. "But when things grew difficult between Niall and Malcolm, he started to rebel against his Da in more ways than one I suppose. When Niall wouldnae become Laird, Malcolm focused on him taking a wife and starting a family. 'Twas yet another thing my cousin felt he was being urged to do, something that was expected of him."

"Niall was so damn lucky and had no idea," she said. "I would've killed to have even one parent who cared so much."

"Aye, to a degree," he said. "Whilst I'm saddened by your hurt, I cannae speak for your upbringing. But I can speak for understanding a lad wanting to find his own way despite the path already laid for him."

"You didn't though," she said. "You became laird."

Rònan remained silent for a long moment before he murmured, "Aye, but mayhap I would have liked the choice."

Nicole was about to respond but stopped. Something inside told her that he was not up for talking too much about it and she got that. Everyone made their choices in life and she, for one, never wanted to be questioned about hers. Which made her reflect on everything she apparently told Niall. She might have said otherwise, but she believed him when he said he didn't intrude on her thoughts. If she had learned nothing else about Niall, it was that he was pretty honorable.

Then there was the real reason.

The bereft sensation she felt when his mind pulled away from hers.

It was a feeling she knew wasn't there before that first night but had somehow formed after it. A wonderful, safe, irreplaceable feeling that left her cold and lonely...and missing him when it vanished.

And he had severed it when she asked.

Instantly, without question, without argument, he ripped it away.

"Nicole?" Rònan murmured.

"Yeah?"

"Are you all right, lass?"

"I have no idea," she answered honestly as she rested her head against his shoulder. "Do me a favor?"

"Aye?"

"Stop sniffing because who arouses me is none of your damned business."

Rònan leaned his head against hers and squeezed her hand. "Aye, I'll try my hardest."

She was about to say thank you when a hot wind blew up and their dismal surroundings changed. The tree limbs and mountain tops burned green and the riverbed flowed red.

"Here they come, lass," Rònan whispered and pulled her closer. "Come to find us in what can only be the Celtic Otherworld's version of hell."

Chapter Thirteen

NICOLE HAD NEVER been a big reader because she didn't have much of an imagination. She was a fighter, a survivor, a girl who knew how to make her way in the world. But that had been a world she understood. One made of busy streets and tough people. One made of Boston smog and predictable outcomes. At least for an inner city girl like her.

What came at her now was far beyond that.

Far beyond anything she could wrap her mind around.

Not just Brae Stewart walked toward them but something indecent. Something made of lewd shifts and grotesque manifestations as it became her backdrop...her fuel. Maybe what made it so surreal was how beautiful Brae appeared draped in black from head to toe as it fluctuated behind her like oily, slick wings she had no control over.

Brae stopped within feet of them, her eyes narrowing on Rònan. "Did yer white angel save ye then, fool?"

Nicole had purposefully not said a word about Rònan's mumbled words when she found him because she happened to know a gorgeous woman with white hair...or white-blond hair.

Jackie.

And if for whatever reason this evil bitch was trying to latch onto her, Nicole had every intention of blocking her first. Not even aware she was doing it, she twirled her ring until the heart of it was facing her palm, turned away from everything heading this way. Honestly, she was surprised the ring wasn't already gone or even her entire finger.

"Say nothing," Rònan whispered.

"She will say what I ask of her, dragon," Brae ground out.

"The name's Rònan, if ye recall." He narrowed his eyes. "Ye knew it well enough when we grew up together."

"Och, Rònan." Brae crouched and eyed him over. "Ye were as fiery then as ye are now, but it didnae do ye much good, aye lad? Now yer chained as ye always should have been."

When Rònan lurched forward, Nicole tried to grab him but it didn't matter. The chain stopped him short. Roaring with frustration, he was forced to his knees as Brae stood and chuckled. "Ye cannae win here."

"Where are we, ye bloody traitor," he growled.

"Where ye belong," she spat before turning her eyes to Nicole. It almost felt like a tidal wave was coming at her as the evil demi-god fluctuated and threw hundreds of frightening faces in her direction at once. But one way or another she had seen shadows of those faces. Their ugliness just as clear in many of the people she'd encountered when growing up. Because of it, she did not shy away.

No, she did her best to look at every evil, demented face.

To show them...it, that she wasn't backing down.

She was pissed that Rònan was so beaten up. She was pissed that Robert wasn't allowed to live a normal little boy life. If those reasons were not enough, she was downright furious that this woman and her pompous, nasty boyfriend had tried to hurt Cassie. So she stood and narrowed her eyes. "What's your plan, bitch?"

"Ye cannae even begin to ken." Brae moved so swiftly that Nicole had no chance to move before the woman snagged her wrist.

"Nicole, where are ye, my lass?"

She released a small breath at Niall's words in her head. Holy hell, it was really him. She just *knew* it. Making no movement, she kept her hand and mind very still as the creature fluctuating around Brae moved closer. Nicole hitched her chin in defiance as the shadow slithered over the woman's arm toward the ring.

"I'll say the same words I've been saying for days," Niall whispered through her mind. *"I'm here. I'm coming. Ye are never alone, my lass."*

Though tempted to tell him she was not his lass, his words were far too comforting as the dark fog slipped and slid over her hand. It felt like someone was rubbing an ice cube over her and her flesh was freezing solid in its wake. As if whatever the shadow was doing was infecting her mind, Niall's words became impossible to understand. But not the last few.

"Ye need to love."

Really? This was like some corny love story gone psycho. Love would save the day? She didn't buy it. Not at all. There was no such thing. Nicole refused to say it, never mind think it. Again, refer to bad movie plot.

"Nicole," Rònan growled, frustration rising in his voice. "I cannae help ye, lass. Not at all."

The chill wrapped tighter around her hand as the shadow tried to work the ring off her finger, twisting it so the heart faced outward. Hell, this hurt. Really bad.

Okay, so she refused to love Niall but she *did* love what he stood for. Protecting those he cared about most. Never giving up. Making sure Robert would never be…

Robert.

She might not have known him long, but she loved the little wannabe king. No doubt about it. So she focused on that. How scared he was and how much she cared about him. How no kid deserved to deal with all the crap he did now, especially being so young. Having been there, done that, she knew better than most. Closing her eyes, she focused on how much she cared about Robert…and even Niall.

He just sort of crept in there.

All the times he protected her. One, two, three, *okay*, so she had stopped counting. But in the midst of everything she recalled being beneath him first on the stairs then in the armory. How determined he was that she learned how to fight. Not like Darach tried to teach her but different. More her style…more cutthroat. Take or be taken in a really bad way.

A way she understood.

A way she respected.

"No," she said through clenched teeth as unwelcomed feelings started to wash over her. "I don't love the brute."

"Nay, ye dinnae," Brae whispered.

"I love Robert the Bruce," Nicole bit out but kept her eyes closed, determined to remain focused on him. She loved the kid good and true but still Niall's face rose up in her mind. How happy he had looked when she enjoyed herself in the Viking King's claw marks the night before. The look in his eyes when they weren't fighting each other but…doing something else.

Something she still didn't understand.

Something she was terrified of losing.

Her throat thickened as she opened her eyes, as she looked Brae square in the face and felt the woman's dark Celtic demi-god slowly but surely try to swallow her whole. All she could do was shake her head and mouth, "No."

Rònan tried to help her. She knew he did. But whatever was happening now had everything to do with destroying her and taking the ring.

"No," Nicole croaked even as she knew she was giving up. She closed her eyes. All she had left was something she didn't understand yet she held on to.

Niall and how she felt about him.

A loud screech started and her eyes shot open. She didn't focus on Brae or even the dark shadow, but the low glow coming from her hand. A glimmer flickered. So low and dull she could barely make it out.

But it was enough to make the darkness start to pull away.

Infuriated, Brae's hand shot out and wrapped around her neck. "Yer a fool! Ye could have saved…" Her words faltered and she screamed, "My Laird always had ye and that has not changed!"

Nicole stumbled back as Brae pulled away and turned. Eyes wide, she watched as the glen slowly filled with color. The mountains became gray and their snowy tips white. Tree trunks turned brown and leaves bloomed and turned green. Crystal blue water started to pour down the dry riverbed.

Life returned from death.

Brae shook her head and kept backing up, eyes enraged before she flung out her arms and the darkness took her. The dark laird whipped her away. As if she had never been there, she was gone in an instant.

Nicole kept stumbling and shaking her head until Rònan caught her. Then, as if she came from a creek as her name implied, Vika raced forward, her hooves roaring through the water. Nostrils flaring, she was nearly as ferocious as the man riding her.

Niall.

Eyes wide, confused, Nicole tried to pull away, murmuring to Rònan, "You have no idea how worried he was about you."

Rònan stepped aside but kept a supportive hand against her lower back as Niall swung off of Vika and raced their way. "Aye, but I think that look on his face has more to do with you, lass."

Nicole tried to step away, but it did no good. Niall yanked her against him so hard she lost her breath. He grabbed her ass and wrapped one arm around her back, pulling her so close she thought she was done for as he murmured, "Ye bloody fool. Ye bloody damned fool."

She meant to push him away but instead wrapped her arms around his waist and shot back, "Took you long enough, Brute."

They held each other tight for several moments before she remembered to say, "Besides being a little beat up, Rònan's okay."

It seemed that was Rònan's opening because he flung his arms around them both and leaned his head against theirs. "Aye."

Niall wrapped an arm around Rònan and pulled him closer into the circle, his deep words emotional. "Aye, brother. I knew ye werenae gone. I just knew it."

Nicole tried to step aside to let the guys embrace, but Niall was having none of it. Instead, she remained smushed between two men that were easily twice her weight. When she peered up between all the muscled arms she swore she saw a glistening in Niall's eyes. So she cozied in and rode out the group hug. She supposed there were worse things in life.

"I dinnae like to break up a good time, but even I cannae keep ye safe in this place for long."

Though Rònan pulled away, Niall kept a firm arm around her waist as an old man with white hair and a cane led Vika past them. There was nothing but a smile in his sparkling blue eyes as he walked. "'Twas a bonnie creek the horse helped save ye at, aye?"

Niall and Rònan seemed equally dumbfounded at they watched the man lead the horse along the creek. He chuckled as he threw over his shoulder, "Come now lads, follow Vika and she will see ye well indeed."

Then he flicked his wrist and the link around Rònan's ankle snapped open.

Nicole had no idea what that meant, but obviously Niall and Rònan did because Niall grabbed her hand and they pursued the old man. The only problem? He vanished.

"Nay," Niall and Rònan said at the same time, looks of awe on their faces.

"What?" Nicole said, trying to keep up. "Who was that?" She kept eying the changing landscape. "Better yet, why the heck did hell just turn into heaven?"

"That was Adlin MacLomain." A heavy frown settled on Niall's face as he turned back. "And dinnae worry over our surroundings." He swung her up onto Vika and looked at Rònan. "Ride with her. I'll catch up."

"Nay." Rònan shook his head. "You go. I'll stay."

"You're injured. I'll run," Niall said before he bolted. "We will do as Adlin asked."

"What the…" Nicole tried to lean down and stop him. With a hearty grunt, Rònan swung up behind her. "Don't bother. When Niall gets something in his head, there's no stopping him."

"I get that," she cried as Vika took off.

There was no chance to tell the brute he was a fool.

No chance to tell him he was putting his life on the line.

Because one way or another, she knew something was off.

"Niall, you jackass!" she yelled as he raced to keep up. "Take my hand. Vika's Wonder Woman. She can carry us all!" But Vika didn't slow and Niall shook his head. When Nicole tried to hold back a hand, Rònan yanked her arms tight against her chest and kept going.

"Rònan," she wailed as Vika ran straight toward a cliff. "You can't leave Niall behind!"

"Run, Cousin, run!" Rònan roared as Vika plowed on.

The cliff grew closer and though the world seemed to grow brighter around them, she knew something was very, very wrong. It was too bright and too perfect.

Just like the idea that she could love.

"No," she cried and tried to fling herself off of Vika but it was too late. The horse was cruising and Rònan was strong as hell.

"Niall," she said softly, looking back as he trailed after them. "Niall," she said a little louder when she realized her gut was right.

Something was wrong. He was fading in more ways than one. From her vision, yes. More importantly, she couldn't hear him.

Screw being cool, she arched and screamed, "You asshole, Niall. C'mon!"

Then it didn't matter anymore.

They sailed straight over the cliff.

Not this again. Nicole plastered herself against Vika's mane and Rònan covered her. This was it. Death. Straight in the face. She should look up. Something. She should be brave.

But she wasn't.

Not at all.

Instead, she pressed her cheek against Vika's mane and cried. Not because she was going to die. Who cared? It was bound to happen eventually. No, what got her was...

Niall.

In that singular moment everything was over, she knew what she wanted. Truly, without question, wanted.

Her brute.

She cried and cursed him the whole way down. Why the hell did she want that dirtbag? Because he was *so* a dirtbag...aside from him saving her time and time again of course. She grit her teeth, shook her head and cried some more.

He was *such* a jerk for sacrificing himself for them like this.

But then it seemed they'd all be dying anyway.

Maybe them faster than him.

Unless Vika pulled another one of her miraculous avoid the water tricks and again ended up at MacLomain Castle.

That was the last thought she had before Vika crashed into the ocean. Fast, violent, water rushed up and swallowed her. Everything ripped away. The horse. Rònan. Liquid sucked and thrashed around her as she sunk. Tumbling. Over and over.

Down.

Down.

Down.

Then all went still as she gazed up at the sun shining through the water high above. Vika drifted closer to the surface, her mane and tail swaying weightlessly. Rònan floated as well.

Strange how none of them struggled. Though everything started going dark, she never stopped searching for Niall. Never stopped thinking about him until everything snapped away and there was nothing but complete darkness and silence.

Death.

Nothingness.

At first.

The distant sound of crashing waves started to echo from far, far away. The whistle of wind on rock. The faint cry of Seagulls. Then everything grew louder...closer. Confused, Nicole cracked open an eye. Vision blurry on and off, she watched a woman with long, black hair walking in the distance. Did she see them? Where was she going? Inhaling deeply, Nicole slowly sat up and blinked several times before her vision cleared.

The woman had vanished. Instead, Vika walked toward them.

The horse was alive.

Nicole patted herself and looked around. So was she it seemed. Then her eyes locked on Rònan. Like her, he was slowly sitting up, out of it as he eyed the rocky shoreline. Desperate, Nicole looked around. Where was Niall? Please let him be here.

Then she saw him.

Further down the beach, he remained unmoving.

"Niall!"

No response. Scrambling to her feet, she ran in his direction then stumbled and fell. Damn was her balance off. Even so, she kept moving, staggering until she fell to her knees beside him. "Niall, can you hear me?"

Shoot, he was turning blue. Nicole knew panicking was the worst thing she could do right now. Putting her ear close to his mouth and nose, she felt for any sign of breathing. Nothing. She watched his chest closely. No movement. So she felt his wrist for a pulse. Again, nothing.

"Shit," she muttered, refusing to give in to fear.

Rònan dropped to his knees on the other side of Niall, alarmed. "Cousin?"

Her eyes met his. "Can you save him somehow with magic?"

"Nay." Rònan shook his head. "I dinnae have the power to heal another."

"Damn." She gestured at him. "Stay back then."

Nicole placed her hands, one on top of the other, on Niall's chest. Careful to stay between his ribs, she pressed down and started to do compressions. About thirty or so every minute.

"What the bloody hell are ye doing, lass?" Rònan said.

"This is our best shot at getting him back," she gasped. "Now let me focus."

When Rònan started to argue, her eyes met his. "Just trust me, okay? I don't wanna lose him any more than you do."

She didn't wait for a response but continued to work on Niall. Tilting his head back, she lifted his chin. God, he was so cold. Too cold. Don't think, just do, Nicole. So she pinched his nose shut, took a breath, put her mouth over his and released two second-long breaths, watching to see if his chest rose.

Nicole ignored Rònan as he muttered something about it being a bloody ill time to kiss.

She resumed chest compressions. Thirty of them, followed by two more breaths. Then she started the whole process over again. Despite how hard she tried to keep emotions at bay, it was becoming difficult.

"Don't you dare leave me, Niall MacLomain," she said again and again as she pressed on his chest. "Damn Wizard of Water, my ass. Not if you let it take your life."

On and on she went.

Somewhere in the back of her mind she knew that it was too late but refused to give up. He wouldn't give up on her. In fact, he hadn't time and time again. So she kept fighting.

The minutes seemed to crawl by as her desperation grew. As she struggled for his life. Fought to bring him back.

"Nicole," Rònan said softly.

"Shut it, Rònan." She shook her head. "He's not gone."

"Och, lass," he whispered.

When he touched her arm to stop her, she whacked him away and kept at it, ignoring the stinging burn of her muscles.

"Nay," Rònan finally said. "Enough."

Damn it. Damn it. Damn it. No.

But this time Rònan wasn't giving her a choice. Before he could pull her away, Nicole pumped a few more times and swore she saw the stone in her ring flicker again. Rònan yanked her off Niall and into his arms. Though she struggled against him, it didn't do much good.

Nicole barely recognized the sound of her own sobs. They almost seemed subhuman. Rònan pressed her cheek against his chest and wrapped his arms around her. The pain raking her was terrible. Different. Nothing she could fight back against. It swamped every part of her, inside and out.

"I can't," she whimpered. "This can't be happening. We've come too damn far."

"I know," Rònan whispered, never letting her go. "I know, lass."

"No you don't," she cried and tried to push away, determined to save Niall.

Then she heard it.

A gurgling sound. Her eyes widened. She *knew* that sound. Yanking away from Rònan, she looked at Niall. Water dribbled from the corner of his mouth.

"Help me roll him onto his side, Rònan!"

This time, he didn't question her but helped. Within moments, Niall began coughing out more water and started taking deep breaths. Heart slamming, she released a burst of nervous laughter as color seeped back into his face. "Christ, he's gonna be okay."

"Bloody hell," Niall gasped and tried to sit up, but Rònan pushed him back down.

"Nay, Cousin. Take a moment."

Niall rolled onto his back, held his forehead and frowned at them as he gasped, "What happened?"

"You died is what happened." Nicole's wobbly smile turned into a frown to match his. "And scared the living shit out of me."

Niall said nothing at first as he took in his surroundings. Yet all the while he eyed her and something fluctuated between them. Whatever it was made her chest tighten and throat thicken.

"Ye dinnae look so well, lass," he murmured and touched her cheek. "Yer eyes are all red."

"That's because she was crying like a—"

"Rònan," she warned, stopping him mid-sentence. "Zip it."

"Zip it?"

"Stop talking."

"Were you crying over me then?" Niall said softly.

"Heck no," she shot and helped him sit up. "My eyes are just stinging from the salt water."

Rònan shook his head at her then clapped Niall on his back, smiling. "'Tis bloody good to have you back with us, Cousin."

Vika neighed her agreement.

Nicole smiled at the horse and spoke within the mind. *Good to see you're okay, friend.*

"Aye, 'tis good indeed to see all are well."

"So where are we?" Niall said, rubbing his hand over his face as he adjusted to breathing.

"My guess is the northern tip of Scotland." Rònan nodded down the shoreline. "And I'd say on Sinclair land based on their plaids."

All three stood as a band of warriors approached on horseback.

"I'd do just about anything to be wearing more than a shirt right about now," she murmured.

"'Tis really more of a short dress on you, lass," Niall said as he wrapped a protective arm around her lower back.

"Aye, 'tis a look more lasses should embrace," Rònan added as he eyed her legs.

"*Really*, Rònan?" She frowned at him. "You're checking me out right now?"

"You cannae blame him," Niall defended, giving her legs a once over as well.

The guys might be making light of the situation, but she felt their tension as the men stopped in front of them. A handsome, older man was the first to speak. "From where do ye hail, strangers?" His eyes went to Niall. "I see ye wear MacLomain colors. That makes ye a friend." Then his eyes went to Rònan. "And ye wear MacLeod colors. That makes ye foe."

Then he looked at Nicole with interest as did every other man. She *really* wished she had on more clothing. But it seemed the head guy wasn't without compassion. He nodded at one of his clansmen. "Toss the lass a blanket."

When the warrior nudged his horse closer, Niall shifted in front of her and shook his head. "Give me the blanket."

When the warrior glanced to his leader, he nodded. So the man tossed it to Niall and backed away. Nicole nodded thanks to the Sinclair and welcomed the coverage when Niall wrapped the blanket around her.

Niall wasted no time introducing them, offering his title first then Rònan's. "He is my cousin by blood. Half MacLeod, half MacLomain. As it has been for over thirty winters, the clans are allies and last I knew, allied with the Sinclairs as well long before that."

"We work toward such an outcome but have not yet achieved it," the man said, still not offering his name. He nodded at Nicole. "And who is she?"

"I'm—" she started, but Niall cut her off.

"She is my wif, Nicole MacLomain."

"Wif?" she said out of the corner of her mouth.

"Wife," he said out of the corner of his.

Hell. No. "Absolutely not—" she said but Niall squeezed her close by his side. She didn't miss the warning.

"Married a fortnight now." He shrugged, explaining her potential denial away. "'Twas an arranged marriage ye see and she's still getting used to the idea."

Oh, she was getting used to the idea all right. The idea of telling him to go blow. But she could admit to feeling relieved when the men began looking at her a little less intensely.

The leader considered them for several long moments before he apparently came to some sort of conclusion. "I am Bryson Sinclair, son of King Alexander Sinclair and Iosbail MacLomain. And ye have just become my prisoners."

Chapter Fourteen

Northern Scotland
1154

NIALL FROWNED WHEN the Sinclair warrior told him what year it was. How the *hell* had they ended up here? Better yet, how had Vika managed to remain dry with not only a saddle but a satchel attached. She had fallen into the ocean so it made no sense.

He would be sure to explore the contents of the satchel later. For now all he could focus on was having Nicole in his arms again. He'd missed her so bloody much and had nearly given up hope of ever seeing her again.

"Did I hear that right?" Nicole murmured incredulously. "Did we seriously travel back in time another hundred and twenty-seven years? And I'm obviously not referring to our layover with the Vikings."

"So it seems," he said softly, keeping his arm locked tight around her waist as they rode Vika. He was surprised the Sinclair had allowed as much. Rònan, still in rough shape, lumbered alongside. At least they were all given blankets to help against the frigid winds. Niall had wanted his cousin to ride with Nicole, but Bryson would have none of it. While he might not like it, he understood the Sinclair's need to be overly cautious. Because, if he wasn't mistaken, they were being taken back to Sinclair Castle.

Back to King Alexander.

Because the MacLomain clan kept its history alive by sharing it with each generation, he knew the tale of Adlin's sister, Iosbail Broun...or MacLomain. How she fell in love with a Sinclair king from another time. Then they saw one another on and off over the years so that the once immortal Iosbail could age at the same rate as

Alexander. What he did *not* know was that they bore children. Why would that have been kept a secret?

"How did you find me and Rònan, Niall? Are Robert and Tait okay? Everybody else?" Nicole whispered.

"Aye, all is well," he whispered back. "I'll fill you in later."

They didn't travel far through the woodland and jagged, sweeping mountains before a large castle came into view. Like MacLomain Castle, it had two moats and two drawbridges. A stately beauty well suited to the Highland King.

As they passed over the first drawbridge, his eyes were drawn to the battlements above. An old woman looked down at them. She might wear the red Sinclair plaid, but he knew she was a Broun and MacLomain.

Iosbail.

When her eyes met Niall's, she nodded. He nodded back. Rònan must have sensed her as well because his gaze turned her way.

"Who is that?" Nicole murmured and Niall realized that she was just as drawn to Iosbail as they were. It made sense considering his lass had Broun blood flowing through her veins. So he explained who Iosbail was. Not only Adlin's sister and former matriarch of the Broun clan but an immortal wizard who started a slow aging process when she met her true love, Alexander.

"Damn," Nicole whispered. "That's amazing."

They had just entered the courtyard when a remarkably fit older man strode out of the castle. Niall would put him past his seventieth winter yet he had a stronger stance then most. He might not be wearing a crown, but there was no doubt who he was.

King Alexander.

"Och, Da," Bryson said as he swung down. "I would have brought them to ye."

"I'm not on my deathbed yet, lad," Alexander said and turned his attention to them as Niall helped Nicole down. "Welcome, I am King Alexander." A twinkle lit his eyes. "So we've more MacLomains and Brouns from another time, have we?" He grinned at the men. "Born of the Next Generation ye are."

Well, at least Niall didn't need to catch him up on anything. No, he suspected Alexander and Iosbail already knew a great deal. As it was, rumor had it they were part of his parent's, aunt's and uncle's adventures.

Niall and Rònan sunk to a knee and lowered their heads as they greeted the King.

"Speaking of the Next Generation," Iosbail said firmly from the top of the castle stairs. "One of them comes."

Who? Niall supposed he would find out soon enough.

Iosbail's eyes shot to Bryson. "Go retrieve he who comes, lad." She nodded back the way they came. "Down by the shore."

"Aye, Ma."

"Please rise, lads," Alexander said to Niall and Rònan. "We are all equal here."

There was nothing equal about them in the least, but Niall respected the man's humble nature so rose. "Ye could be putting yer clan in danger by bringing us here," he began, but Alexander shook his head sharply.

"I know the risk."

Did he really?

The King kissed the back of Nicole's hand. "Greetings, lass." Then he held out the crook of his elbow. "Allow me?"

"Absolutely." Nicole smiled and slid her arm into his. "I'm Nicole by the way. Never Nicki, Nics or any other variation. Just Nicole."

The king didn't bat a lash at her odd greeting. "Nice to meet ye, Nicole."

She glanced at Vika. "What about my horse?"

"She will be well cared for," he assured and led her up the stairs.

Niall was sure to grab the satchel before they took the horse away.

Iosbail nodded at Nicole as Alexander stopped and kissed the back of her hand as well. Deep love passed between the elders before the King led Nicole inside. Meantime, Iosbail's attention turned to Niall and Rònan as they arrived at the top of the stairs. She eyed them up and down with blatant approval. "More strong MacLomain lads."

"'Tis good I suppose that Adlin sent ye my way." She urged them to follow. "It seems ye've a nasty beastie after ye indeed, aye?"

"Aye," Rònan said. "One that we cannae assure willnae follow us here."

"Nay, I dinnae suppose ye can." She nodded at a servant and he brought over three mugs of whisky. One, of course, was for Iosbail. "Come, warm yerselves by the fire. Yer chambers are almost ready."

"So we arenae prisoners after all?" Rònan said, a grin on his face. "Yer lad made it sound otherwise."

"Aye, 'twas best he treated ye such until I landed eyes on ye meself."

Niall felt edgy when he looked around the hall and couldn't locate Nicole. "Where did the King bring my lass?"

"Above stairs," she said. "My King tends to like to get to know the lasses who wear the rings. Especially yer lass's. 'Twas once the ring of someone he was quite fond of."

"Who?" Rònan asked.

"That doesnae matter right now." Iosbail took a few hearty gulps of whisky and again gave Niall a good eying over. "Yer William's grandson to be sure though ye've the look of your Da."

"Aye, William was my grandfather." Niall felt a jolt of melancholy. "I miss him."

"Aye," Rònan agreed. "He was a good man."

"All me MacLomains are," Iosbail murmured, her Irish lilt becoming more obvious. "As are me Brouns."

"No disrespect, 'tis truly a pleasure to meet ye, but I should be with my lass," Niall said. "She shouldnae go unprotected."

"And ye think she's such with me Sinclair?" Iosbail bit back, eyes sharp and assessing despite her advanced age.

"That was not what I meant—" he began.

"'Tis exactly what ye meant," Iosbail said. "'Tis a MacLomain gene ye come by naturally that ye think none but ye are suited to protect yer lasses."

Niall supposed he looked a little sheepish because that was precisely what he thought.

"'Tis understandable he feels as much," Rònan defended. "'Tis not every day a lass saves his life." He took a swig and cracked a grin. "Though 'tis more frequent that a lass brings him to his knees with a good pinch."

"Is that right?" Iosbail chuckled and eyed Niall. "Yer Broun did such then?"

"Och, aye, bloody nails on her." But Niall was more concerned with what else Rònan had said. "What do ye mean she saved my life?"

"She beat on ye good she did. Then kissed breath right into ye whilst holding yer nose then beat on ye some more. 'Twas nearly impossible to finally get her to stop." Rònan snorted and eyed Niall. "Do ye two often hold each other's nose whilst kissing? 'Twas a bloody odd sight."

Niall looked skyward and shook his head. "Ye really need to visit the twenty-first century more often, Cousin. She was performing what they call CPR. A way to save without magic."

A host of emotions blew through him as he mulled it over. Thankfulness. Admiration. But more than anything a need to hold her again. He seriously didn't like her being out of his sight.

"How did ye find Nicole and me anyway?" Rònan said to Niall.

"Nay." Iosbail shook her head, wise eyes never leaving Niall. "That will be a conversation for later."

Both clearly understood that what Iosbail said was not to be questioned. She was to be respected every bit as much as her brother, Adlin.

So they chatted about things of little importance. Autumn's harvest. The holiday preparations and the current going on's of the Sinclair clan. Niall finally had a chance to peek in the satchel and was pleasantly surprised to see its contents. It was something for Nicole. But how did it get there? Uncle Grant or Adlin were surely behind it. Or at least making sure it made it this far.

It wasn't too long before Iosbail nodded that they follow her. "'Tis time for Niall to be with his lass." She led them up the stairs. "Dragon-shifter, the King and I need to speak with ye for a bit."

Niall and Rònan glanced at each other, curious. She led them down one of several long torch-lit corridors and nodded at a spacious chamber. "Rònan, clean yerself up then come below stairs. Alexander and I will be waiting."

Rònan had no chance to respond because Iosbail kept walking. She might be older, but she could move right along. Niall followed her up into a tower not all that far from where they left his cousin. Iosbail stopped at the top of the stairs, gestured down a narrow hallway then winked. "Ye'll find yer bride that way."

"She isnae my bride," Niall explained. "I only said that to keep her safe."

"I think 'tis a fine idea that she remain such for now." Iosbail headed back down and he swore he heard her murmur, "'Tis only a matter of time till 'tis true enough."

Niall pondered that as he strode down the hallway. The interesting thing? He was not so opposed to the idea. He was sort of thrown off kilter by the revelation. But somehow he and Nicole suited one another and he knew without a shadow of doubt that life with her would never be dull.

Then there was the alternative. Life without her.

The concept tore through him and he shook his head in denial.

He hadn't known her long and she drove him insane half the time but...life without her?

Niall might have been lost in thought, but his breath caught when he stopped at the doorway of the large, circular torch-lit chamber and his eyes locked on her. Yet again, he had come upon her bathing. This time, the tub was considerably larger and she wasn't snoring.

Arms resting casually on either side of the basin, she curled one finger. "C'mere you. There's room enough for two."

No need to be told twice. He undressed and headed her way. Something about his lass soaking wet aroused him to no end. All that glistening, smooth skin.

Her eyes flickered over his already semi-erect cock as she scooted forward enough that he could slide in behind and rest his legs on either side of her. Though a fire burned brightly, the chamber was still cool enough that steam rose from the water. When Nicole leaned back against him, he pretty much figured he had died and traveled on to his idea of the perfect afterlife.

As if she had been far tenser than she let on, Nicole released a deep breath and leaned her head back. "It took you long enough."

"'Twas not all that long," he murmured, resting his cheek against the side of her head. "Did ye miss me then?"

"Not really," she said, voice a little breathless when he slowly slid a hand across her stomach then rested it on her hipbone.

When she went to grab the soap, he moved faster and scooped it up. "I think I owe you a good scrubbing, lass."

"Why's that?" she murmured.

He kept his accent thick. "Did ye not save me?"

"I owed ya one." She gasped when he ran the soap around her breast then pinched her nipple in passing.

"Thank ye," he whispered, paying just as much attention to the other breast.

"Think nothing of it," she whispered and squeezed her thighs together when he abandoned her hip and started exploring.

"Wait," she said softly. "I need to talk to you." She half-heartedly shoved his other hand away and released a throaty groan when he kept fondling her breast. "And I can't focus when you do that."

"Then 'twas probably unwise to invite me into yer bath to begin with, lass." Because he was no longer semi-erect and seconds away from finding a way to slip inside of her.

"Seriously, Niall." She turned enough that her eyes met his. Beautiful cedar eyes that burned with the reflection of the fire. "Though I'm obviously not mad at you anymore over the whole erased memory thing, I want to know…"

When she trailed off, trying to find the right words, he took a guess. "You want to know my response to what you shared?"

She shrugged and her expression grew guarded. "Yeah…maybe."

There was no need to drag the moment out. He gave her a ready, truthful answer.

"I think you're the bravest lass I've ever met." He remained still so that she understood there was nothing sexual about what he said, about what he felt. "And I told you as much that night."

"Why brave?"

"Because you faced everything in your young life with courage. You didnae let those who misunderstood you lessen your opinion of yourself. And you learned how to protect yourself." He cupped her cheek. "Mayhap overly so."

"Not much choice," she murmured. "What about the other stuff I said?"

"What about it?" He arched his brows. "I dinnae care how old you were when you lost your virginity and I think there's nothing wrong with you taking off your clothes for money. 'Tis a means to survive and nothing to be ashamed of."

"Not everyone would agree."

"I'm not everyone." He brushed his thumb over her chin. "And neither are you."

Her eyes held his. "It wasn't always easy."

Nicole spoke of her profession. "Nay, I cannae imagine it was." His words grew whisper soft as he dusted a finger over her cheek. "Yet you remain so strong."

"Heck, yeah," she whispered.

Nicole searched his eyes for several long moments and he prayed she would stay with him. Not pull away…

And she did. She stayed right with him.

"Sorry I threw rocks at you," she said softly.

He kept stroking her cheek, words just as soft. "I had it coming."

"Them," she reminded. "There were quite a few rocks."

"Aye." He grinned. "You've got a good arm on you."

"Yeah, I used to play a little softball." She grinned as well, tension leaving her body as she settled against him. "I wasn't half bad either."

"I would think not." He rubbed the soap between his hands then urged her to sit forward again so he could lather it into her hair. "Where did you learn CPR?"

Nicole hesitated a moment then spoke. "I was a lifeguard at one of the city pools for a while along with several other part-time jobs." She moaned as he massaged her scalp. "That's when a friend of mine saw me in a bathing suit and said I should start stripping. I could make a lot more money and work fewer hours."

"How much were you working?"

"I have no idea." She sighed as he continued scrubbing his fingers through her hair. "Sixty, seventy hours a week? Maybe more."

"Doing what?"

"Everything." She chuckled. "Bartending, waitressing, janitorial stuff, even sweeping up hair at the hairdressers. Anything to get the rent paid and afford some nice clothes on occasion."

"You're a survivor," he murmured.

"I just did what I had to do." She leaned her head back as he began rinsing her hair. "So there were definite perks to stripping. More sleep and…"

When she hesitated, he said, "And?"

"Well, it wasn't half bad having a job where nobody knew when I was having issues with my hearing. It was hard managing through it at the others jobs," she said. "But I've always loved dancing so if my hearing went I'd just keep on swaying my hips. The manager cued me when the song was over."

"Then the people you worked for treated you well?"

"Yeah, actually. They were all right, especially the other girls. They were super supportive and believe it or not treated me with more kindness than most."

As he had the night she first opened up, Niall bit back emotion and pulled her against him again. He had never met another like her and knew he never would again. She might have thought she was special in all the wrong ways at points in her life, but he knew she was special in all the right ways.

Though it was always hard to know how Nicole might take things, his curiosity had been growing and growing since their time at the mountain. Since talk of it being a place that promoted fertility. So he led into the topic as evasively as he could manage. "You strike me as verra independent. Were you ever hoping to start a family of your own? Mayhap have a wee bairn or two? You didnae seem overly fond of the idea of becoming pregnant at the mountain."

She hesitated but not for long. "Well, damn, Niall, I'd just slept with you for the first time and things were still a little rocky between us."

That *almost* sounded as if she was of a different mind now.

She kept talking before he could respond. "Actually, yeah, having a kid eventually wouldn't be so bad. I wouldn't mind giving them a better upbringing than I had." He heard the smile in her voice. "I'd probably spoil 'em rotten. Naturally, I'd make sure they appreciated things but..." She sighed. "I'd want them to have everything I didn't. Especially a mom and dad."

A sense of rightness blew through him at her words. He could easily imagine starting a family...with her.

"What about you?" she said so softly it was almost a whisper. He was surprised to see her grip tighten on the edge of the tub as if she was tense about his response.

But there was only one way to answer whether or not she wanted to hear it. Truthfully. "Aye. I do want wee ones." When had that happened? Because children had been the furthest thing from his mind before he met her.

But not now.

Bloody hell, not now in the least.

Before he even realized what he was saying, he murmured, "I dinnae want ye to leave Scotland, lass. Stay here with me."

He might not have intended to say it, but he meant it.

He wanted her. Here with him. Always.

When she stilled and remained silent, he brushed aside her hair and peppered light kisses along the side of her neck. "I would care for ye always," he whispered between kisses. "And ye would be free to be exactly who ye are."

Niall realized his poor wording a few seconds too late. Before he could correct himself, she pulled forward and started rinsing off. "Thanks but I can take care of myself." She shot a look over her shoulder. "And I'm not sure if you realize it or not but there's a pretty good chance that who I'll be is a deaf girl trying to adjust to living in a silent world."

Before she could get too huffy and bolt away, he pulled her back against him again, locked an arm firmly around her waist and spoke telepathically. He reminded her that his voice was within her mind. *"Nay, lass, 'twill never be a silent world so long as I'm alive. Ye can flee back to the twenty-first century, but I'll always be with ye one way or another if ye need me. That willnae ever change."*

Giving her no chance to respond, he lifted her to a standing position, whipped her around and spoke aloud. "And what I meant to say was not 'I would care *for* ye always' but 'I would care *about* ye always.' I dinnae care if you go deaf, blind or any other ailment befalls you, I mean to remain your friend and more if you've the mind to let me. I willnae coddle you but support you, ye bloody stubborn lass."

Again giving her no chance to respond, he cupped her cheeks and kissed her. Hard. Long. And damn thorough. If he couldn't get through to her one way, then he would get through to her another. He needed her to understand that he had never been more serious. That he wanted her in ways unfamiliar to him. In ways that he refused to ignore any longer.

Their tongues tangled as she melted against him. Her mind brushed against his like wind rippling over the still sea. Soft and caressing until it became choppy with the arousal flaring within. Both groaned, hands stroking as they struggled to get closer.

When she pulled away, breath harsh, he was relieved to see not defiance but dewy lust in her eyes as she licked her swollen lips. "I can hear your thoughts. So many." Her chest rose and fell. "But I'd really like to try out the one…"

Niall had no idea what she was talking about until she ran her hands down his sides then dropped to her knees. Bloody *hell*. His head fell back and he groaned when she started doing things to him that had fire shooting up his spine far too quickly. Barely coherent, he wrapped his hand into her hair and stared down through half-mast eyes.

He had never seen anything so beautiful.

Mayhap *this* was his perfect afterlife instead.

But even a perfect potential afterlife could be interrupted.

"What's taking ye both so long," Rònan called as he appeared at the top of the stairs and started walking down the hallway.

"Get the bloody hell out of here," Niall roared.

Rònan stopped short and his brows shot up when his eyes locked on them.

"Now," Niall growled as Nicole pulled away and kept her face averted.

"Och, ye bloody lucky bastard," Rònan muttered and spun away. He strode back the way he came, tossing over his shoulder, "The King has summoned ye both so hurry up."

Elbow braced on the side of the basin, Nicole had a hand over her mouth as she shook her head and chuckled. At least someone found humor in all this. Not him. He would rather put a blade to Rònan's neck for stealing away what was bound to be one of the best moments of his life.

"Bloody bastard, my arse," he muttered as she climbed out of the tub. "Piss poor timing."

Sinking down, he made quick work of bathing as she toweled off. Watching her didn't help his already raging arousal so by the time he set to drying off as well he was fighting a foul mood.

"Cheer up, sweetie," Nicole said as she worked at the sashes on her dress. "The day's not over yet."

Niall growled under his breath as he wrapped the Sinclair plaid around his waist and went over to her. "Let me help."

Nicole allowed him to finish tying her laces and eyed him with a smile.

"You appear far too pleased that we were interrupted," he grumbled.

"Naw, I wish we weren't." She shrugged. "I guess I'm just in a good mood is all."

His eyes met hers and his frustration started to fizzle away. "Aye?"

"Yeah," she murmured, looking at him in a whole new way. "Not sure why."

Only then did Niall realize what was different. There was no wariness remaining in her eyes when she looked at him. Strength and challenge, yes, but that was just Nicole. Who she was. The heart of her. No, what he saw now was…acceptance. Of him. Her. Them.

Any aggravation he'd felt faded away entirely as a surge of hope made his chest tighten yet again. He wanted to say so much at that moment but had no desire to say the wrong thing and scare her away. So he showed her instead by pulling her close, wrapping a hand behind her neck and kissing her. Not hard and fast like before but slow and easy. Aye, they may have been summoned by the King of Scotland, but his heart was too busy being summoned by something else altogether.

"I was told to escort ye down so I'm waiting," Rònan called up the few scant stairs he likely went down.

Nicole grinned and murmured against Niall's lips. "I guess we're outta time, Brute."

"So it seems," he whispered but kissed her some more before pulling away. Yet he could not help eying the massive bed as he yanked on a tunic and continued wrapping his plaid. "We should be on that and nowhere else."

"Soon enough." She slid on shoes, muttering, "Man, I miss a decent pair of heels."

Niall smiled as he plunked down on the bed and started to pull on boots. He remembered well the impractical shoes she had shown up in. Or at least the one shoe. But he thought it best to keep her mind off of the twenty-first century and potentially leaving him for as long as possible. "I think Rònan is jealous."

"Jealous." Nicole took a small sip from a mug perched on the table. "Of us?"

"Aye. I think he has a thing for you."

"I think he has a thing for all women." She shook her head. "But maybe not for long."

Niall kept lacing up his boots. "What makes you say that?"

"Well…"

When she paused, he looked up and arched a brow in question.

"Can you keep a secret?"

"I think we both know I can and far too well."

"Right." But she didn't seem phased by the reminder. Instead, she plopped down next to him. "Back when I was in that dank place they brought Rònan, he was suffering through a fever and thought I was some chick with white hair. He was totally into me…well, her."

Before he could respond, she frowned. "Speaking of that scuzzy otherworld, how the heck did you get there? I've been so wrapped up in saving your life then…" Her eyes drifted down to his groin. "Other things, that I totally spaced it." Her eyes shot to his. "You're sure Robert's okay? And Conall? Did he die? Because he was seriously getting his ass whipped."

"Aye. They're all fine. You saved everyone, lass. At least for now." He pulled her to her feet. "As to how I got there, I imagine that's why the King summoned me so you will soon hear."

"Niall." She stopped him when he tried to pull her after him. "Tell me now, please."

Caught by the concerned look in her eyes, he cocked his head. "Why?"

He was surprised by her honesty.

"Because I'm in a super foreign place and I'm…scared." She swallowed. "That was rough stuff with Brae and her evil sidekick."

That took a lot for her to admit and he knew it.

The King of Scotland was just going to have to wait a few more minutes.

So he pulled her back down onto the bed and explained the best way he knew how, knowing full well the information might just push her away entirely. "'Twas Kjar who helped me…then Fionn Mac Cumhail."

When she looked at him in confusion, he continued. "You and Rònan were brought to the Celtic Otherworld. At least a corner of it. But the Otherworld regardless."

"Yeah, I sorta figured."

He pulled her hand onto his lap, bracing himself for the impact of his words. "Nicole, you've been gone for three fortnights as time passes here...or in my era."

"Three fortnights?" she whispered.

"A month and a half as you would say it."

"Fuc-fudge, no," she murmured, eyes growing wider. "You're screwing with me, right?"

"Nay," he murmured. "The Vikings sent us on our way and the wee Bruce remains at the Mother Oak with all of the Next Generation, Fionn, and Kjar to protect him."

"Kjar too?" she asked, relief in her eyes.

"Aye."

"Okay." She nodded. "That's good. He's with the best of the best." Then her eyes met his. "And Heidrek and little Tait are safe?"

"Aye," he assured. "Nothing will get by the Viking King and his brothers."

"Except Brae Stewart!" she pointed out. "Why the hell was Tait even there to begin with when Naðr said all dragon-shifter kids were at the fortress?"

"Because 'twould have been unwise to put all of their bloodline in one place," Niall said. "Kjar was with Tait and that was enough for not only Naðr but the wee one's Da, Kol."

"So how did Brae end up there?" Nicole kept frowning. "And how did you end up in the Celtic Otherworld?"

"We still dinnae ken how Brae arrived there, but I do know how I got to you."

"How?"

Niall rallied himself for her reaction. While it had meant everything to him, it might make her run away as fast as she could.

Not meaning to, his brogue thickened with his emotions. "Ye had to love, lass."

"Love?" she murmured. Her eyes tore from his and she stared at the floor, whispering, "I remember that. I remember your voice in my mind. I thought it had to mean loving you, but then I realized it could mean Robert."

That worked for him so he tried to pull his hand away before she got too close...before she heard the thoughts he tried to repress.

Her hands clamped tightly around his and she blinked several times before her eyes shot to his. "Oh my God."

He might have tried to block her, but something had changed.

They were too connected now.

She knew.

"You sat in that oak in the mountain day after day trying to…communicate with me?" Her eyes grew moist. "Find me?"

Lying to her would be pointless. So he did not.

"Aye," he whispered. Try as he might, he couldn't push the memories away. All the long hours fearing for her life. Terrified that she was dead. The endless guilt he felt because he had not stopped her. Had not kept her safe. He had failed and she was gone. With her, a part of him he never knew existed.

"How did you finally make contact?" Her brows drew down. "How was it that I finally heard you?"

Niall tried to speak, but the words died on his lips.

"Love," Rònan said softly from the doorway. "Ye finally realized that ye loved him as much as he loved ye and the ring heard it."

"Oh, shit," she croaked and stood. When she wobbled, he pulled her back down so she wouldn't fall. Giving her space, knowing full well those were the last words she wanted to hear, Niall made sure she was safely sitting and walked to the fire.

"Ye should stay by her side, Cousin," Rònan began, but Niall interrupted him.

"Nay, 'tis not what she wants."

"No," Nicole said, voice thick. "It's not."

Her words might have well been a million axes thrust into his gut.

"What I mean is," Nicole started but she was cut off by Iosbail.

"'Tis no kin o' mine that makes me King wait such as ye are."

All apologized, but Rònan was the one to save the day. Arm held out to Iosbail, he said, "Might I have the pleasure of walking with ye, lass? 'Twould do my heart good."

"Och, I ought not." Iosbail twisted her lips as she peered up at him. "But ye said it graciously enough ye did."

Nicole and Niall stared at each other for several long, lost moments before they trailed behind Iosbail and Rònan. Niall didn't dare say a word to his lass and it appeared she felt the same because she remained silent. They were at an impasse that neither understood.

Yet it was an impasse that had saved them both.

Her from the Celtic Otherworld

Him from…what? But he knew.

Endless grief.

Because what he felt when she was taken, what he had felt when he thought she was lost to him forever, was incomparable. A feeling so soul-deep that the idea of losing her again made him sick to his stomach. Aye, she might return to the twenty-first century but at least he would know she was alive and well. Mayhap not with him but *alive*. And that was all he cared about.

There were few people in the great hall. A bagpipe played softly and food had been laid out. But none of that mattered as his eyes went to the man standing in front of the fire.

Gods and damnation, it was Alan Stewart.

Brae Stewart's father.

Chapter Fifteen

IN ANY OTHER reality—mostly a twenty-first century one—Nicole would have already downed the mug of whisky handed to her. But this was not any other reality and drinking was about the last thing on her mind. You would think having been to hell, in one form or another, she would want to drown her sorrows in liquor but no. The truth was she wasn't sad in the least. Confused maybe, but not sad. She wanted Niall alone so they could talk more. So she could understand what was happening between them.

But it seemed that was not going to happen any time soon.

It was easily an hour later and they were well past dining and making pleasant chit-chat. Not that she ate much or even talked all that much. Neither appealed to her in the least. Niall had shared his story about how he arrived in the Otherworld. What he could not explain however was Adlin's arrival. Vika, naturally, had not strayed far from Niall so it made sense he would have ridden her into the afterlife, such as it was.

Maybe in his late fifties, Alan Stewart was as handsome as she imagined he might be having met his daughter. The only difference? He was super kind where his offspring clearly wasn't.

While Nicole might be eager, no, desperate, to get Niall alone, compassion won over as she eyed Alan. The vacant, searching way he looked at the fire when the conversation turned from him told her a lot. He had no idea why his daughter went rogue. Worse than that, he was struggling with news of her twin brother, his first born son, Cullen. Apparently Brae had murdered him and he had, of all things, become an angel. While that was pretty darn cool, what he did to stop his sister was not.

It seemed Cullen had embraced evil and become a warlock to fight her. That meant his wings were clipped. Long story short, he'd been banned not only by God but by Fionn Mac Cumhail into the twenty-first century. Nobody knew what became of him after that.

"I guess we're all a little out of it," Nicole said softly, sitting next to Alan.

He offered a forced smile in greeting. "To say the least, lass."

Though Nicole wasn't sure she should tell him her doubts about Brae because it was probably nothing, her heart went out to him. "Is there any chance Brae could've been forced into what she's doing?"

She might have been trying to keep it between them, but everyone went quiet at her words.

"What say ye, lass?" Iosbail said.

"I don't know." Nicole shook her head. "Maybe it was nothing but when Niall showed up, Brae called me a fool and started to say I could save something. That was all she got out before she went all…" Her eyes darted to Alan. "Well, she went with the evil guy she's hooked up with." She frowned at everyone. "Why would she have said I could save something when she not only wanted my ring but wanted me dead? It makes no sense."

"What of the look in her eyes?" Alan sat forward. "Did she seem lost, desperate, scared?"

"I don't know. Yes." She shook her head. "No." Then she flinched. "Maybe."

"'Twas fast and too much," Rònan said, coming to her aid. "There was no making sense of any of it for even I, a dragon-shifter, never mind a lass from the future who only just came into all of this."

"Aye," Niall agreed as he sat beside her. He obviously understood the glimmer of hope she was trying to give Alan. "'Tis something this, aye? Mayhap Brae struggles even as we do?"

"Mayhap," Iosbail murmured, eyes on the fire.

Like they all did, Nicole heard the doubt in her voice and it pissed her off. Unlike everybody else who *had* to be thinking the same thing, she spoke up. "Don't be so dour and evasive, Iosbail. Say what you're thinking. Alan deserves as much."

The old woman's eyes shot to hers. "Ye've a sharp tongue on ye, lass."

"Ye've no idea," Niall and Rònan said at the same time, grinning at Nicole with pride.

"Fine then," Iosbail muttered, pacing in front of the fire, clearly pleased that her King looked at her with such unabashed admiration. "I'll say it as I see it." Her eyes went to Alan. "Though it pains me, dinnae get yer hopes up, my friend. Evil is verra good at what it does and will use trickery at every opportunity. Use yer good sense to come to a conclusion. Why did Brae leave behind ye and yer good wife to travel to the wee Bruce's era? And how was it ye never knew yer bonnie son had become an angel to begin with?"

"Congratulations, by the way," Nicole said to Alan because she would be damned if Iosbail sunk his ship entirely. "It's not too shabby that your son became an angel. He must've been a super good guy."

"Aye," Alan said, welcoming her kind words. "He was a good lad, indeed." But his eyes soon swung to Iosbail's and Nicole saw that though he might be heartbroken, he was a leader and realist by nature. "I willnae get my hopes up unnecessarily, but I will pay close attention for I will always believe the best of my bairns. What would ye and yer King suggest I do next?"

"Wait and keep yer eyes and heart open, m'Laird Stewart," Alexander cut in, clearly seeing the benefit in keeping Alan's spirits up. "'Tis always a good chance yer bairns might reach out to ye and yer wife. Mayhap even Cullen from the future. If either does, contact Fionn Mac Cumhail. Ye know how."

"Aye." Alan nodded. "I do and I will."

"They'd be bloody fools to contact ye," Iosbail said under her breath.

"Good wife." Alexander held out his hand. "Come sit with me and stop yer fretting, aye?"

"I'll not stop my fretting, husband," she shot back.

Nicole pressed her lips together, careful not to show amusement when the King moved fast, scooped up Iosbail and plunked back down. "Ye'll sit with me if I say ye'll sit with me."

Way to go older generation. Nicole smirked at Niall when his hand clamped over her thigh and he shook his head. But she couldn't shut her mouth any more than Iosbail could. "I guess we Brouns have spunk in any century."

"Bloody hell right," Iosbail muttered as she snuggled closer to Alexander. "'Tis good to see that didnae change."

Alexander nuzzled his face against the side of Iosbail's neck. "I would hope not."

Apparently wanting to pursue where her husband was going, Iosbail waved them all away. "Off ye go. We've had enough talk for this eve. The morrow is another day."

To hell with evil swooping down and killing them all. Iosbail wanted to get laid.

"Now that I've seen the darker side in a real bad way I've gotta ask," Nicole said. "How safe *are* we here because—"

"Yer protected by my brother and me, so safe enough." Iosbail's eyes narrowed on Nicole. "Now get yer wee arse up to bed and leave me and mine be, aye?"

Um, okay. *Not.* Nicole was about to bite back with her thoughts on Iosbail's one-track mind, but Niall and Rònan pulled her after them. Niall had her hand and Rònan kept a hand on her lower back.

When Nicole stopped short, Niall arched a pointed look at her. "I dinnae mind throwing ye over my shoulder again, lass." He lowered his head slightly and gave Rònan a relenting look. "And if ye manage to bring me down with a pinch, my cousin will pick up where I left off."

Rònan winked when she glared at him. "Except a good pinch willnae bring this dragon down."

They meant it. Damn them. She looked at Alan. He was already heading in the opposite direction so there was no more helping him for now. Frustrated, she shoved past Niall but made sure he and Rònan heard her. "Asswipes."

"I thought she was working on her cursing," Rònan said as she headed for the stairs.

"Aye, but mayhap 'tis easier to slip when the wee King isnae around."

"Even so, 'twould be a good habit to overcome," Rònan mentioned.

"Shut your traps," she said as she headed up the stairs.

"Our traps?" Rònan said.

"Our mouths." But there was a smile in Niall's voice as he grabbed Nicole's hand only a few stairs up. "Come, lass. We want to show you something."

"We do?" Rònan said.

"Aye, ye bloody pagan." Niall nodded at the hall then the door. "I dinnae know where ye stand on religion, Nicole, but 'tis the eve before a celebrated day in these parts." He gestured at all the spruce and berries strewn about. "'Tis the day before Christmastide for the Sinclairs as they are for the most part Christians."

Nicole blinked and looked around. No way. "Are you telling me it's Christmas Eve?"

"Aye." Niall smiled. "Is that good for you, lass?"

Good for her? She had no idea. It was never a holiday that meant much because family didn't exist. Until the last few years. And the only reason for that was because of her friends. They made Christmas fun.

"Sure, it's good," she murmured and let him pull her after him and Rònan. "So what's going on?"

"Nothing." He smiled as he led her out the door. "Just snow."

Snow? While she found the heavy flakes cool enough especially considering she had never seen them fall outside a medieval castle, they were nothing new. "Sorry to break it to you guys but I grew up in Boston. Snow's kinda common."

"Aye." Niall said. "I know."

"I should leave ye two be," Rònan said, though there was a hopeful look on his face.

"Nay," Niall said as they walked down the stairs. "'Tis a time meant for friends and ye are Nicole's friend, aye?"

"Aye," Rònan agreed.

Niall was like a kid as he pulled her around a corner at the bottom of the stairs, down a hallway and up another winding set of stairs. By the time they reached the top, the snow was falling harder but half the moon still shone over the distant ocean.

Torches flickered and wind whipped as Niall pulled something from his pocket. "This somehow made it into the satchel attached to Vika. I suspect Cassie must have slipped it in at MacLomain Castle. Anyways, she wanted to make sure you were alone when you received it." He glanced at Rònan. "But I thought 'twould be best to give it to you with good friends around."

"Okay," she said slowly. Nicole knew Cassie. If she wanted her to be alone there was a reason for it. But Niall looked too excited. So did Rònan.

"'Tis something Cassie and your friends, Erin and Jaqueline saved a long time to purchase for you." Niall pressed a small object into her hand. "Though I'm pagan, I know they would say, "Merry Christmas.""

Nicole looked at them warily as Niall stepped back.

Both he and Rònan looked so expectant.

Opening her hand, she looked at the device. Heat born of strong emotion swamped her. It was the highest tech hearing aid on the market. Tears welled, but she blinked them away, embarrassed. Damn them. Her friends should not have done this. They were all struggling in one way or another and nobody had enough money. But that was not what bothered her most right now.

No, it was that her upcoming disability had been laid bare.

It was coming and there was no stopping it.

Worse than that, her friends weren't here to give it to her.

Instead, men that she had only just met. She might like them. A lot. Still. This was too uncomfortable.

"Thanks," she murmured and shoved it back into Niall's hand. "But no thanks."

Nicole flew downstairs and made her way to their chamber, grateful neither man was on her tail. Mostly because she was crying and that irritated the living hell out of her.

What were her friends thinking doing this for her? What was Niall thinking giving it to her with Rònan there? Better yet, why the heck did Cassie give it to Niall to begin with? She knew better. She knew how Nicole thought.

Didn't she?

Angry, she wiped away tears, took a swig of whisky but cringed and set it aside. She didn't want alcohol. She just wanted escape. From this. Her past. Present. Possibly even her future. Just her feelings in general. All and all, she wanted to escape from the shitty cards she'd been dealt in life.

Crawling onto the bed, she curled into a ball and got busy feeling sorry for herself. Something she had not done her entire life. She wasn't a fan of people who cried 'oh poor me' and had sworn to never be one. But here, so far away from twenty-first century life and all the prying eyes, she let go.

By the time she was done her eyes were swollen and she could barely breathe through her nose. Drowsy, she must have dosed because when she sniffled again, there was a warm body against her back. Nicole peeked over her shoulder. Of course, it was Niall. Fully clothed, body wrapped tightly around hers to the best of his ability, his eyes were wide open.

"I'm not up for company," she whispered, voice catching.

"I've been here for hours."

"I don't care. I'm not up for company."

"But mayhap I am," he said softly and tightened his arm around her waist. "Mayhap I need to ken why 'twas my Da who arrived here after us but stayed away. Why he didnae check on me once to see if I was well."

So he intended to ease into the conversation about her behavior by putting the spotlight on his issues first.

Nicole swallowed, eyes holding his as she peered over her shoulder. What was she supposed to say? "Maybe Malcolm's tired."

"Mayhap." He propped up on an elbow when she rolled onto her back. "Or mayhap I've disappointed him again somehow."

"Do you live your life like that?" She searched his eyes. "Wondering if you've disappointed your dad yet again?"

He shrugged. "I dinnae know." He tugged her closer, almost as if he didn't want her to flee. "I could ask you the same. Do you live your life running away when faced with anything having to do with your hearing?"

And there it was.

"Listen, Niall, I'm not into comparisons or trying to relate to other people. You've got your problems. I've got mine." She sighed. "So I've got no answers for you except that if I were your dad I'd steer clear and let you work out your own bullshit. As I see it, you've found a safe place to hide behind your, what...honor? Pride? Good enough I suppose but still, you're hiding in a way." Her eyes held his. "So unless you're ready to be straight with him and say what's on your mind, stop bitching."

When he frowned, she arched her brows. "Sorry, but Malcolm strikes me as a straight shooter. Maybe not when it comes to his son, but I'll bet that'd change if you got the balls to not pussy-foot around him but tell him where you stand without offending the guy. Tell him how you feel. Don't hold back. Be you and be proud."

"I have," he murmured. "Many times."

"Pfft," she scoffed. "I'd say you didn't *explain* but *told* him how things were gonna be. Your way or the highway." She shrugged. "Sorry, but you sort of strike me as the type to do that."

"Aye, mayhap," he granted. "But what of you, lass? You're tougher and more courageous than anyone I know yet you pretend you're not going deaf. Even though you fear it, it simply doesnae exist. You're avoiding it."

Before she could pull away, he locked his arm more securely around her and narrowed his eyes. "To my mind, you're *pussy-footing* around your problems just as much as I am mine."

"The difference?" she retaliated, eyes just as narrowed. "Yours is tangible and family. Mine is just a personal problem."

"Yours is *just* as tangible." He kept his voice low and even. "And something that involves your family. Cassie, Erin, Jaqueline." Before she could talk, he shook his head. "And me, Rònan and all my cousins, all the MacLomains. Everyone who cares about you."

Not quite sure what to say, she did what she always did.

Downplayed things.

"I'm going deaf. No biggie. Nothing that needs friends or support or anything else. Not in light of all the crap happening. Cassie's blind. That's huge and sucks big time. Focus on her." Nicole curled away, for the first time not interested in arguing. Not with him. Not right now. "I wanna crash. Leave me alone."

Relieved, she squeezed back annoying tears, grateful that he seemed fine with leaving her be.

Or at least she thought so.

She should have known better.

Nicole seethed through her teeth when he rolled her onto her back, came over her and propped his elbows in such a fashion that her arms were pinned by her side. Yet all the while he managed to keep a less-than-ferocious look on his face as he wedged her tight against the bed and met her eyes.

"I'm sorry that I gave you that Christmas present with Rònan around. I thought 'twould make you happy to have us both there. Either way, 'tis time for you to face what's ahead because 'tis coming, Nicole. And no matter how far you run, you cannae escape it. What you *can* do, is allow me and even my cousins to help you through it."

Though tempted to get mad at him, to spark a fight to detour from the conversation, she just couldn't seem to find it in her. She was tired of all the anger and resentment. Yes, her friends had been a solid network of support over the years but she'd always felt like she needed to be strong for them. That losing her hearing was nothing compared to their troubles.

But maybe it was something after all.

Niall must have sensed she was finally relenting because he sat up against the headboard and pulled her onto his lap. He wrapped his arms around her waist and eyed her with tempered compassion. Just enough to let her know he cared but not enough that she felt the need to whack him upside the head.

"I want to know what the doctors have told you about your hearing," he said softly. "And I want you to be truthful."

Nicole sighed but didn't push away. "They've never really given a solid diagnosis except that it's likely hereditary. There's all sorts of modern day technology that can help me hear vibrations and stuff when my hearing goes entirely." She shrugged and stared at the fire. "But I've always had this deep-down feeling that they won't work for me."

"Have you learned sign language?" he asked.

"I'm surprised you know what that is."

"When I heard what you were facing, I learned all I could."

Her eyes met his. "So, what, you grilled Cassie?"

"Nay, she was coping with blindness and I didnae want to bother her. So I traveled to the future."

"You were in the twenty-first century after Cassie left?" Her eyes widened. "When I was there?"

"Aye," he murmured. "Forgive me for staying away. We werenae on the best of terms."

Wasn't that the truth.

Unexpected warmth curled inside her. "I can't believe you did that."

"I wanted to better ken who I was sworn to protect," he said and she knew he was hedging. "It only made sense."

Nicole eyed him. "Was that the only reason?"

"Aye," he said before he shook his head and cupped the side of her neck. "Nay, 'twas not. I had a deep need to ken your plight. To ken what made you the lass you were."

"And what sort of conclusions did you come to?"

"The same sort that I came to that night at the MacLeods," he said. "That you're a fighter and verra brave."

She grinned a little. "So my looks had nothing to do with it?"

"Nay, I didnae have much time to see your looks on the battlefield." He grinned as well. "I was too busy being dropped to my knees and defending your drunken arse."

Nicole chuckled, glad he was keeping what could have been a difficult conversation light. "Yeah, that was definitely bad timing." She traced her finger over the stubble on his strong jaw. "But I think you're lying about not checking me out. I think you thought I was hot."

"I would've had to be blind to think otherwise," he murmured when she traced the pad of her thumb over his lower lip.

Nicole adjusted her backside a smidge as arousal flared.

"Och, lass." He stilled her with a hand to her hip. "I'm not finished talking with you yet."

"I think that you are for now," she countered seductively, lowering her lashes and licking her lips as she hiked up her dress and straddled him. "I'll tell you anything you wanna know later." She ran her hands up beneath his tunic. "After."

"After," he murmured as she dragged her fingers up his chiseled abs and over his pecs. God, she loved touching him. The feel of hot skin over steely muscles. She brushed her lips across his as she lightly scraped her nails back down.

But merely sampling his lips was just not enough.

As soon as their mouths opened and their tongues connected, it was spontaneous combustion. They groaned as the kiss deepened. Nicole tore at the plaid wrapped over his shoulder then started pushing up his tunic. Their mouths separated just long enough for him to pull it over his head.

Then their lips were back together, desperate to stay connected, desperate to keep tasting and exploring. Like it had been in the Viking King's cave, Nicole felt an immense closeness. A feeling that she had never felt with anyone else. A craving to catapult far beyond simple sex and find that place where only they seemed to exist. That wonderland of wickedness and carnal bliss that had her breathing hard just thinking about it.

"Niall," she whimpered into his mouth, desperate to get closer.

He seemed to understand because he pushed his plaid down just enough as she hiked up her skirts. When he eased into her she almost blew apart it felt so good. Trembling, she grabbed onto his broad shoulders and struggled for breath as their eyes locked.

At that moment she knew her thoughts were as much his as his were hers and it only intensified all the sensations and emotions whiplashing through her. The connection was so strong she went multi-orgasmic right then and there as the muscles in her stomach and thighs started to flutter wildly.

She had never felt anything like it.

Fully impaling her, Niall made no movement with his hips but wrapped a hand into her hair and pulled her close for another long, heartfelt kiss. One that seemed to meld them together more thoroughly than they already were. Slow and easy then fast and passionate, the kisses egged on the building sensations in her belly. The little waves of pleasure that had her quivering against him.

This time when sound faded she knew it had nothing to do with her affliction and everything to do with him. A buzz made entirely of the blood rushing through her veins as anticipation grew. As their worlds wrapped together and twisted into scalding flame.

Lost in everything she felt, Nicole released a long, low groan when he grabbed her backside and started to move. Not much. Just a scant fraction in and a scant fraction out. He went so incredibly deep that her womb contracted in pleasure and she started to grind ever-so-slightly.

Niall's head fell back and he whispered, "Bloody hell," as he watched her from beneath hooded eyes. "You're so beautiful."

As his thoughts twirled with hers, she truly felt it. Beautiful. Inside and out. The way he looked at her. The way he seemed to see things nobody else could. How pleasing he found all those unfortunate quirks of her personality. Her toughness and defiance. Her challenging nature. To him, they were all the best parts of her. The things that made her into the woman he desired above all others.

The woman he loved.

Amazingly enough, she felt no need to run or flee but instead let the deep emotion wash over her. In its own way, it was the most freeing moment of her life. Letting someone in like this. Letting someone other than her friends into her heart.

Into her soul.

As if he sensed her acceptance, his pupils flared and he began to move faster. Matching his pace, she braced her hands more firmly on his shoulders and met his thrusts. Smooth, well-matched, they moved together in such synchronization that she knew their minds were anticipating the others.

Nicole gasped when he rolled her onto her back, never losing contact. With one hand wrapped around a bedpost, he thrust faster and faster. Legs wrapped around his waist, she grabbed the post as well and braced herself. Blazing heat flared beneath her skin as she watched him. The straining muscles. The sweat soaked skin.

They were hungry and eager and way out of control now as he worked her body into a frenzy. Flashes of how he saw her flickered in her mind. Wild. Desperate. Crazed. Gorgeous.

Ready.

"Nicole," he whispered aloud then into her mind. He said her name as though he intended to say it a thousand more times. As though it belonged to him and he wouldn't have it any other way.

She was shocked by how much she like the possession. By how much she liked being his.

"Niall," she whispered back aloud then in his mind. Because it worked both ways and he needed to know it. He was every inch hers. At least right here. Right now.

Somehow her word mingling with his sent them both sailing over the edge. When he roared and locked up against her, her body seized. Completely out of control, her muscles clamped tight. All of them. Her stomach, thighs, calves, arms, everything. It was almost frightening in its intensity.

He pulsed and trembled against her but her body seemed suspended in some sort of limbo. She knew it was the start of a powerful orgasm and gripped the post and his shoulder as tightly as possible.

"Niall," she gasped, needing his eyes on hers.

Hearing the desperation in her voice, he lifted his head and their eyes met. It was *that* connection, the utter safety she found in his gaze, that unlocked her body and she detonated. Burst wide open. Screamed. Saw a zillion fireworks zipping everywhere. Sharp tingles swarmed over her skin and she swore her heart stopped. Jagged breath ripped from her lungs as she struggled for breath.

"Shh," Niall whispered and cupped her cheek. "Dinnae fight it, lass."

Fight it? There was nothing to fight. Yet she supposed in some strange way there was. She was letting go. Letting him in entirely. Nicole cupped his cheek as well when he pressed his forehead against hers.

A few more jagged gasps tore from her before pleasure whipped through her like heat-lightning over a raging sea. Then the flood truly let go and she started shaking. But with Niall as her anchor, she could ride the waves and find true release without fear.

Once she gave in to the safety and certainty of that, she was able to ride out the climax of her life. Or should she say climaxes. Because there were several. Too many to count. However many there were, they carried her to another plane and she lost touch with reality.

In fact, she downright passed out.

Or so she assumed because the next thing she knew, dim daylight flooded through the windows and snow drifted in as animal skins flapped in the wind. Niall was spooned against her back. Nicole smiled when she realized she was wearing his tunic. The fire on the hearth must have been fed because it crackled invitingly. But that wasn't what caught her attention. No, it was something else entirely.

Something that warmed her to her very core.

It sat in the corner, blazing with festive lights.

For the first time in her life, she was waking up to a Christmas tree.

Chapter Sixteen

NIALL WATCHED AS Nicole climbed out of bed and made her way over to the tree. Pleased by how happy she looked, he smiled as she crouched and fingered the branches. He sat up, rested his arms on bent knees and remained silent so that she could enjoy the moment.

But he should have known better.

Sensing him, she peered over her shoulder. The smile she shot his way was one of a kind. "Did you do this?"

"Aye." He kept smiling, unable to help himself. "Rònan and I."

"Hell," she whispered and turned her gaze back to the tree. He knew she fought tears as she again fingered the small pine's magically lit branches. "It's amazing. Thank you."

Sensing that she would like him there, Niall got out of bed, wrapped his plaid and joined her. Crouching, he took her hand and nodded beneath the tree. "Those are for you."

Her eyes went from under the tree to him and back again. "Are you serious?"

"Aye. Go ahead, pick them up. They should suit your size perfectly."

Hands trembling, she picked up the ornately carved dagger and round shield before standing. He stood as well and nodded at the shield. "That's from Rònan. He wanted to honor our Viking ancestors who kept you safe so had it made to resemble theirs. Out of wood. It's lightweight enough for you to hold without growing weary and was dyed to match the colors of your Broun clan's plaid."

Clearly emotional, she eyed the shield. "This is amazingly awesome." She shook her head. "Too much."

"Nay." Niall shook his head too. "Never enough for the lass who protected Scotland's future king, saved Rònan from hell then went on to save me. Those were his exact words. He cast his own dragon spell on it so that it might protect you as fiercely as you have all of us."

"Damn," she murmured, shifting it around as she adjusted to its weight. "A dragon spell? What exactly does that mean?"

Niall shrugged. "'Tis hard to know, but I'd say 'tis a verra good thing."

"I'll bet." Her gaze went to the dagger, eyes growing wider as she took in the Celtic symbols curving up its blade. "And this?"

"That is from me," he said softly. "Forged as the last of the moon was covered and the wild winds blew through the glen. Forged as the sea went from calm to crashing." He traced a finger over the symbols. "Tied by not only my magic but by Iosbail's and her brother Adlin's too, these have the power to protect ye from great evil. Darkness cultivated in the Otherworld."

"I get why their magic could do that." She swallowed as her eyes met his. "But how does yours?"

"Because I've been there. When I went after you and Rònan," he said. "As such, my magic is now tied into it."

"That sounds intense," she whispered, eyes dropping to the well-forged blade. Her fingers traced over the scroll along the hilt. "These tiny symbols are words, aren't they?"

"Aye, in Latin," he said. "The most powerful language of magic."

"What do they say?"

Niall had been very careful choosing them. They had to tell her that he cared, but she was her own person. That he would always be here to protect her but had faith that she could protect herself as well.

"*Bellator, si quando opus vires magicis meis tibi ducitur.*" His eyes met hers. "Warrior, if ever in need, the strength of my heart and magic is yours to lead."

Nicole held his gaze for several long moments before she blinked a few times, swallowed hard then looked at the blade. Though she pretended like she was scratching her cheek, he didn't miss the small tear that she wiped away before she whispered, "Hell, Niall. Who knew you were so sweet?"

Clearing her throat, trying to hide her emotions, she swiped the blade a few times. "This feels perfect." Her eyes went to his. "When did you guys find time to have these made?"

"Och, lass, we wouldnae trust another to make these," he said. "We made them ourselves. You slept many hours before I came back to the chamber last night. We started then. After you fell asleep again, I went back down and continued to help. Having done her romping, Iosbail was able to lend her magic."

"But how was Adlin there?"

Niall only grinned and shrugged, offering an evasive answer. "How is Adlin anywhere?"

"You tell me." But there was a twinkle in her eyes. "Just kidding." She gestured at the blade and winked. "After this, you're allowed to have a few secrets."

"Am I then?" He might be beyond happy to see her smiling, but the lass aroused him to no end when she wore his tunic so he pulled her into his arms. He wanted a good morning kiss.

"No, you're not really allowed to have your secrets but it seemed like the thing to say," she murmured as she stood on her tiptoes and wrapped her arms around his shoulders. Blade in one hand, shield in the other, her lips melted beneath his just as readily now as they had the night before. He had no idea how long they kissed save she gave into it as thoroughly as him.

Only when they finally pulled apart did she see the last gift beneath the tree. The one she needed to see and accept the most.

Niall carefully took the blade and shield from her as she stared at it. It was hers to pick up if she was ready to accept it. If she was the true warrior he knew her to be, she would. Then again, he thought her every inch his heroine even if she did not.

He understood confusion and trepidation.

He understood denial and defiance.

Nicole slowly sank to her knees and kept staring at it. Niall set aside the weapons and debated whether or not to give her space. Her thoughts were scattered so he had no sense of direction. Mostly her friends swirled through her mind. The hard times they'd had. The good times. Even the in-between times when she didn't see them for months and worried they might be losing touch.

Niall made his decision based on that last thought. On her fear that her friends might vanish because life got too busy. Crouching beside her, he put a comforting hand on her shoulder and reminded her that her true friends would *always* be there. Her days of being abandoned were long past.

Her eyes met his and she nodded. She understood.

Now she just had to make her move.

Would she, though? Was she ready to conquer her number one fear? Niall remained silent and kept his thoughts still. This hurdle was hers alone.

Long seconds or mayhap even minutes passed before she took a deep breath, nodded and simply said, "Okay," before snatching up the hearing aid he had tried to give her the night before. "Okay," she repeated and stood, still staring at the object.

Niall stood as well and kept his words soft but firm. "Like the blade and shield, 'tis a way to lend you strength, lass. A weapon of sorts."

Her eyes rose to his. "A weapon?"

"Aye." He closed her hand around the small device, slipping into his brogue as he spoke from the heart. "Until Fate takes ye where she shall, this will help with the transition and keep ye sharp to yer surroundings where mayhap ye might not have been otherwise."

"What about magic?" she said softly. "I know it couldn't help Cassie but is there any chance…"

"Nay," he said, preferring to be blunt rather than give hope when it was beyond him to give such. A lass like her deserved nothing but the truth so that she might move forward with her eyes wide open and her courage well rallied. "What ails ye is something beyond magic. 'Tis part of yer destiny."

Nicole stared at him for a long moment. He didn't need to hear her thoughts to know how conflicted and frightened she still was. But she was, if nothing else, brave so she clenched her jaw then the hearing aid, a strong set to her chin as she kept his gaze. "Thanks for being honest, Niall." She nodded. "I mean that."

"Aye," he murmured as her eyes turned back to the tree.

"You've done a lot for me and…" She shook her head, her emotions swamping his mind though she tried to get them under control. "And I'm not really sure how to show you how much I appreciate it. Outside of my friends, I haven't dealt with a lot of your sort in my life."

Niall shook his head, upset. He made her sit beside the table then crouched in front of her. Holding her hands, he made sure she was looking at him when he spoke. "Nicole, I dinnae need you to show me how thankful you are. I already know it. And I hope you know how thankful I am for all you've done for me."

Before she could respond, he continued. "All I needed from you was what you just showed me. That you were able to accept the device. Gods know, you have and always will face all the evil you've been thrust into with courage." He cupped the side of her neck while still squeezing her other hand. "But now I know that you can face your worst fear. *That* is everything. It means the enemy can use nothing against you."

He nodded, so damn proud. "You are your own warrior from here on out. A lass who is not only a Broun but a MacLomain by right. Let nothing stand in your way."

Nicole notched her chin a little as his words sunk in. "I always have one way or another," she conceded, a bit of her spunk simmering to the surface. "Before all the evil that is."

Niall grinned and granted, "There has been more of that than usual."

She eyed the hearing aid. "I suppose it couldn't hurt to try this out on occasion."

"Why not now?" he said softly. "'Twould not be so bad to have in place if you need it."

"Yeah, maybe." If he wasn't mistaken, there was an octave of excitement in her voice as she tucked it into her ear. "I really don't need this right now," she murmured as she kept fiddling with it until her eyes widened and she whispered, "Oh my *God*."

Niall wished her friends were here. That they could see the look of awe on her face. She might have been able to hear things before but he wondered how much she had to strain to do so. Or maybe she'd just become so used to her reality that it seemed normal.

"Everything sounds so much clearer, louder," she whispered. "I guess I don't have to be so strict about people calling me Nicole anymore."

"What do you mean?"

"That's why I never allowed people to call me by a nickname." She shrugged as if it were no big deal. "I was always able to catch my name based on its second syllable. The 'cole' sound. It was distinctive enough I guess."

Niall was caught off guard by the surge of emotion he felt. How saddened he was that she had gone so long without hearing things as she should have.

"What?" she said, her eyes on his face. "Everything okay?"

He made damn well sure those thoughts were shut off from her and nodded. "'Tis just hard to imagine how you must've been hearing beforehand."

Her eyes narrowed as if she didn't quite believe him, but thankfully her attention was drawn to the door. "Rònan!"

Niall was surprised he hadn't sensed his cousin coming but probably shouldn't be considering how wrapped up in Nicole he was. He stepped aside as she flew into Rònan's arms and gave him a big hug.

"Thank you for the shield," she exclaimed. "Totally awesome."

Grinning, Rònan held on to her for as long as possible. "Anything for ye, lass."

When Rònan's hand snaked toward her arse, Niall narrowed his eyes. His cousin grinned and kept his hand where it belonged. At long last, they pulled apart and joined him.

Nicole's eyes were wide as she stared at Rònan. "Check out your hair! Totally works for you."

Refusing to let what the enemy had done bother him, Rònan cut off all his hair.

"Aye? It looks all right then?" he said to Nicole, clearly pleased with her compliment.

"Definitely." She kept studying him. "Your eye looks a lot better today." She cocked her head. "Wow, it almost looks completely healed."

"Aye, 'tis my dragon blood," he said. "Though it cannae heal others it tends to heal me fairly quickly."

Niall poured everyone mead and nodded at the food a servant had brought in. "Let us break our fast together this fine Christmastide morn, aye?"

"Aye," Rònan agreed. He plunked down but not before his eyes went to Niall's back. Better yet, the nail marks left behind from when he and Nicole coupled together at the mountain. "Och, lad, I see yer lass is as wild in bed as she is on the battlefield."

Niall didn't miss the envy in his voice.

"You bet your ass I am," Nicole said, grinning as she sat.

He realized that Rònan showing up had lent her a reprieve from all the intensity. Only concerned for her well-being, he found contentment in her revived spirit and smiled as he handed her some bannock.

After that, they enjoyed their meal, chatted and laughed far more than they probably should have considering the circumstances. It was a few hours that none of them would likely get again anytime soon. An escape. A place where they could enjoy getting to know one another within the comfort of a castle and under the protection of Iosbail Broun…or Iosbail MacLomain depending on who you asked.

"So you're gonna play a Christmas carol on that thing," Nicole finally said to Rònan as they all lounged back with full bellies. Niall had wrapped a fur around her shoulders and pushed aside the animal skins so she could enjoy the falling snow in combination with her Christmas tree.

Rònan lifted the bagpipes and grinned. "Aye, lass. Anything you like. I might not be inside your head like my cousin, but I can repeat a tune if you think it."

Nicole shrugged, but he saw the casual humor in her eyes go soft and turn to something else. "I always did like Carol of the Bells. The words almost seemed to be sung by someone stuck on the outside of Christmas looking in on all the magic of it. There but not quite there."

"Aye," Rònan murmured. "And you've a love of a version by a Celtic woman group from your time."

"Yeah," Nicole said, a little surprised. "I do. They're pretty great."

Rònan nodded and lifted the pipes. "Let's see then."

Niall had seen his cousin do a lot of things, including killing ruthlessly time and time again in battle, but he had never seen him take up the pipes as he did now. As if he wanted to give back something even he didn't fully understand.

So when he started playing, Niall was taken aback by the sound. By the pure feeling. It was bloody powerful. Because of his magic, Rònan even managed to backdrop the sound with the echo of violins to mimic the sound of the music she admired so much.

By the time he was finished and the last note trilled away, Nicole had a faraway look in her eyes. Niall kept his mind separate from hers, determined that she might enjoy wherever the music took her.

Rònan's words slipped into his mind. *"She is happy, Cousin."*

"Aye, thank ye."

"Why do ye thank me when 'twas ye that caused such?"

"'Twas yer pipes."

"Och, nay, the happiness in her runs far deeper than a turn of the pipes could ever take her."

"Sorry, guys, but I've gotta go to the bathroom," Nicole said, cutting into a sentimental moment as only she could.

Niall grinned. His lass didn't hold back in the least.

Rònan nodded. "I'll show you the way."

"Nay, lad." Niall snorted. "Ye'll do no such thing."

Nicole nodded at the screen on the other side of the room "Pretty sure that's where I go." She shook her head. "I only know that because Jackie reads so many historical romances. I've learned far more than I ever wanted to know about the Dark ages. Or Golden ages. Or Regency period. Or Medieval period. Whatever." She stood. "Seriously, I gotta go."

"Aye," both men said and nodded at the screen.

Her eyes flickered between them before she nodded. "Sure, okay. Be right back."

Rònan and Niall had only been talking for a few moments when Nicole piped up. "Um, here's the thing. You guys need to get out of here. This is officially too weird."

"We dinnae care in the least if—"

"Leaving now," Niall said as he yanked on boots and dragged Rònan out. "Should we wait or meet you below stairs?"

"Downstairs works," she called. "Thanks."

Rònan waited until they reached the bottom stair before he nudged Niall and grinned. "So she was happy when she awoke, aye?"

"Verra." Niall smiled and stopped. "Again, many thanks for the shield and for caring so much, Cousin."

"Aye, 'twas my pleasure." Rònan kept walking but stopped when Niall leaned against the wall. "Are ye coming then?"

"Nay, ye know I mean to protect her," Niall said. "Coming this far is only because she deserves her privacy."

"Aye." Rònan nodded and leaned against the opposite wall. "Then I'll wait with ye."

Niall nodded his thanks and eyed Rònan, curious. Because his cousins' thoughts brushed his on occasion and Niall's more than the others, he knew his dragon kin had not slept well the night before. Almost as if he was haunted. "Ye told me that ye remember verra little of what happened in the Otherworld prior to Nicole arriving. But do ye not recall the things ye said to her when she got there?"

None would catch it if they didn't have MacLomain blood and a certain eye toward the way Rònan could turn into himself, but Niall knew better. His cousin was shying away from something.

"A lass came to me. A bonnie lass if ever there was one." Rònan closed his eyes and shook his head before his gaze once more met Niall's. "She said she could smell my scent...my fire. Her touch was soothing, gentle. She relieved me of great pain, Cousin."

"Did she give you her name?" Niall frowned. "Hell, ye should have already been in the twenty-first century to see if one of these Brouns were yours!"

"Nay." Rònan shook his head, disturbed. "She flitted in and out, there was no direct connection. But 'twas her face that somehow eased me from whatever the bloody bastards did to me there."

"Aye, 'tis hard to imagine what ye suffered."

Rònan shrugged as if it were no big deal, but Niall didn't miss the unease that flickered in his eyes. "I did manage to convey one thing to her, though."

"Aye? What was that?"

"My oath that I would find her," Rònan said. "That I wouldnae abandon her."

Niall frowned. "I dinnae ken."

Something crossed his cousin's face that alarmed him. Downright confusion.

"Rònan?"

"Aye?"

"Why did ye promise this lass ye would find her?" Niall said. "Where is she?"

"With the wee King." Rònan's eyes suddenly glazed over. "Calling for me from far away."

Worried, he grabbed his cousin's shoulders and shook him. "Rònan, are ye with me, lad?"

Rònan's eyes remained unfocused as he looked at something only he could see. "'Twill be the end of them both if I dinnae save them."

"Rònan?" Nicole said and hurried down, obviously having heard them. She already had on her dress and boots.

"What's going on with him?" she asked when she got to the bottom. Hearing aid in place, she held her shield and dagger. "Is he all right?"

Niall started to nod but knew she deserved the truth so shook his head. "Nay, lass. He speaks of the lass he saw in the Otherworld."

"Okay." She nodded. Though upset, she seemed to come to a quick conclusion and handed him her weapons "He needs a woman's touch. He needs to connect. I don't know how I know, but I do."

Niall had no idea what to make of that but certainly would not fight it. He stepped aside so she could cup Rònan's cheeks.

"Hey, do you see me, Rònan?" she said. "Are you with me?"

"'Tis ye, lass," Rònan murmured and tried to focus on her.

"Yeah, it's me." Nicole clamped her hands tighter, stood on her tiptoes and pulled his head down so he was forced to look in her general direction. "And I need you right now. Nicole needs you. Nobody else. You *hear* that?"

"I hear ye, Jaqueline," he whispered. "And I will save ye."

"Oh my God," she whispered and glanced at Niall, distressed. "I was right. It's Jackie."

"'Tis nothing we can worry over at the moment, lass." Niall shook his head. "If he doesnae remember saying her name we will wait till we're with the Bruce again then share. If we do so earlier, 'tis verra likely Rònan will go rogue trying to save her and we cannae have that right now."

Nicole nodded. "All right."

She tried to get through to Rònan several more times, but it didn't work.

"I will save ye," he kept saying.

Apparently fed up, Nicole pulled back and slapped Rònan hard. "Snap out of it."

There's no way a slap would bring his cousin back. Or at least that's what he thought. But something about the connection forged between his lass and cousin seemed to work because Rònan blinked several times and caught Nicole's hand before she slapped him again.

After a few more blinks, he frowned. Both Niall and Nicole waited with baited breath as his cousin slowly but surely came out from beneath his spell.

"Are you with us, sweetie?" Nicole finally asked.

"Aye." Rònan made light of it. "Where else would I be?"

"Good question." Nicole leaned her forehead against Rònan's chest and breathed a sigh of relief.

Rònan rested his chin on top of her head, still a little out of it as whatever magic seized him let go. Not pleased in the least that either of them were connected to this dark magic, Niall touched her lower back, came close and clasped Rònan's shoulder. "How do ye feel, Cousin?"

"Good enough," he rumbled, but there was an octave of discontent in his voice as he stepped away.

He wasn't good enough in the least but completely confused. Just as much as they were.

"Rònan, what happened?" Nicole asked. "Did you see the woman with white hair again? Is that who you made the oath to?"

"Oath?" Baffled, Rònan shook his head and readjusted his plaid, clearly discontented by the exchange. "An oath means signing away your soul. I would never make an oath to anyone beyond my kin."

"But ye did," Niall cut in. "Ye made an oath beyond the one ye already gave the wee king upon his birth." He looked his cousin dead in the eyes. "Ye made an oath that ye would find a lass, that ye wouldnae abandon her."

"Och, nay," Rònan bit back, throwing short words over his shoulder as he strode down the hallway. "Ye didnae hear correctly. I wouldnae make an oath to someone I dinnae know."

Frustrated, Niall started to pursue but Nicole shook her head. "Wait."

So he did. She ran upstairs then returned with his tunic. "If we're gonna get to the heart of this, get dressed."

"Many thanks, my lass," he muttered and pulled on his tunic. Only when he started wrapping his plaid correctly did he realize she had not corrected him. Maybe it was because she was lacing up her own boots and too distracted.

But he knew better.

They had come far together and though the bloody stone at the heart of her ring didn't match his eye color, neither of them much cared. Like him, she had her own mind and would not be swayed by Fate or anybody else telling them who they should love.

To hell with destiny and magic.

When their eyes met, he knew they were a team.

Dagger and shield in hand, she stood. "We need to stick close to Rònan."

"Aye." He brushed his lips over hers then got moving. "Let's go."

By the time they joined Rònan in the great hall, Iosbail, Alexander, and Malcolm were already there.

Iosbail's eyes went to Nicole's blade. "'Tis a fine dagger ye have there, lass."

Nicole grinned and nodded. "Thanks." She winked. "In more ways than one." Then she looked around. "Where's Alan?"

"The Stewart has returned home." Iosbail gave her a pointed look. "With far more hope in his heart than when he came thanks to ye." The older woman shrugged. "But I suppose a wee bit o' hope never hurt anyone."

Niall was surprised to see Alexander sitting before the fire with a fur wrapped around his shoulders. Coughs wracked him and he shivered. Only then did he understand why Bryson had told his father the day before that he would have brought their guests to Alexander. The King was unwell. He suspected it had taken a tremendous amount of magic to seem so fit before.

When Bryson entered, Iosbail nodded. "'Tis almost time then." Her eyes went to Niall. "Ye and yers sit at a table whilst I say my goodbyes."

Niall, Nicole, and his cousin exchanged frowns as they sat and received mugs of mead. Why was she saying goodbye? Malcolm stood beside the hearth with his head bent. Bryson sat beside his father and rested his hand on his shoulder. Iosbail knelt at the King's feet and took his hand as her eyes met his. "How fare ye, my love?"

When another cough wracked him, she put a hand to his chest and shook her head. He stopped coughing and sighed in apparent relief. "Better when yer near, my lass," he murmured. "Always better."

Only then, as Iosbail's eyes grew moist, did Niall realize what was happening.

King Alexander was dying.

Having figured it out as well, Rònan lowered his head in respect. When Niall's eyes met Nicole's, he knew she understood too.

"'Twas a good life we've lived together such as it was, aye, me King?" Iosbail murmured and cupped Alexander's cheek.

"Aye," he said weakly. "I still remember the day ye showed up at this verra castle set to murder me."

"Aye, but 'twas lucky ye were that I wed ye instead."

"Forced into it ye were," Alexander reminded.

"As were ye." A wobbly smile came to her lips. "But in the end 'twas the verra best thing that could've happened."

"Aye." He took his son's hand and met his eyes. "Ye've made yer Ma and me verra proud, lad. This is all yours now. Take good care of the Sinclairs, ye ken?"

"Aye, Da." Emotion was obvious in Bryson's voice. "I love ye."

"And I ye." Alexander's eyes swung back to Iosbail and it was clear he was growing weary, that the end was near. "I love ye too, my lass."

"Our love is eternal." A tear escaped as she once more cupped his cheek. "Until we meet again, aye?"

"Aye," he whispered as his eyes slid shut and he leaned his cheek into her touch.

The room grew very, very quiet as King Alexander drew his last breath then passed away peacefully. Iosbail let his head rest back and put her head on his lap. Her tears were quiet as several minutes went by and she said goodbye to her love.

When she was ready, Bryson helped her stand. Chin set, Iosbail cupped her son's cheeks and eyed him for a long moment. "Ye've been a good lad and I love ye something fierce. Now do right by me and yer Da, aye?"

Shocked, Niall realized she was saying goodbye to Bryson as well.

"Aye, Ma." Tears rolled down his cheeks. "Always."

They embraced for several long moments before Iosbail pulled back, wiped away her tears and stood up straighter. She eyed Bryson long and hard before she nodded then turned from him. Surprisingly strong considering everything, Iosbail's eyes locked on them. "All right, 'tis time to send ye on yer way. Bryson hasnae the magic to defend against what seeks ye."

Iosbail tossed them furs and nodded that they follow her. The snow had lessened some, but it seemed the wind had increased. Cold and driving, the visibility was poor as she led them to the armory. As well stocked as the MacLomains, the Sinclairs had room upon room full of weaponry.

"Take whatever ye like," Iosbail said as she went into another room. She reappeared within moments and headed Niall's way. "I believe this is yers, Highlander."

"My favorite sword," he exclaimed and nodded his thanks as he took it. He thought it lost when he fought on the shore at the mountain. "How did ye get this?"

"It doesnae matter." Her eyes stayed with his. "'Tis a fine blade Colin MacLeod gave ye. One that did verra powerful things at one point in time. Now, because of Adlin and I and even Alan Stewart's magic, 'twill help ye and yer cousins through all that lies ahead."

"Will it then?" Niall said softly. "Why the Stewart's?"

Sadness flickered in Iosbail's eyes. "Because 'tis his blood that seeks to do ye harm so 'tis only right that his magic help fight it. 'Twill make it more powerful."

Niall nodded. Though thankful for the Stewart's help, it saddened him that Alan helped strengthen a blade that could very well kill his offspring.

"When the time comes ye must give it to Rònan." Iosbail's eyes went to his cousin. "Then the time will come that ye must give it to Darach, aye?"

"Aye," Rònan said and eyed the blade with curiosity.

Niall had always been sort of surprised that Colin had given him this sword considering it played such a big part in defeating Keir Hamilton so long ago. But he assumed it was because Niall had such a longing for it whenever he visited.

He still recalled the day his uncle had gifted it to him. Interestingly enough it had been the Christmastide of his thirteenth winter and he thought himself in love for the first time. Back in the days before he avoided love to spite Malcolm of course.

Niall had wanted to spar with it that day so that he might impress the lass. He remembered the odd look Colin had given him in the MacLeod armory. The stern tone of his voice when he said, "So ye think that blade can win ye love, aye, lad?"

"I do," Niall said.

"'Tis always hard to know if a blade can win ye such a prize." Colin removed it from the wall and eyed Niall. "Mayhap when used under the right circumstances. But 'tis important that when love comes that ye willnae run from it but welcome such a gift. That ye will commit to it truly and with all yer heart."

"I will," Niall promised, convinced that the lass he had designs on was as good as his anyway.

Colin again eyed him for a long moment. Apparently he saw whatever he needed because he handed Niall the blade and nodded. "Then this is yers. Might ye care for it well."

Niall had never been so happy. Though he and the lass had lain together, love was never theirs. Regardless, the blade was and had remained so all these years. Yet as it turned out the sword had not won him love. He glanced at Nicole. That had happened all on its own. So if he had to part with the blade to keep his brethren safe, he would do so willingly.

"Many thanks for its safe return," Niall said to Iosbail. "I will see it given to Rònan when 'tis time."

Niall wondered *how* he would know when that moment arrived but figured the blade's magic would tell him. Or so he hoped.

Iosbail nodded then headed out of the armory. "'Tis almost time to leave. Niall, ye and yer Da pick out a few more daggers then join us in the stables."

When he urged Nicole to stay, she shook her head and squeezed his hand. "I think I'm safe enough with Iosbail and Rònan. See you in a few minutes."

Her eyes went to Malcolm and she offered a small smile before she left.

Niall frowned as he headed into a room full of daggers. He knew she wanted him to speak with his father. Likely Iosbail did as well. Malcolm was already strapping several blades to his body as Niall pondered which ones to choose.

"'Tis a good selection this," Niall murmured.

"Aye," Malcolm said.

Though he didn't look his father's way, he sensed that Malcolm eyed him. And while tempted to keep to small talk, he finally asked what had been weighing on his mind. Or at least hinted toward it.

"I didnae see ye yesterday," Niall said. "Why are ye here?"

"Because yer my son and I intended to travel on this journey with ye as much as possible," Malcolm said. "Ye might be a lad full grown, but that doesnae mean I dinnae want to protect ye any less than I did when ye were a wee one."

"I can protect myself," he mumbled while testing the weight of a blade. Despite how determined he was to remain silent, Nicole's words from the previous night kept flickering through his mind. "I can also protect others quite well and make good decisions despite what ye might think."

"I have long known that ye can make good decisions, Son," Malcolm said softly. "And whilst I might not have realized it at the time, I see ye made a good one when ye gave Logan the lairdship. The two of ye in yer current positions have worked well together and made our MacLomains strong indeed."

Niall had not expected that. He had expected a fight.

"Furthermore," Malcolm continued. "Every decision ye have made since, everything ye have done, has made me verra proud."

Baffled, Niall's eyes went to his father. "I dinnae ken yer change of heart."

"My change of heart?" Malcolm shook his head and frowned. "Ye havenae seen inside my heart for a long time, lad. Not since Logan became Laird and I didnae support yer decision as I should have. After that, ye turned from me and did what ye would."

Niall narrowed his eyes as he strapped on a few daggers. "Mayhap I wouldnae have if ye'd said ye'd forgiven me for turning away the position of chieftain."

"I tried several times but ye made a habit of becoming scarce," Malcolm said. "Either leading yer men or visiting the Hamilton and MacLeod castles. Ye might not realize it, but ye sit still about as well as yer cousin, Darach." His father sighed. "And ye tend to hold on to bitterness as well as I did in my youth."

"Bitterness," Niall murmured, trying to swallow the idea that his Da might have been attempting to reach out to him all this time. That he might have been avoiding such a thing without realizing it. Ready to take Nicole's advice, he met his father's eyes. "Did ye feel as if I rejected ye when I rejected becoming laird?"

Their eyes held for several long moments before Malcolm finally murmured, "Aye, 'twas exactly how I felt. 'Twas foolish that."

"Bloody hell," Niall whispered and shook his head. "Aye, 'twas." He kept frowning. "Why did ye not seek me out when ye arrived here? 'Twas truly dangerous entering the Celtic Otherworld."

"I might ask the same of ye, Son. Ye knew I had arrived." Malcolm cocked his head. "But then it has become normal to evade me, aye?" Before Niall could say anything, his Da continued. "I didnae seek ye out because I didnae want to upset ye whilst ye were busy discovering love. All those long days ye spent in the Mother Oak trying to find yer lass were not only verra difficult for ye but for me and yer Ma. It has always been our greatest hope that ye'd find the sort of love she and I share. A true connection."

"I barely saw ye all that time," Niall said.

"Ye barely saw beyond yer need to save her and though 'twas partly because of yer honor to keep her safe 'twas mostly because ye love her so fiercely. Ye only came from that tree to eat and sleep," Malcolm said. "But know that when ye did I was never far off. I kept an eye on ye always."

Niall's brows drew together as the stark truth dawned on him. "I trained my whole life to protect the wee Bruce but instead of staying by his side I left him behind to save the lass."

"A lass he wanted saved as much as the rest of us," Malcolm reminded. "And ye must never forget, by saving her ye also saved the future King. For if the enemy gets their hands on just one of those rings, there will be graver trouble than there already is."

"'Twas the glow inside the stone that kept the beast at bay," Niall murmured.

"Aye, for now," Malcolm said. "It doesnae like the love attached to it and Nicole's ring seems to be developing just such a spark." His father's eyes never left Niall's. "So ye see, though ye thought ye abandoned the wee King, ye did right by him by pursuing love. By saving it so to speak."

Niall kept eying his father and felt something shift. Or better yet fall away. A sense of...defensiveness? Of being on edge without realizing it. Nicole was right yet again. It had become habit to steer clear of his father. To not bother with confronting him about anything because it would do no good. Malcolm saw things one way. He saw them another. But now he realized that at the heart of them, they really weren't all that different and perhaps saw things pretty much the same way.

Malcolm clasped Niall's shoulders. "I am sorry for being upset with ye for not choosing to become Laird. More than that, I'm sorry that I didnae sit yer arse down years ago and tell ye I felt as much. Though I sought ye out to simply be around ye, it seems in our own way we avoided one another equally."

Niall scowled, but it wasn't because he was frustrated with Malcolm. No, it was because he should have confronted his father long before this. "And I'm sorry I didnae talk with ye sooner, Da. 'Twould of mayhap made life much easier for us both."

"Though 'twas always more my place to make sure this conversation happened 'tis good that ye are saying what yer saying now. That we're…"

When Malcolm broke off, emotional, Niall nodded. "None of it matters because we're saying what's in our hearts now, aye, Da?"

"Aye," Malcolm whispered and pulled Niall into an embrace. "And we always will from this point forward."

"Aye," Niall whispered and held him just as tightly.

"I love ye, Son."

"I love ye too, Da."

When Malcolm finally stepped away, his eyes were moist. Niall supposed his must be too.

"Come, lad. 'Tis time to join the others."

Niall nodded and followed.

By the time they made it to the stables they were covered in snow. Nicole stood in Vika's stall. Her gaze met Niall's when he entered. She didn't need to search his eyes long to see what she hoped for. With a small smile, she hugged him and whispered, "I'm glad we both faced what we needed to."

"Aye." He brushed his lips over hers. "We did, lass."

Iosbail appeared at the stall door. "Ye and yer lass must ride Vika together."

"Aye, I'll get her saddled," Niall said. Nicole followed Rònan when he gestured at her.

"How fare ye, friend?" Niall said into Vika's mind.

"Good, lad. Happy to see ye and yer lass well."

"As well as we can be considering the good King has passed on."

"Aye, 'tis sad that. But such an end often leads to many beginnings."

"What do you mean?"

But Vika went silent as Nicole exclaimed from further down in the stables. "Oh my God, what the heck is Eara doing here?"

Niall frowned as he joined the rest of them. Sure as heck, the light horse with a pale blond mane and tail that had been at the Colonial in New Hampshire was *here*.

Iosbail shrugged, completely evasive. "I dinnae know, lass." Her wise eyes went to Rònan. "But she is yours to ride."

Chapter Seventeen

WHILE NICOLE WAS certainly upset that Eara was here when she was fairly certain the horse was somehow connected with Jackie, she was more concerned about Iosbail. She couldn't imagine the pain the woman was suffering considering she had just lost her husband. More than that, she got the distinct feeling that Iosbail had just said goodbye to her son for the final time as well. But much like Nicole, Iosbail kept her feelings well hidden. Or should she say her deepest feelings. Because hell if they both didn't let the whole world know what their surface feelings were.

The snow had lessened some by the time they left the stables. Malcolm and Iosbail rode their own mounts. Rònan was on Eara and Niall and Nicole on Vika. She found it interesting that Eara was the largest of the horses considering Rònan was the largest of the men. His muscular build met Niall's, but he still had his cousin by a few inches. Ironically enough, Jackie was the tallest of her friends so Nicole had to wonder.

No, that was wrong. She didn't wonder at all.

Deep down she knew Eara was Jackie's.

And Jackie, of course, was the woman Rònan had sworn an oath to.

But hell were they a miss-matched pair if ever one existed. Rònan was as boisterous and rowdy as Nicole. Jackie? The polar opposite. They might make a physically striking couple, but it was *impossible* to see them ever connecting. Jackie preferred quiet, soft-spoken academic men. She cared little for looks but valued intelligence above all else. Not to say Rònan wasn't intelligent. He was. But soft-spoken? Quiet? Nicole shook her head. God help them both if they were heading in each other's direction.

"Rònan and Eara seem to be at odds," Niall murmured in her ear as they followed everyone over the second drawbridge.

Nicole bit her lower lip as Rònan tried to get Eara to stay behind Iosbail. Instead, the horse tried again and again to veer off. "'Tis an ill-trained beastie," he kept muttering.

"She but has her own mind," Iosbail assured over her shoulder. "Be gentle with her and she will listen, laddie."

"How'd it go with your dad, Niall?" Nicole said softly.

"Verra good." He squeezed her hand. "And I think I have you to thank for that."

"I only nudged you along." She glanced over her shoulder at him. "You did the rest, hon."

His warm eyes met hers. "So I'm not 'brute' anymore?"

"Oh, you'll always be that." She cocked the corner of her lips. "C'mon now, it defines all my favorite parts of you."

He was about to reply when Iosbail stopped just after they entered the forest. There was nothing around but a small stream nearly caked over with snow. She turned her horse so that she faced them. "This is where we must part, my friends."

Malcolm met her eyes. "'Tis time then?"

"Aye." Iosbail's eyes had a fresh sheen of moisture in them. "Did ye think I'd be long without my King?"

"Nay," Malcolm said softly. "Ye go to give my Da, William yer magic before ye pass on, aye?"

Oh, wow, what? When Nicole glanced over her shoulder, Niall's eyes were on Iosbail.

"Aye," Iosbail responded to Malcolm. "How else is he to meet his love Coira and go on to have ye and Grant?" Her eyes went to Niall. "Which, naturally, will lead to ye and without ye there couldnae be what blossoms betwixt ye and yer lass."

Niall nodded, emotional.

Malcolm swung off his horse, strode to within feet of Iosbail, dropped to one knee and lowered his head. "I bid ye farewell, Matriarch. And I thank ye for yer devotion to yer kin." Emotion thickened his voice. "Most especially to my Da, William."

Niall swung off Vika and joined his father. Rònan soon followed. All were on bended knee with their heads lowered in respect.

"Och, rise up my kin, ye've done me proud." Her eyes met Nicole's. "All of ye."

Before Nicole could say a word, Iosbail turned her horse and nodded at the stream. "Follow me."

The men were back on their horses in a flash. Niall grabbed the reins and said, "Hold on tight, lass."

Nicole knew that meant they were going to scoot fast so she leaned down and grabbed Vika's mane, speaking within the mind to the horse. *"Where are we going?"*

"Home," Vika said. *"Make sure ye know right where yer weapons are, aye?"*

"Hell, yeah. That's sorta protocol by now."

Vika offered no answer as she jolted after Iosbail but Nicole sensed the horse was pleased with her response. So they flew toward the stream. Some might even call it a creek. Though snow barely fell, the wind whipped stronger than ever as Iosbail's horse leapt over the water...then vanished into thin air.

"Ohhhh." Nicole knew what that meant. She kept her head down as Rònan and Malcolm's horses leapt as well and vanished. While tempted to close her eyes, she just couldn't do it as Niall said, "Here we go, lass!" and Vika leapt.

Unlike her previous times on this horse, she didn't suffer from pure terror as everything fluctuated around her. Instead, this was by far the most beautiful leap to *wherever* they were heading. And the sight that met her on the other side was nothing short of astounding. Though dimly lit, the sun's rays rose over distant mountains as a lake churned wildly beneath them. This place looked familiar...sort of.

"Where are we?" Nicole started, but Vika had already stopped and Niall was swinging down. It would not have mattered if he responded because that old familiar buzzing started in her ears.

"Nicole, can ye hear me?" echoed in her mind.

Robert? Nicole's ears popped as though she was in a plane gaining altitude too fast. She ignored the sensation as complete chaos erupted around her. Not only the mega dark shadow laird but the three shadows or *Genii Cucullati* rushed at them. If that wasn't enough, so did far too many enemy warriors to count with Brae Stewart at their lead.

Seriously not good.

Though tempted to pull out her hearing aid because the sounds were already too much, she didn't. It was there for a reason. So she grabbed her dagger and shield.

"Stay by my side, lass," Niall said. When her eyes met his with defiance because she thought he didn't think she could handle herself, he shook his head. "Defend me as I will defend you."

The world might be crashing down around her, but she felt an unusual but very acute sense of relief. He saw her as his equal. "You got it, Brute."

Niall grinned even as his eyes grew wild. He truly loved to fight and it showed as he muttered, "Come on, ye bloody bastards," as his sword met the blade of the first man who rushed them.

Nicole might be worried about Robert, but she knew a crazy grin lit her face when Machara rushed into the mix with a host of MacLomain, Hamilton and MacLeod warriors at her back. The MacLomain woman grinned and nodded at Nicole moments before her blade met another's.

Nicole didn't hesitate another moment but rushed into the fray.

Niall had stuck several blades into her pockets so she used those first. Tucking her main blade into her side pouch, she grabbed another and started slashing. Suddenly, as warriors came at her, she wasn't fighting the enemy but her past.

When a guy swiped his sword at her, she leapt back, ducked and came in fast. A trick Darach had taught her. She skimmed the dagger across his side. When he tried to spin away, she tripped him. Before he could gain ground, she cut his Achilles tendon. He cried out in pain and dropped.

That was for her blood parents who never looked back when they gave her up.

When Machara drove a warrior back so hard that he stumbled, Nicole gave him a good roundhouse kick, then lodged a knife in his throat when he fell to his knees.

There were great foster homes in Boston, but *that* was for the ones she had ended up in.

She heard the roar of fighting around her, even the dark laird growing closer, but for some reason his words were a weak whisper in her mind. *"Dinnae leave me, lass."*

Nicole didn't give two shits about what he did and did not want. She was out for vengeance. For Robert. Her friends. The MacLomains.

For herself.

So when the next warrior rushed her, she didn't mess around. She whipped her dagger. It caught him in the chest and he fell.

That was for all the kids in school who made fun of her when she couldn't understand what they were saying. Their endless, cruel taunts.

Machara's grin was crazed as she eyed the man Nicole had just taken down. "'Twould be my honor to fight back to back with ye, lass."

"Right, like they do in the movies." Nicole nodded. "Sounds good."

She thought at first it wouldn't work but hell, Hollywood had something figured out because when they went back to back and started fighting, they were solid. Thrashing, slicing, fighting, they were taking them down.

Yet somehow in the fray, a guy got ahold of her and they were separated. Nicole scrambled, but he was fast. Faster than the others. When he dropped her, she wasn't quite quick enough to get away. He had her locked tight and they were outside the main battling. Now nothing was going to save her but herself.

She had yet to draw the blade Niall had given her and the shield Rònan gave her was pinned to the ground.

"Och, yer a feisty wee lass, ye are," the enemy murmured against her ear.

Nicole realized that she had just ended up in the very position that Niall had her in back in the armory at MacLeod Castle. She was vulnerable as only a woman could be.

Could she do what she had with him and get away with it?

Or was she asking for trouble that there was no escape from?

Only one way to find out.

So she relaxed, wiggled her ass and murmured in the most feminine, damsel-in-distress voice she could muster, "Let me go. I'll do anything."

Then she prayed. *Please* let him take the bait.

Like clockwork, the guy stilled. "Anything?"

"Anything."

She barely drew a breath before he flipped her, wedged her legs apart and leered down. "Aye, then, lass."

Though Niall's words in the armory came back to her about being fully prepared to defend herself if she egged this sort of thing on, his words in her head now were much louder. More furious. Straight from the heart. *"Ye better bloody well handle things correctly, lass, because I cannae get to ye."*

Oh, she would. Nicole offered the man holding her down a soft smile and spread her legs wider. Sensing her willingness, he worked at lifting his plaid. She almost snorted. War might be echoing around them, but this douche was willing to slake his lust rather than fight for his cause. Then again, he was fighting for evil so that said everything. No need to use her magical blade, she released a throaty moan. When he glanced at her, she drove a dagger up through the soft spot beneath his chin.

That was for her stripper friends. Better yet, it was against the men who hurt them one way or another. For the most part, guys were fine and just looking for a good time when they hit the clubs. They tipped and treated the ladies well. Then there were the few who didn't. Who thought women existed to please them, didn't tip and one way or another went after girls in a real bad way.

Nicole shoved the enemy aside when his eyes went blank and sprang to her feet.

"Fight on, warrior," whispered through her mind. Iosbail?

With nothing left but Niall's dagger and Rònan's shield, she rushed into a scant fray. Most were behind her and falling fast. The bad guys that is. When she looked back, she almost wished she hadn't. The mortal enemies might be falling, but Brae, her monster boyfriend, and the creepy shadows were full throttle.

Niall's mind slammed into hers as he fought alongside his cousins. *"Go, Nicole. Run!"*

"Heck if I will," she muttered and started back toward them.

But suddenly Grant was there and unlike his predecessor arch-MacLomain wizard, Adlin, he didn't deal in jolly. Eyes glowing blue, caught in some sort of slow-motion wind, he roared, "Ye listen to yer MacLomain and run!"

Though determined to fight alongside Niall, whatever Grant did made her heels spin and she started running. Fast. Hard. When she rounded the corner of the mountain, she stopped short.

No wonder she semi-recognized this spot. It was the lake on the backside of the mountain that the Viking ship appeared on. They had returned to the 'mystical mountain of fertility' as she called it. But where was Robert? He could only be within the mountain. Under the influence of Grant's words, she raced along the shore toward the waterfall but slowed the closer she got.

Deep down, she knew Robert was safe.

But Niall was not.

Though she desperately wanted to stop, her feet tingled to keep going. Yet she fought it. She and Niall had come too far and she *refused* to leave him behind. Because of the hearing aid, she caught sounds she never would have before. The cries of pain still echoing around the side of the mountain. The grunts and groans. The pure anguish of not only the enemy but allies.

"No, no, no," she cried and pushed against Grant's compulsion because she knew that's exactly what it was. Sure, the wizard meant to keep her safe but he also meant to keep her ring out of the enemy's hands.

To hell with that if it meant her friends would die for it.

But even as she turned and saw everyone come around the corner, she was being sucked toward the mountain. The horses had already rushed by and ran through the waterfall. But not her friends. Rònan and Machara.

Most especially, Niall.

Not about to give up and let Grant somehow pull her away from protecting them, she shook her head. "Fuc-fudge no!"

She couldn't fight magic like Grant's, but maybe something else could. So she dropped to her knees and tried to dig her magical blade into the sand to stop herself. Yet she couldn't get it lodged. Her friends raced along the shore. While no enemy warriors followed, something far worse did.

Brae, the dark shadow laird and his minion Otherworld shadows.

All had rushed into the mountain which left Machara, Rònan, Malcolm, Grant and Niall.

And based on their stances, they intended to fight until the death.

Nicole never gave up trying to dig her blade into the ground so she could help.

Based on the cry of rage and her rushing forward, Machara intended to go down first. Nicole wailed in denial as the shadows swamped her. Though she didn't seem to care in the least, someone else did. Whipping around the corner on horseback, Conall leaned over, scooped Machara around the waist and sped toward the waterfall.

Though that gave her a modicum of relief, Nicole's fear only increased when the others became the sole target of Brae and the dark, foggy laird.

"Noooo," she kept murmuring as she fought against Grant's compulsion. While she understood his need to protect her, her need to stay and help was too great. So she started to use both the shield and dagger to keep her grounded.

"Get the bloody hell to safety, Nicole," Niall and Rònan roared into her mind.

Hearing them made tears fall. Stupid, defiant tears. So she screamed right back within the mind. *"Over my dead body."*

After that is was a complete horror show made not of warfare but of magic. Nicole realized in that singular moment that she was in *way* over her head. She supposed it was a good thing that Grant was heading in her direction. It seemed his final stance would be protecting her.

The evil guy who had been in her mind roared forward. Niall was tossed. So were Rònan and Malcolm. Struggling to fight him they went for their weapons, but his darkness was too great. Water churned. The spectacular sunrise struggled as it splintered through blackened clouds. Even Nicole could feel the dark, powerful magic inundating around her.

This was insane.

How would they ever fight this?

But somehow she knew when Niall jumped in front of them and raised his sword sideways. He would die protecting everyone if given the chance. So would she. They might be half a lake away, but their eyes met.

Understood.

Nicole's breath caught. It wasn't just about protecting but so much more. It was about love. Not just a deep love for one another but everyone that meant anything to them. The people they knew.

The lives that had changed theirs. It was about mistakes and new beginnings. It was about no more avoidance but only acceptance.

More than anything, it was about embracing change.

It had come and it was theirs.

They were kindred. One. Always had been. Always would be.

"Screw this," she mouthed and once more dug her blade and shield into the sand to stop herself.

"Aye, lass," he mouthed back and kept his sword held high.

Whatever passed between them at that moment changed everything. Brae Stewart staggered back. The three spirit shadows twisted away. The wind that whipped died and the sun rays gave way to a bright, pale purple twilight. The waters calmed as Niall in his red Sinclair plaid kept his blade raised, as ready to defend as the dark demi-god was determined to destroy.

The rest might have meant to defend him, but they couldn't get close.

No, he was caught in magic.

At first she thought it meant the enemy had him but soon realized it meant something else entirely. Not only did the Celtic symbols in her blade ignite with dark blue but the prisms of her shield as well. Yet she knew that wasn't what gave them the most power. No. Though terrified for his life as the darkness swamped down on him, Nicole's eyes fell to her hand and she smiled.

Outright, unabashedly smiled.

The stone in the center of her ring shone brightly. Dark blue.

To match Niall's eye color.

There were weapons then there was *the* weapon. Though she would have sworn it was the worst plot possible in any book or movie, it was the best plot imaginable in their story. Whatever happened with her ring fed into not only her blade and shield but into Niall's eyes and even his sword. He might have been able to control water before but now?

Now it was everything.

Nicole didn't mess around trying to save everyone because she knew they would be just fine as she raced toward the waterfall. Niall loved her and his wrath, his element, was crashing down. The lake swirled up and became a massive, watery weapon against Brae and her laird. It was unstoppable.

A roar swallowed the heavens as evil tried to attack one final time but had no chance against…

Love.

Nicole held back when the others rushed through.

The dark laird roared again, trying desperately to get past the magic she and Niall had created, but he was going nowhere fast. Apparently now that her ring had ignited, he no longer had control over her because she heard his words struggle within her mind then zap out entirely. Within moments, the dark laird wrapped around Brae and they both vanished.

Nicole gasped when Niall scooped her up and raced through the waterfall. The fury of their nemesis' departure made the ground shake, but it didn't last long.

"We are safe," Grant announced even as he continued to weave what she assumed were protective spells.

The second Niall lowered her; she wrapped her arms around him and pressed her face against his chest. "I'm so glad you're okay."

"Aye, I could say the same of you, my crazy, wee, lass," he murmured.

"Och, ye two had me worried out there," Rònan said and embraced them both.

When Rònan started sniffing, Nicole warned, "Stop it, Rònan."

Rònan only offered an indefinable sound before inhaling a few more times.

Nicole chuckled, mumbling, "You guys really like group hugs, huh?"

"Well, ye cannae blame us," Niall rumbled. "Ye are a bonnie lass if ever there was one."

"Aye," Rònan agreed.

"Nicole!"

"Alrighty, time to let me go, guys," Nicole managed before they stepped away. When she crouched, Robert flew into her arms and she held him tight. "Hey, kiddo, good to see you!"

"Aye!" She heard the tears in his voice. "I thought ye truly gone for good when ye protected me and went with the evil lass."

"Nah. You can't get rid of me that easily." She pulled back enough so that she could tilt up his chin and meet his eyes. "Besides,

I was too darn proud of you not to make it back so I could tell you how amazing I think you are."

"I am?" He sniffled a little and rubbed away some tears. "Why?"

"Because..." She made sure her voice and expression were very serious. "Remember what I told you back in the Viking cave? I asked you to steer clear of the bad guy and you did. You listened to those who tried to protect you because you knew you could trust them."

He brushed away the last of his tears. "Just like I trusted you."

Nicole nodded. "That's right."

Robert stood up a little taller and nodded. "Thank ye for everything ye've done for me, Nicole."

"Anytime, kid." She ruffled his hair and grinned.

Nicole no sooner stood before Darach was there. He spun her once and grinned before he gave her a big hug. "'Tis bloody good to see you alive and well, lass."

"Good to see you too, sweetie." She hugged him and laughed. "I wish you could've come along for the last part of the ride."

"Och, nay. Someone needed to keep an eye on the wee King." He pulled back but kept his arms around her, still smiling. "Besides, I couldnae have gotten past Niall if I wanted to."

"Probably not," she agreed.

"Enough with that, Cousin," Niall muttered and pulled Nicole free even though he patted Darach on the back. She found it amusing he was fine with Rònan putting his hands all over her but not Darach.

Niall took her elbow and nodded at a tall, stunning redhead. She might be older with traces of silver in her hair, but she was still rocking it. "Nicole, this is my Ma, Cadence."

Ah, Leslie's sister.

"Nice to meet you," Nicole started but Cadence pulled her in for a tight hug before she could finish.

"So nice to meet you too, Nicole." Then Cadence held her at arm's length. "Thank you for taking such good care of my boy."

"Well, it was really more the other way around," Nicole said with a smile.

"Don't be so humble." Cadence's eyes narrowed a fraction. "You're a Broun. That means it worked both ways."

Not going anywhere near arguing with Niall's Mom, Nicole only grinned. "I suppose it did one way or another."

"I'd say so." Cadence glanced at Malcolm and Niall clapping one another on the back and smiling. "After all, you managed to do something I've been trying to do for years." Her eyes went back to Nicole, voice soft. "Again, thank you."

Cadence squeezed her hand and pulled away.

"'Tis time for everyone save Malcolm, Niall, and Nicole to join the others in the cave at the Defiance," Grant said, his gaze narrowed on the slim hallway that ran in the opposite direction.

Nicole gasped when she looked that way.

Vika stood beside the creek that ran through the cave further down.

But that wasn't the kicker.

It appeared someone was with the horse.

Though Nicole had no idea how she knew, she was positive it was the woman she saw on the shores of Northern Scotland when they traveled back in time.

Chapter Eighteen

WARMTH UNCURLED IN Niall's chest as they made their way toward the small stream. Though the waterfall roared even closer here, Grant dimmed the sound as they approached. The woman waiting for them might have been old the last time he saw her, but his grandmother was now young as she smiled at them.

Coira MacLomain.

One of the four original MacLomain wizards.

Wide-eyed, Nicole remained silent.

Coira cupped one of Grant's cheeks and one of Malcolm's as she stared at them fondly. "My lads. How I've missed ye."

Niall squeezed Nicole's hand and offered a soft smile when she glanced at him.

"And we've missed ye, Ma," Grant said. "More than ye know."

"Aye," Malcolm agreed.

She looked at her sons for another long, affectionate moment before she pulled away and turned to Niall and Nicole. Her eyes went to Niall first. "Ye've grown up into a handsome lad ye have. Tall and strapping like yer Da." A warm smile curled her lips. "And like yer Grandpa, William."

Niall nodded, eyes damp. "'Tis good to see ye again, Grandma."

Nicole's eyes only grew wider when Coira's gaze turned her way and she introduced herself. "'Tis nice to finally meet ye outside of the horse, Nicole."

"You too," Nicole said slowly as she began to realize. "Like Cassie's horse, Athdara was merged with someone, so were you...with Vika?"

"Aye." Coira nodded. "Harnessing the magic of our Viking ancestors."

"Wow," Nicole whispered and glanced at the horse. "How is Vika still here then?"

"Because 'twas a different harnessing of power than what was done with Athdara." Coira brushed her hand fondly over the horse who munched on a spare bit of grass. "I joined with her from the afterlife." Her eyes went to Nicole. "Vika was alive and well before and remains so if ye'd like to keep her, lass. She will care well for ye, indeed."

"I'd love to keep her." Nicole's eyes went from the horse to Coira. "So…was that you I've been talking to telepathically all this time?"

"Aye." Coira nodded. "But Vika's soul was there as well and has bonded with ye. Her voice will be different, but I think ye'll find she's well suited to ye." His grandmother winked. "She's got a wee bit o' a wild streak in her."

Nicole grinned. "Sounds just perfect."

"I cannae stay on any longer." Her eyes flickered between Niall and Nicole. "Ye both did verra well and the wee Bruce is still safe." Then her eyes dropped to Nicole's hand. "My ring has found true love once again." Her eyes met theirs and a warm smile came to her lips. "I wish ye both a lifetime of happiness."

Nicole blinked several times and looked at her ring, whispering, "I'll be damned."

"Not damned." Coira smiled. "But much loved."

Nicole's eyes grew moist and she nodded.

Coira's gaze went to Malcolm's and held before they went to Grant's. "Watch over yer dragon nephew. 'Tis the darkest of danger ahead for him and a bright light that will lead him straight toward it."

Niall wrapped his arm around Nicole's waist when he felt her tense.

"I will see him well cared for, Ma," Grant assured. "With my dying breath if need be."

"Och, hopefully it willnae come to that," she murmured and stepped away. "I love ye all, but I must go."

Everyone was emotional as she turned away and started walking along the stream toward the waterfall. Sun glistened through the water and caused diamond chips of light to scatter everywhere. Niall knew it wasn't his imagination when an ethereal image shimmered within the water and held out his hand to her.

His grandfather, William.

She took his hand and they vanished.

Everyone remained silent for several long moments before they got their bearings. Malcolm patted his shoulder as he went by. "I'm off to be with yer Ma. Join us in a bit, aye?"

He smiled. "Aye, Da."

Grant came next, expression as nostalgic as his father's had been. "You did verra well, lad." His eyes went to Nicole. "You both did the MacLomain's, Hamilton's and MacLeod's proud. The Brouns too I'd say. Well done, indeed."

"We couldnae have done it without you, Uncle." Niall embraced him. "I'm sorry if I grew angry with you on occasion."

"'Tis naught to worry over, lad. Your heart was always in the right place." Grant pulled back. "Me and my kin of the Next Generation may have helped here and there but 'twas the love you two found that kept safe not only the wee King but your kin. Be proud."

Grant smiled at Nicole. "When you're done here with your lad, join us at the Defiance. My wife, Sheila looks forward to meeting you." He chuckled. "Like you, she's been enjoying a wee bit o' Christmastide lately."

"Has she?" Nicole cocked her head. "But it's late summer here, isn't it?" She frowned. "Oh, wait, maybe fall now because of that time gap when I was in the Otherworld."

"Nay, 'tis not Christmastide here yet." He kept chuckling. "We've just been busy playing Mr. and Mrs. Claus to some friends in the future is all."

"Huh?" Nicole asked, but Grant had already turned and was heading down the hallway.

Her eyes went to Niall. "What'd he mean by that?"

"Trust me, lass, Grant is becoming as evasive as Adlin was so dinnae ever expect an answer to that."

"So he wasn't talking about my friends?"

"Nay." Niall shook his head. "That I can tell you with assurance."

Nicole eyed him. "Yeah?"

"Aye," he murmured and pulled her into his arms.

Yet she remained tense. "We need to tell Rònan that he said Jackie's name back at Sinclair Castle. That she's likely the woman who's in trouble."

"I already did." He wrapped his hand into her hair. "He knows."

"Really?" she said, voice growing softer as he pressed his arousal against her.

"Aye," he whispered, so damn glad to have her safely back in his arms. Even gladder that the stone in her ring matched his eye color so that she knew he was hers.

"Nicole," he began but the words died on his tongue he felt so strongly.

"Yeah?" she whispered.

Not used to expressing such deep emotions—to confiding how much he felt—he bided his time. "How is your hearing?" He recalled all too well what being caught in so much dark magic had done to Cassie. "Has it worsened?"

"I don't think so." Tentative, she took out the device. Nicole bit her lip. Though fear flashed in her eyes, she quickly blinked it away. "Nope, everything sounds about the same."

He knew it. The magic had progressed her condition. But she'd come too far to revert to her old ways, so he shook his head and wrapped his hand firmly around the back of her neck. "Your days of denial are over, lass. Be proud that you know how to face this now."

She ground her jaw and held his gaze.

"What can you hear?" he said, trying his best to enunciate each word so that she could read his lips if she needed to.

"I can still hear you." Nicole straightened her shoulders, clearly unwilling to give in to fear again. "But it's faint."

His eyes fell to her hand. The stone had stopped glowing. Interesting. So he lifted her hand. "Put the device back in your ear, lass."

"I don't know." She frowned. "Maybe this is it, Niall. Maybe the device got me through until I took it out. Maybe—"

He put a finger to her lips and shook his head. "Just put it back in."

Niall lent her all the strength he could as he gazed into her eyes. "And remember, even if the device does nothing, you will always hear me within the mind. That willnae ever change."

Nicole stared at him for a long moment before she rallied her courage. "Okay, you're right."

Not hesitating another second, she put the device back in her ear...and smiled.

"It works," she exclaimed.

His eyes fell to the ring. It once again glowed brightly. As he suspected, somehow the power of their love was tied with the love and support she shared with her friends back home. So he told her as much.

"Unreal." Her eyes went from the ring to him. "That's kinda *really* cool."

"Aye," he agreed, truly happy for her. Though he desperately hoped she would stay in Scotland with him, he didn't want to push her. Even so, it couldn't hurt to remove any potential reason she may have to return to the future. "I'd imagine the power of the ring will also keep the device's battery charged."

Nicole grinned and eyed the ring. "Nice perk."

"'Tis," he murmured.

"Niall?" she whispered as her eyes met his and they became lost in each other's gaze.

"Aye, lass?"

"Do you know how much I love—"

"There ye are," Rònan said as he poked his head around the corner.

Niall frowned at his cousin. "We would have joined ye eventually. Is it too much to ask for a few moments alone with my lass?"

"Nay." Rònan shrugged. "But ye never really asked for a few moments alone so I assumed ye wouldnae mind me popping by to say farewell."

Nicole frowned. "Where are you going?"

"To the future." Rònan frowned as well. "Though I wish ye'd both told me sooner that I gave ye the lass's name at the Sinclair's, I ken yer need to wait." His frown only deepened as he looked at Nicole. "But now I know 'twas yer friend, Jaqueline, I need to make sure she's safe. I'm taking the horse, Eara with me."

"When did ye last go to the future, Cousin?" Niall asked, concerned. As far as he knew, it had only been once years ago.

Rònan shrugged. "It doesnae really matter, does it?"

"Mayhap not," Niall conceded, but something about it made him uncomfortable. "I wish ye had more often, my friend."

"'Twas no need," Rònan said but Niall sensed his cousin's discomfort.

"But now there is," Niall said softly.

"Aye," Rònan said just as softly. "Now there is."

"Well, I think that's awesome," Nicole said and hugged Rònan. "My friends could use a guy like you around. I mean seriously, Darach's there as much as possible and he's a wicked flirt."

Rònan pulled back and frowned again. "He is, isn't he?"

"Aye." Niall shook his head as he embraced his cousin. "With a particular love for twenty-first century lassies, I'd say."

Nicole chuckled. "I second that."

Rònan looked at her as he patted Niall's back and stepped away. "Aye?"

"Yup." She grinned and winked. "Add in his heart of gold and watch the heck out."

"Yet Cassie is with Logan and you're with Niall," Rònan reminded.

"That we are." She sort of flinched. "But Darach and Jackie, well…"

"Jackie?"

"That's Jaqueline's nickname."

"Ah." Rònan's expression grew troubled. "What about her and Darach?"

"I dunno." Nicole shrugged. "They seemed sorta into each other."

"Did they really?" Rònan said under his breath before he nodded. "Aye then, I must go."

"Travel safe, Cousin," Niall said.

"Love you, sweetie," Nicole added.

Rònan nodded and started to stride away before he stopped short and turned back. He eyed them for a few seconds before Niall spoke up. "Is everything all right?"

"Aye," Rònan said slowly, almost carefully, before he walked back. His eyes flickered between them before landing on Nicole.

"What?" she said, as confused as Niall by his cousin's cautious aloofness. It was so unlike Rònan it was almost comical.

"Well," Rònan began and swallowed. When he sniffed, Nicole's eyes widened.

"Did you *seriously* just come back here to tell me I'm turned on by Niall?"

Niall almost grinned but sensed Rònan's tension. "What is it, Cousin?"

Rònan kept eying them before he sighed. "I dinnae know if 'tis my place to say as much but 'twould give me much pleasure to be the first to share."

When they looked at him with confusion, Rònan met Nicole's eyes. "You saved more than a single wee one on this adventure of yours, lass."

"Yeah, I know," she said. "Not just Robert but Tait."

"Aye," he agreed. "But more than that."

"I wouldn't exactly call Heidrek wee but sure, yeah, him too."

Niall's eyes narrowed as he began to understand.

"Aye." Rònan nodded then shook his head. "But nay."

"Out with it, Rònan." Totally baffled, Nicole narrowed her eyes as well. "What the heck are you talking about?"

Rònan placed his hand against her stomach, eyes deadly seriously as they met hers. "This wee one, lass."

It felt like the ground fell out from beneath him as Niall's eyes locked on his cousin's hand.

Nicole's eyes went round as saucers as she looked from her stomach to Rònan. "Are you trying to tell me I'm *pregnant*?"

"Aye," Rònan murmured. "Because of my dragon blood I can smell such." There was tremendous pride in his eyes as they held Nicole's. "Though newly made, already the bairn has a fierce heartbeat. The heart of a warrior, I'd say."

"Get out," she whispered and put her hand over Rònan's.

"Aye, I'll leave," he murmured.

When he tried to pull his hand away, she grabbed it and shook her head. "It's an expression, hon. It means, 'wow' or 'amazing.'"

Niall couldn't agree more as he watched a tear roll down her cheek. He wasn't sure what part had him soaring more. That she carried his bairn or the light in her eyes knowing that she did.

"I don't understand," she said softly, holding both of their hands. "Kol told me I wasn't pregnant."

"You werenae when last he saw you," Rònan said. "But you are now without doubt."

"So it happened at the Sinclair's?" Niall said. "Why did you not sense it there?"

Rònan shrugged, but there was wisdom in his eyes. "I dinnae know much of these things, but I'd say it takes a moment or two for your seed to take root, lad."

Niall's eyes met Nicole's and it felt like the world faded away. Nothing existed but them and...new life. They knew Rònan said goodbye and left, but all they could see was one another.

"Nicole," he whispered as he placed his hand over her belly.

"Niall," she whispered back as she put her hand over his.

"What think ye of this?" he said softly, unable to stop his brogue.

Another tear rolled down her cheek. "What do *you* think of this?"

"I asked ye first."

"You did." She nodded and shrugged. "But I want to hear your answer first."

Niall understood that she *needed* to hear it. She *needed* confirmation.

"I think I'm the luckiest bloody lad alive," he whispered.

"Yeah, I think you are too." Her voice was wobbly as she pulled him closer. "But I suppose I'm pretty lucky too."

"Aye?" he murmured, walking her back a few steps until she was against the wall and he knew she was safe and sound between him and the mystical mountain. "Why?"

"I think it's pretty obvious."

He brushed the pad of his thumb over the erect nipple straining through the material of her dress. "Only one thing's obvious, lass." His purposefully innocent eyes met hers. "Is there more?"

"You just want to pull it right outta me, huh?" she murmured as her hands rode up his chest.

"Aye," he murmured back. "But I can see as always you're determined to be stubborn."

Nicole shrugged a shoulder and gave a crooked grin. "I don't know how else to be."

Neither did Niall, but he knew this moment deserved more than them not being absolutely truthful with one another. So he said what needed to be said.

"As I told you back at the Sinclair's, I want you to stay here with me in Scotland, Nicole." He clenched his teeth before he said the entirety of what she needed to hear. "But I willnae hold you back if you want to go home." His eyes dropped. "Even in light of our wee one."

He hated giving her the option to flee but knew she deserved it. His was a lass who should never be held back. They might have connected when fighting the enemy. He might have felt true love.

But had she?

Nicole remained silent for far too long as she fiddled with the collar of his tunic. He imagined she was trying to figure out a way to run, but he was never more wrong.

"I think you can do better than that, Brute," she said softly.

"Can I?" he whispered, hope surging.

"I think you should give it a shot," she whispered back.

"Aye, then." Not needing to be told twice, he cupped her cheeks and looked deeply into her eyes. "I love you, Nicole. With everything I am and everything I never knew I was. Dinnae leave. Not ever. Stay with me. Let us start a family together. Let's spoil our wee bairn together and give him or her a Ma and Da that will love them unconditionally."

Another tear rolled down her cheek. "That was much better."

"Aye?"

"Yeah." She swallowed. "I wouldn't be opposed to teaching a little brute how to use his dagger."

He worked at a smile, gratefulness making it hard to speak. "And I wouldnae mind teaching a wee feisty redhead how to swing her sword."

"Damn, okay," she whispered and closed her eyes, but not before another tear rolled. Then her eyes shot open. "There are a few conditions, though."

"Love shouldnae come with conditions."

"No, but I play by my own set of rules."

"Aye." The corner of his lip hitched up. "What are they?"

"No coddling when I lose my hearing. Not ever. Because on occasion I'll need to take this thing out of my ear and go natural. When I do, you better never go soft on me or I'm outta here."

Niall nodded. "Agreed. No coddling."

"And, pregnant or not, I still want to fight against this thing trying to get Robert."

When he frowned and pulled his hands away, her eyes widened. "I'm serious. I'll play it safe and hang back if I'm not needed but if things get heavy, I'm in it, babe. I made a promise to that kid just as much as you did and I won't have anyone, including you, telling me I can't help."

Everything inside him rebelled against her request, but he understood that Nicole was only being Nicole. She couldn't be anything else. And would he want her to be? No. Everything she was made him love her more and more. So how could he deny her? What he could do was try his best to keep her out of harm's way then pray that the gods kept her and his bairn safe after that.

So though it took everything he had to say it…he said it.

"I will never hold you back, lass. If you need to fight, I'll be right there fighting alongside you."

She cupped his cheeks and searched his eyes. "Do you mean that?"

"Aye." He kept his eyes locked with hers. "I mean it."

"You do, don't you." She nodded and pressed her lips together. "Thank you."

Before he could speak, she pressed her thumb against his lips and shook her head. "My turn." Nicole released his cheeks and pulled him closer until she could whisper in his ear. "I love you, Niall." She kissed his cheek and murmured, "I seriously just love the hell out of you."

Deep emotion overwhelmed him and Niall closed his eyes, whispering, "Aye, 'tis bloody good to hear."

She peppered kisses along his cheek until her lips met his. The kiss they found was different and new. The first of its kind. Soft, gentle and seeking even though they had already found what they were looking for. Still, it was precious and all theirs because they shared it with a new life.

The waterfall roared and sunlight speckled around them as moist mist blew in and their passion only intensified. As always, they could not get close enough.

The war against evil had not been won, but all their mini-battles were over.

Robert the Bruce was still safe and no ring had been taken by the enemy.

The future of Scotland remained unchanged.

A Highlander maintained his honor.

A twenty-first century woman faced her fear.

Niall and Nicole had fought, struggled and outright battled but still found their way into one another's heart. Right where they were always supposed to be.

As it turned out, love finally found them.

More than that, it had definitely saved the day.

The End

Determined to confront the beautiful woman who reached out to him in the Celtic Otherworld, Rònan heads for the twenty-first century. But what he finds when he arrives is the last thing he expects. Two Broun lasses are supposed to be there, but only one remains. And not the one he was looking for. Yet the enemy is hot on his heels. Now he is torn. Does he protect the one he's with or the one he swore an oath to save? Find out in *Oath of a Scottish Warrior*.

Previous Releases

~The MacLomain Series- Early Years~

Highland Defiance- Book One
Highland Persuasion- Book Two
Highland Mystic- Book Three

~The MacLomain Series~

The King's Druidess- Prelude
Fate's Monolith- Book One
Destiny's Denial- Book Two
Sylvan Mist- Book Three

~The MacLomain Series- Next Generation~

Mark of the Highlander- Book One
Vow of the Highlander- Book Two
Wrath of the Highlander- Book Three
Faith of the Highlander- Book Four
Plight of the Highlander- Book Five

~The MacLomain Series- Viking Ancestors~

Viking King- Book One
Viking Claim- Book Two
Viking Heart- Book Three

~The MacLomain Series- Later Years~

Quest of a Scottish Warrior- Book One
Honor of a Scottish Warrior- Book Two
Oath of a Scottish Warrior- Book Three
Passion of a Scottish Warrior- Book Four

~Calum's Curse Series~

The Victorian Lure- Book One
The Georgian Embrace- Book Two
The Tudor Revival- Book Three

~Holiday Tales~

Yule's Fallen Angel

Available exclusively in the *Alpha's Unwrapped Multi-Author Boxed Set*.
21 brand new paranormal holiday stories from NY Times & USA Today best-selling authors.

~Forsaken Brethren Series~

Darkest Memory- Book One
Heart of Vesuvius- Book Two

~Song of the Muses Series~

Highland Muse

About the Author

Sky Purington is the best-selling author of eighteen novels and several novellas. A New Englander born and bred, Sky was raised hearing stories of folklore, myth and legend. When combined with a love for nature, romance and time-travel, elements from the stories of her youth found release in her books.

Purington loves to hear from readers and can be contacted at Sky@SkyPurington.com. Interested in keeping up with Sky's latest news and releases? Visit Sky's website, www.SkyPurington.com to download her free App on iTunes and Android or sign up for her quarterly newsletter. Love social networking? Find Sky on Facebook and Twitter.

68846100R00150

Made in the USA
Middletown, DE
02 April 2018